Ormerod's Landing

Leslie Thomas was born in South Wales in 1931 and, when his parents died, he and his younger brother were brought up in an orphanage. His first book, *This Time Next Week*, is the autobiography of a happy orphan. At sixteen he became a reporter on a weekly newspaper in Essex and then did his National Service in Malaya during the Communist bandit war. *The Virgin Soldiers* tells of these days; it was an immediate bestseller and has been made into a film with Lynn Redgrave and Hywel Bennett.

Returning to civilian life, Leslie Thomas joined the staff of the *Evening News*, becoming a top feature writer and travelling a great deal. His second novel, *Orange Wednesday*, was published in 1967. For nine months during 1967 he travelled around ten islands off the coast of Britain, the result of which was a lyrical travelogue, *Some Lovely Islands*, from which the BBC did a television series. He has continued to travel a great deal and has also written several television plays. He is a director of a London publishing house. His hobbies include golf, antiques and Queen's Park Rangers Football Club.

His other books include *Come to the War*, *His Lordship*, *Arthur McCann and All His Women*, *The Man With the Power*, *Onward Virgin Soldiers*, *Stand Up Virgin Soldiers*, *Tropic of Ruislip*, *Dangerous Davies: The Last Detective*, and *Bare Nell* – all of them published in Pan.

20p

D0237356

Also by Leslie Thomas in Pan Books

Fiction
Virgin Soldiers
Orange Wednesday
The Love Beach
Come to the War
His Lordship
Onward Virgin Soldiers
Arthur McCann and All His Women
The Man with the Power
Tropic of Ruislip
Stand Up Virgin Soldiers
Dangerous Davies
Bare Nell
Non-fiction
This Time Next Week
Some Lovely Islands

Leslie Thomas

Ormerod's Landing

Pan Books London and Sydney

This is dedicated to my son Mark

First published in Great Britain in 1978 by Eyre Methuen Ltd
This edition published 1979 by Pan Books Ltd,
Cavaye Place, London SW10 9PG
© New Lion Dealings Ltd 1978
ISBN 0 330 25778 1
Printed and bound in Great Britain by
Richard Clay (The Chaucer Press) Ltd, Bungay, Suffolk

author's note

The occupation of secret agent is bizarre and sometimes frankly comic. Professor M. R. D. Foot in his official history of the British Special Operations Executive in wartime France describes an 'atmosphere of adventure and daring often with a touch of light opera thrown in'.

He records that the initial raid attempt on occupied Europe after Dunkirk resulted in the three British participants having to row home. (It took thirteen hours.) Churchill called it a 'foolish fiasco'.

Plans to drop the first parachutist agent into France were marred by his last-moment refusal to jump. A later raider dropped on the roof of a police station. A third, a Frenchman, jumped and then quietly went home to his wife for the remainder of the war. Another parachutist hung in a tree all through a dark night, to discover at dawn that his feet were inches from the ground. Peter Churchill was horrified to have ebullient and noisy Frenchmen, like football supporters, taking him to a rendezvous at a secret air strip.

Agents, not infrequently, spoke imperfect French, or none at all. One, questioned by the Gestapo on a train, and unable to speak French, pretended to be a dolt and got away with it. Another, who did speak the language, blithely told the Germans he was a British Officer carrying a radio transmitter. They laughed and let him go.

One operative, wearing an English overcoat and smoking a pipe, met his secret contact in public with the words 'How are you mate?' A resistance leader 'hiding' among a group of plain-clothes Gestapo men in a bar was loudly sought out by some downed RAF men – *in uniform* – and seeking asylum.

The French also had their oddities. Before 1940 they entrusted at least part of their espionage plans to two men – one nearly blind and the other stone deaf. During the German Occupation they used a submarine to land agents, a vessel impotent in normal operations – a fault in its tubes sent its torpedoes in circles!

In the realm of the outlandish, then, George Ormerod, whose tale is told here, was not alone . . .

'It is not Policy to use a good intelligence agent for a dangerous mission involving sabotage. He is more valuable lying low, making contacts and gathering information. Others, more readily replaced, should be used for violent or dubious projects . . .'

Intelligence Directive
August 1940

one

The little-known island of Chausey lies between Jersey and the Normandy coast. Two kilometres in length and seven hundred metres at its widest, it has a population of about fifty. It is cast about with islets and many rocks. Of all the Channel Islands group, it alone is part of France.

At dawn on September 20th, 1940, at the ebb of the highest tide of the year (a prodigious rise and fall of forty-one feet) a nervous London police officer and a young French school-mistress, who was also a trained killer, landed on the island. It was the first Anglo-French raid on Occupied Europe follow-ing Dunkirk and the collapse of France.

Two nights later the infiltrators – Detective-Sergeant George Ormerod, aged thirty-five, of 'V' Division Metropolitan Police, and Madame Marie-Thérèse Velin, aged twenty-six, from the village of St Luc-au-Perche in Lower Normandy – were put ashore, *by the Germans themselves*, at Granville on the main-land. By then they were accompanied by a thin, ugly mongrel called *Formidable*.

Their adventure has never been told before, not because it has been concealed by the Official Secrets Act, or any other such bureaucratic device, as so many have, but merely because the two people most concerned had never felt the need to talk about it. In addition, as with other early escapades of its nature, the documentation is missing from the files, a fact which gives rise to the suspicion that the operation was tacitly 'disowned'.

I first heard the strange story of the Dove and the Dodo, as they were called, from Madame Velin herself, twenty-three years after it took place. She was then living on the French Pacific Island of New Caledonia, about twenty miles from Noumea, its capital.

I was *en route* to London after a newspaper assignment, covering the visit of Her Majesty the Queen and Prince Philip to Australia. New Caledonia is a little over two hours flying from Sydney and I had gone there for a few days holiday.

It was at a dinner party on my second evening that I first heard the name of Marie-Thérèse Velin. My host, a young doctor doing his National Service in the colony, was treating her for a tropical ailment which caused temporary spasms of blindness.

He mentioned that she had been a member of the wartime resistance in France and had settled in New Caledonia as a school teacher in the early nineteen-fifties. It was suggested that I might like to accompany him on a visit to her the following day, as she spoke good English but had little opportunity of doing so on the island.

I agreed and in the late afternoon, when the day had cooled off a little, we went out from the town and into the copra country beyond, the road running straight between miles of coconut plantations, until we eventually came to a sedate cottage overlooking a shell beach. On the veranda, looking out over the sea, was Marie-Thérèse Velin whose name was to remain with me for a long time after that day.

When I first saw her that afternoon in 1963 she appeared much older than she was. The illness which was then in its second month had drained her face and her blindness had returned to remain for two further days. She looked quite small sitting there in her bamboo chair and her hands, laid on her lap, were veined and delicate. She held them up at one point to make some comment in the conversation and I noticed that it was possible to see the light around the edges of her fingers and thumbs. I did not know then that she had once been described, by allies and enemies, as a dangerous woman.

She was obviously pleased in a quiet way that I had come to see her because she enjoyed conversing in her good but painstaking English. We remained for a couple of hours, trying to tie up fragments of her memories of England to the places that I knew. At one point I mentioned the Channel Islands and for a moment her face lightened to a smile. 'Have you ever been to the Channel Island of Chausey?' she asked eagerly. 'It is the only one of the islands that is still French. The English have taken the rest long ago.'

Not only had I not been to Chausey, I had never heard of it. The smile remained with her. 'Not many people know,' she said in a playful whisper. 'We Normans keep it a secret. Go there one day. It is delightful. I went there once.'

If I imagined that this might be the opening of some reminiscence I was mistaken, at least for that day. But three days later, with my doctor friend, I once again drove to the bamboo house by the sea and there she was still, sitting, staring out to the horizon she could no longer see. Her eyes were a good deal improved that day, however, and we had a very cheerful afternoon during which we ceremoniously drank Chinese tea and ate colonial French *pâtisserie*. After talking for a while she rose and said: 'I will show you something I have hidden, like a secret. I do not show it to many people in New Caledonia. In some way it does not belong here in the Pacific.'

With that she went gracefully into the cool house and returned with a small leather case which she opened to reveal a medal. On the face of it was the two-barred cross of Lorraine. It was, she said proudly, *La Médaille de la Résistance*, awarded only to members of the French underground movement.

Naturally I asked her questions about her part in the movement, but she politely declined to enlarge on it, merely showing how pleased she was that I had enjoyed seeing the medal. However, I was conscious that she wanted to tell me something, something connected with England and with the medal, and I was right. On my third visit to her house, the day before I was due to fly from Noumea, she quite abruptly began to tell me the story.

'I was one of the first agents of Free France to be landed in my country after the German Occupation, you know,' she said, glancing to see my reaction. 'I was with an Englishman. A man codenamed Dodo. His real name was Ormerod, George Ormerod. He was a policeman. It was only September 1940, just a few weeks after the British deserted from Dunkirk.'

My journalist's desire not to spoil a good story prevented me from querying this version of history. I was glad because the next thing she said was: 'The Englishman was a London policeman. I was going to make a check on possible resistance groups in Normandy, to help to form them and organize them, because these were very early days and little had been done to oppose the Germans. My companion was going to Paris to arrest a murderer.'

It was one of those moments when you swallow but say nothing. She went on: 'We were landed by a British submarine on that same island of Chausey which I mentioned to you the other day. It was necessary to kill some of the enemy. After that the Germans very kindly put us ashore on the mainland and we had a strange and dangerous journey through France to Paris. We did not always – how do you say it? – "get on" very well because we were both so different. He was a petit bourgeois, a Conservative and a policeman as well, and I was a radical, I suppose almost a Communist in those days. But we lived together, sometimes very dangerously, for some weeks, and there was a feeling, a bond, between us. I often think of him now,' she laughed. 'He was so ... old fashioned.'

'And he was going to Paris to find a *murderer*?' I asked incredulously. *'Paris?'*

'Yes Paris, with all the Germans there. But he was very determined and one-minded about it. Just as I was about my mission. Very often the two objects got in each other's way. And he did not like killing Germans.'

At this point she took the story from the start and talked for about two hours about this strangest of adventures. I was almost conscious of my eyes widening as she related the tale. Viewed now it seems extraordinary. But she spoke of unusual times.

When she had finished – and after a long pause and silence – I told her I would like to write something about it and saw immediately how the alarm jumped to her face. 'Oh no, please Monsieur,' she remonstrated. 'I am telling you because you are English and in many ways it is an English story. Not because I want you to write it. That would be terrible.'

Every journalist knows the sinking feeling when someone blithely tells him they know of a plan to steal the Crown Jewels, or blow up Parliament, and then pleads with him to keep it confidential. But it was impossible for me not to agree. I promised I would write nothing and she believed me and thanked me. Then she said: 'One day perhaps you can tell it. When I am dead.' Then she smiled that distant smile, a smile apparently intended for someone far away beyond the horizon, and added: 'But first you must find George Ormerod – my English policeman – and ask him too.'

I returned to England and pushed the story from my mind, certainly from any professional point of view. After all it was only one amazing thing in the war when many amazing things had happened every day before breakfast. At first, however, from private curiosity, I checked the name and history of Detective-Sergeant George Ormerod in the records of the Metropolitan Police. He was there all right but with no clue to the extraordinary escapade of 1940. He retired in 1965 with a pat and a pension.

But that was as far as I took it. After all, I had a promise to keep.

Then last summer in Paris I went to the Museum of the Order of the Liberation in the Boulevard Latour-Maubourg, a poignant collection of mementoes of the Occupation of France and the Resistance Movement. On a day when I have no doubt the Louvre was crowded and people were frenetically ascending and descending the Eiffel Tower, I was the only visitor in that sad gallery. Marie-Thérèse Velin had returned to my thoughts.

That evening, on the impulse, I took a train to Granville in Normandy, where Marie-Thérèse and George Ormerod, those odd companions, were so obligingly landed by the Germans. In a bar by the harbour the following night I saw what I next sought, a group of blue-overalled fishermen, middle-aged to elderly, the sort who looked as if they had been in the town in the wartime days.

After a few cognacs and some general conversation, I tried the subject. Casually I said: 'I met a Frenchwoman a few years ago in New Caledonia. Her name was Marie-Thérèse Velin. She told me she had come here to Granville during the war as a Free French agent.'

It was first time lucky. Immediately the expressions changed, especially that of one of the older men. The others looked at him oddly. 'The Dove,' he muttered. 'She was called the Dove. Her name is not popular in this place.' He shook his heavy, grey head and swallowed the rest of his cognac.

'I was here then, in Granville,' he confirmed. 'We had returned defeated from the war and she came here and she wanted us to fight. There was no sympathy for fighting, you understand. France was crushed, in pieces. The Germans were here. And she wanted us to fight! She was brave, I suppose, but she was dangerous, Monsieur, very dangerous. We are not fond of her memory.'

He put his elderly, wooden hand on my shoulder and led me to the door overlooking the stone harbour. It was two in the morning and there were a few doleful lights along the quay. 'Over there,' pointed the fisherman. 'Where the third light is. That is the place where she landed in Granville. The mad thing is the Germans brought her themselves. In their own boat!'

'I know,' I said. 'She told me. There was an Englishman with her.'

He nodded. 'A decent man,' he shrugged. 'I don't know why they sent him.'

He closed the door against the night on the harbour and we went inside again. There were more cognacs at the bar. It was obvious that he was going to tell me his version of the story and he did. The others listened, making the occasional comment and observation, but in the main listening like children who know a tale by heart but are fascinated to hear it again. When he had finished we were all silent and I was looking through the bottom of my glass. 'She is back in France now,' he concluded to my surprise. 'She is dead you know. She is buried in her village near Mortagne in the Perche country of Normandy. There are some people here in Granville who would have seen her in her grave a long time ago.'

In the September of that year, by now fascinated with the story of the Dove and Dodo, I returned to Normandy and attempted to retrace the journey they took in 1940. It was the same season, the countryside was full and brown with the harvest, cider apples were red in the orchards, and the misty mornings gave way to delicate days.

Although there were, naturally, some changes in the landscape, they were easily detectable and my surroundings on those autumn days must have been much as theirs would have been. The battles of the summer of 1940 had stopped west of Dunkirk, when the French had surrendered, and from Granville through the Bocage region and the Perche, Normandy was physically unscarred. Four years later the time for battle came in that countryside. In 1940, war or no war, the harvest still needed to be gathered and the cider apples brought to the presses. The French defeat had not stopped the flowers blooming or prevented the trees turning gold. But the land was full of weary soldiers returning, relieved but betrayed, to their homes. For them the war was over.

At the end of this journey I went to the village cemetery at St Luc-au-Perche, south-west of Mortagne, and without trouble found the dignified tombstone of Marie-Thérèse Velin sitting quietly amid all the model-village vaults in which the French take such a morbid delight. The inscription gives merely her name and the dates 1914 to 1966. An impatient rush of September leaves came across the stone as I was reading it. I felt a certain strangeness in this little Normandy cemetery in the autumn evening. I bent forward to brush away the leaves from her name but a fresh touch of wind did it for me. It seemed a long way from the Pacific Ocean.

The death of Marie-Thérèse Velin had released me from my promise not to write her story, but now it was necessary to seek out George Ormerod and, if possible, to persuade him to tell his part of the adventure.

It is rarely a complex matter to discover the whereabouts of a former policeman. The force tends to keep a general eye on the movements of its retired members if for no other reason than paternal concern for their welfare. It took me only a day to find that Ormerod, now in his early seventies, was living with his wife Sarah in a block of maisonettes especially designed for elderly people at Stevenage in Hertfordshire.

The following morning I drove north from London and had no difficulty in finding Abacus Court, Stevenage, a well-planned area with the old people's accommodation – maisonettes for couples and bed-sitting rooms for single residents – grouped around a sheltered garden.

It appeared that ex-policeman Ormerod never availed him-

self of any of the communal amenities offered by the establishment, preferring to stay within his own solid front door.
His wife was a semi-invalid and the other residents rarely saw
her. Ormerod himself would sometimes walk to the local inn,
The Antelope, stay half an hour and then return. He also did
the couple's shopping and took their washing to the launder-
ette in the High Street.

Having reconnoitred, I decided on the frontal approach, but
with some apprehension. Ormerod having been a cautious
policeman, and now a virtual recluse, would hardly stand in-
dulging in a chummy chat. It would be necessary for me to
tell him my business clearly and quickly. I rang the bell. He
took two minutes to answer it. He must have been on the
lavatory because I heard the flush go. When he arrived at the
door and opened it he was still tucking his old-fashioned striped
flannel shirt around his trouser top. 'What is it?' he asked
uncompromisingly.

He was a tall man and upright too. He had obviously been
broad in his time, although age had withered him down. The
grey hair was cut very close around his powerful head. The
face was lined but he had a good healthy look about him for
someone who, by reputation, rarely went out. Perhaps he sat
in the sun by an open window. His eyes were pale, almost as
grey as his hair. He had all his own teeth. 'I want to ask you
about France in 1940,' I said baldly.

His eyes lifted and he started to say something, then stopped
as if he could not frame the words. Then he said 'Bugger off,'
and closed the door in my face.

From my reporter's experience I knew that a second knock
would either go unanswered or would result in an even ruder
dismissal. I went away. For an hour I sat in the pub, The
Antelope, and thought about it before retracing the way to
Abacus Court. I rang at his bell and he came to the door
angrily as if he had been waiting in ambush. 'I told you to
bugger off ...' he began.

Quickly I said: 'I have seen Marie-Thérèse Velin.'

That stopped him. His face changed. My hopes rose. He
glanced behind him into the room. 'Can you come out?' I
suggested quickly.

14

'Of course I can,' he replied roughly. 'It's not a bloody prison.' His voice went quiet. 'There's a pub called The Antelope. I'll be in there about seven tonight.'

I heard a woman's voice from within. He closed the door on me without a further word.

By seven o'clock I had been in The Antelope for half an hour. I was sitting in a corner but Ormerod spotted me as soon as he came in. I started to get to my feet but he ignored me and went straight to the bar and ordered a pint of ordinary bitter. The barman recognized him and nodded a 'good evening' but he was obviously known as a customer who did not indulge in a lot of conversation. The beer was drawn and Ormerod, after taking a first drink from the top of the tankard, turned and came directly towards me. He sat down and put the drink on the table in front of him. He did not look into my face. Staring to the front he said abruptly: 'All right. When did you see her?'

'Some time ago,' I replied cautiously. If I had told him how long ago I thought he would probably have got up and walked out. 'I'm sorry to tell you she is dead now,' I said. 'She is buried in France. In Normandy.'

He nodded. 'At St Luc-au-Perche,' he said, pronouncing it awkwardly. 'Yes, she would be.' He drank some beer. 'She wasn't very old,' he said thoughtfully. 'She was nine years younger than me, you know.' He added a nostalgic word – 'Then.' His more conversational tone gave me hope. It was his first sign of friendliness.

'I met her in New Caledonia,' I said. 'A few years ago.'

'Where's New Caledonia when it's at home?' he asked. 'Can't say I've ever heard of it.'

'It's a French island in the Pacific,' I told him.

'Yes, she would,' he said thinking about it. 'She always said she wouldn't be able to live in France unless it all changed.'

I nodded. 'She was a governess for a group of French families,' I said.

'How was she then?' he asked suddenly. He looked at me awkwardly. 'How did she look?' There was almost an embarrassing tenderness about the question.

'She was ill,' I told him carefully. 'In fact she had periods of blindness. It was a temporary sort of thing, some tropical disease. But she was very nice. Small, neat. Like she was in the days when they called her the Dove, I suppose,' I said that purposely.

He smiled slightly. 'The Dove,' he repeated. He took a reflective drink from his tankard. 'You seem to have gone into this a bit thoroughly,' he said. 'Did she tell you much?'

'A good deal,' I nodded. 'But I promised her I would do nothing about it while she was alive. I've been in France and I've seen her grave, and I've been to the bell foundry at Villedieu and to Bagnoles de l'Orne and the Catacombs in Paris.'

At once he looked at me with some alarm. 'What do you mean you "wouldn't do anything about it"?' he inquired suspiciously. 'What's that all about? What are you thinking of doing about it?'

'I'm a writer,' I said simply. 'I want to write the story.'

'Christ,' he muttered. 'You won't get anything from me, son. Not a bloody word.'

'Why not?' I pressed. 'It's all a long time ago. You came out of it with great credit. In fact, it looks to me that you didn't get the recognition you deserved. What's your objection?'

'To start with,' he said, his voice a hard monotone, 'it was a complete balls-up.' He paused. His glass was almost drained. He sensed that I was about to offer him a drink and he shook his head. 'I don't want anything written,' he said. 'And that's that. Final. I was married then to the same wife I've still got. She's a sick woman and I don't want to see it in print that I went to France and killed people and especially that I went with this other woman. That would upset her.'

'Even now?' I tried. 'After all this time?'

'Even now,' he said. 'A lifetime's only short. And for us it's not all that long ago. I don't want her to know. Understand?'

'How did you manage to keep it from her the last time?' I challenged hollowly.

'Told her I was going on a special police course,' he said.

Astonished, I said: 'You mean you could go to France, go all through that, all the killing and everything, and come back and act as if you'd been to school?'

'I could and I did,' he said firmly. 'And that's how it's going to be.' He got up and I knew there was nothing I would be able to do to stop him going. 'If you want to write your story,' he said with almost a sneer, 'you'll have to wait until I'm dead too.'

For two weeks I left the matter to rest. There seemed little I could do. Then, as a last throw, I wrote to George Ormerod asking him to reconsider the matter, pledging that he could read the written manuscript and make any changes he wished to make, and offering him a thousand pounds for his co-operation. I told him that this would be a fee for his services, for I would need to have some extended tape-recorded sessions with him, but I guessed that, even knowing him as little as I did, his policeman's instinct would be to smell it as a bribe.

It was no surprise, therefore, when only silence followed the letter. I had to console myself with the thought that one day I would be able to write the story, albeit only from the version related to me by Marie-Thérèse and by my own inquiries in France. But even without his side of the story, that would have to wait until George Ormerod was dead.

Then three months later he wrote to me in the mannered way with which I was to become familiar. 'My wife died on Nov. 23rd,' the letter said. 'We had been married since September 7th, 1939, four days after the outbreak of the hostilities with Hitler. Since she has gone I have occupied myself with writing an account of what happened to me and to Madame Marie-Thérèse Velin in North France and Paris in 1940. It is quite long, about a hundred pages, and is true as far as I can properly remember. In those days, in France, of course I could not keep a diary in case I was captured by the enemy, but when I returned to England I privately wrote up the whole thing and kept it hidden. It is from the notes I made then that I have done this new account. I have also written up the circumstances which took place in this country before going to France in September 1940. There are also a few old photographs.

'My niece and her husband are coming back from Canada to buy a house at Chelmsford and they want me to go and live with them. I don't want to go to them empty handed and I don't have any money except my pension. So I will take the one thousand pounds you offer me in return for all the notes I have. But this is all there is and I do not want to make any tape recordings. If you agree, send the money and I promise to send the information by return. If you think it fair I would also like to ask for another five hundred pounds if the book you write is a success.'

It was a plain man's letter, very touching in its directness and simplicity. At once I sent a reply with a cheque and waited eagerly for the return package. It arrived within four days. I opened it. His account was held in a loose-leaf binder, a hundred pages of close handwriting. On the cover he had pasted a gummed label upon which was written: 'Journal of some Operations in German Occupied France 1940.' I held it as if someone had sent me the Holy Grail. Then two envelopes fell from the binder. The first contained a dozen or more photographs of himself, Marie-Thérèse and other people all taken in France. Almost breathlessly I picked them up one by one, touching the edges only. They were brown and not very expertly taken but they were more than I could have ever hoped for. Marie-Thérèse in a baggy dress carrying a sub-machine gun; Ormerod sitting at the entrance to a cave; Ormerod and Marie-Thérèse on Chausey Island sitting in the sun; and then, heaven help me, a friendly photograph of a cheerful German staff officer with the caption hand-written on the back: 'General Wolfgang Groemann at Bagnoles. Just before he was killed. A good man.'

The second envelope contained a brief note. It said: 'Thank you for the money. This is all the stuff there is. Please do not contact me again unless the book is a success and you want to send me the other five hundred.'

two

George Ormerod's journal, from which I have reconstructed the singular adventures of the Dodo and the Dove, began like this:

'In September 1939, I was a Detective-Sergeant in the Criminal Investigation Department of the Metropolitan Police (V Division) covering the south-west area of London, Wandsworth and Putney. When the war was declared I got married (September 7th) to Sarah Ann Billington and right away volunteered for the army. On 20th September I was called up to the Royal Artillery and I went to Woolwich for training and later to Aldershot to await drafting with the British Expeditionary Force to the Western Front in France.

'Nothing very much seemed to be happening in the war (this was called the Phoney War period) and in February of 1940 I was discharged from the army because the London police force was finding itself short of experienced men and it was thought better that I should be doing a job for which I was suited.

'So on February 8th, I left the army with a good character and went back to the CID. I got a flat in Fulham and Sarah, who was working in a solicitor's office at Putney, and I settled down there. I was glad to be back in the police because I was always devoted to the work. They used to say I was dogged and I still am. Once I get my teeth into something there is not much that can make me let go. This is what happened in the case of the murder of Lorna Smith, but it is the way I am made and it was the way I saw my work. In fact you could say that this particular murder case became so important to me that it put everything else out of my mind for months, even the war.

'Lorna Smith was a decent girl of eighteen who was found dead in the mud on the banks of the Thames, not far from Wandsworth Bridge on March 18th, 1940. She had been brutally raped and murdered, strangled with one of her own stockings. I knew the girl personally and also her parents. They kept a grocer's shop and dairy at Fulham. I have never seen two people so distressed in my life. I thought they would never get over it. For myself, I was livid, plain bloody angry, that this young girl's life should be snuffed out by some animal who couldn't control himself. God knows there were enough whores operating in London at that time, you could hardly move for them in the West End, so why he had to take it out on a decent-living kid like that, don't ask me.

'I got myself assigned to the case, on account of knowing the family, and for weeks I hardly stopped working even to eat or sleep. Sarah, my wife, got very upset about it. She thought it was something else. (She was always a shade suspicious because she'd had some dealings with the CID in her work at the solicitors and she did not have all that high opinion of their morals.) I remember she said to me one night when I got home pale and played out: "Are you sure it's not a living girl that's taking up all your time?" That was the nearest time I ever came to hitting her in all our years of marriage.

'About the middle of May I got a strong lead. A soldier stationed at the camp in Richmond Park got drunk in the Queen's Head pub in Kingston-on-Thames one night and a barmaid overheard him say he knew who had done the killing of Lorna Smith. She reported what she had heard and the next night I went to the pub myself, bought this soldier three or four Scotches (I said I wanted to do something for the war effort) and then took him to Putney police station for questioning.

'He was a pimply little bastard called Braithwaite, a private in the Catering Corps, though I wouldn't have liked him to cook my dinner. At first, naturally, even though he was drunk, he denied ever making the remarks about Lorna Smith. Then he admitted he had said it but was telling lies, just trying to make an impression on his listeners. I was not going to have that. I had come too far to stop now. All I had to do was close my eyes and see that girl lying on the mortuary slab and remember her father having to identify her and my blood boiled.

'So I leaned on Braithwaite, not brutally (of course) but enough to make him change his mind again. He started to cry. He must have been a great soldier, but I suppose they took all sorts in those days. And he sobbed it all out. One night in the billet in Richmond Park, the soldier in the next bed had come in late and drunk and had fallen down at the side of the bed and started to pray to God for forgiveness for doing somebody to death. Most of the others in the barrack room were asleep – it was a Thursday which was pay night and they'd all been out to the pubs – and only Braithwaite remembered it in the morning. Even he had not taken much notice until he read in the *Evening News* that the girl had been murdered.

'But he did not do anything about it, although he noticed that the other man was very pale and unusually quiet for about a week. This man was a soldier called Albert Smales, twenty-six, formerly a labourer of Preston in Lancashire, who, incidentally, had a long police record for violence against women and girls. About two weeks after the murder Smales had put himself forward to volunteer for a draft to France with the British Expeditionary Force, was accepted and went within the next few days.

'Right away I applied for permission to go to France and see the man, but my superiors were all horror-struck. There was a war on, they pointed out, and a war that was just beginning to liven up. The Germans had begun to attack all along the front and they were breaking through in Belgium. If we wanted Smales questioned then let the army Special Investigation Branch do it. There was no chance of my going.

'In the end a request was put in to the SIB office of the military police in France where it must have raised a laugh, because by this time the army was a bit of a shambles, pulling back towards Dunkirk, and nobody knew where anybody was. To try and pick up one man, no matter what he was accused of, was impossible and they said so. Very rudely I recall.

'All I could do was to fret around getting on everybody's nerves, my colleagues, my wife, and even, I regret to say, Lorna Smith's parents. Everybody seemed to want to close the business except me. I wasn't going to let it drop. In the end I got permission to go to Preston to see Smales' family – a right collection. All the male members had done time for something or other, the sister was on the streets and the mother had a go at that when a customer turned up who was not all that particular. I obtained from them a picture of Albert Smales in uniform (well, truthfully, I lifted it from their mantelpiece, but I thought anything was fair with that class of people), and on the way back south in the train I kept taking out that photograph in its frame and staring at it. A clergyman got in at Crewe and, thinking I was looking at a picture of my soldier brother, the silly old fool said he would pray for him. The bastard needed somebody to pray for him.

'To me Dunkirk was even more of a miracle than it was to most people. Here was fate bringing my quarry right back to me, if he was alive, which I thought he was because they never got themselves killed in battle, that sort. As soon as they began to bring the soldiers back from the beaches I asked for permission to go down to Dover, Folkestone and other places on the coast to try and pick up Smales.

'This request was met with a very sharp refusal and all the usual catch-phrases like "Don't you know there's a war on?" and they sent me out to look for German spies and parachutists disguised as old ladies and vicars. (There was even a ridiculous rumour went round at this time that the enemy had dropped midgets in children's clothes to act as saboteurs. Some lunatic seriously suggested that I should go around the playgrounds and the parks looking for Nazi dwarfs.)

'I was much more interested in finding a full-grown murderer. I tried again with my bosses but now they turned really nasty and the Detective-Superintendent, a man called Lowe, blew me up and said that I only had it on hearsay that Smales had anything to do with it at all, now would I bugger off and look for fifth columnists.

'That decided me. I took some leave I had due to me and under my own steam I went down to the south coast where there were camps for all the men who had disembarked from Dunkirk. You never saw such a shambles. If the Germans had followed them they would have been in London by midday. And all the fuss! Everybody patting everybody on the back as if it were a great victory instead of a defeat. You'd have thought they had all swum back.

'Anyway for three days I had no dice at all. I went to all sorts of camps and army offices making my inquiries. The reactions I got varied from complete indifference to nasty tempers. How dare I look around for an ordinary, unimportant murderer, when the whole future of civilization was at stake? That sort of blind attitude. There they all were drinking their millions of cups of tea and eating their sandwiches provided by middle-aged ladies who wanted to kill Hitler, but nobody knew nor cared about Private Smales.

'Eventually, on the last day of my leave, I had some luck. I discovered the unit he had been attached to and right away I found that some men from that unit were in hospital in Canterbury. So off to Canterbury I went, taking with me cigarettes and apples, the sort of thing it was fashionable to give to soldiers in those days.

'I flashed my police warrant card about a bit but it was only grudgingly that they let me into the hospital. They did not think that any business I might have had could be important enough. The war seemed to have dulled people's idea of simple public duty. I know the murder of Lorna Smith was not as glamorous as Dunkirk but, to me, it was more important. After all Dunkirk had now all been cleared up. This case had not.

'But my luck had turned. There was a soldier in one of the beds, a boy only about eighteen, who had what looked like a nasty hole in the top of his arm, and it was he who told me about Smales. "Didn't like him," he said after I had shown him the photograph. "Nasty bully type of bloke. Throwing his weight about, getting drunk, even reckoning he'd done people in."

' "He said that?" I said, trying not to sound too eager. "Can you remember what he said about it?" He looked at me in a funny way and then shook his head. "No, nothing definite. Nobody believed him anyway, just general bragging, like. And he didn't hang around to do any of the killing when the bleeding Jerries arrived. He just hopped it."

' "Deserted did he?" I said. This gave me some sort of funny hope that the military would give me a bit more assistance.

' "Yes," said the lad. "Cleared off about the third week in May when it was getting nasty. I don't know how he got away or where he went. Paris, I expect. The dodgers always went to Paris."

'I talked to him for another half an hour, trying to get something more from him. But it was not much use and after that the ward sister came along and started to get shirty with me for plugging away at the boy. So I left him all the cigarettes and apples I had brought and made to go out. It was not much use because from the door I saw the sister taking them away from him. She came charging down the ward after me and shoved the lot into my arms again. "Take these with you," she said, really nasty. "He can't smoke and he can't eat apples."

' "Oh all right," I said, a bit hurt. "Why can't he?"

'She looked very annoyed. "Because he's got a bullet lodged in his lung, that's why," she sort of rasped at me. "If I'd known you were from the police I wouldn't have allowed you to talk to him at all. You've exhausted him. *You* ought to try being in the army. Can't think why you're not anyway."

'This was the trouble with people in those days, you see. Unless you had a uniform they thought you ought to be tarred and covered with white feathers. Nobody ever stopped to think that if the police did not act normally while everybody else was playing soldiers then there would be a lot more Lorna Smiths lying dead in the mud around the country.

'As I went away with my apples and cigarettes I was feeling disappointed, thinking that I was even further from getting Smales. Even if he had returned from Dunkirk then I had no more leave to find him. If he had stayed in France then he would soon be in a nice cosy prison camp for the rest of the war, doing fretwork and body-building. He wasn't the type to escape and certainly being inside was no change for him.

'I had to go back to everyday police work, checking up on stolen ration books, questioning people who were reckoned to be signalling to enemy aircraft by opening their blackout curtains. Thrilling stuff like that. And there was, of course, the unending excitement of checking little old ladies and vicars to make sure they didn't have concealed guns or bombs.

'In July I managed to get permission, after a lot of trying, to go back to Preston to interview Smales' family again. This time the journey took the best part of three days there and back and I was only in their house for twenty minutes. But I got something for my trouble. His mother, who wasn't too sure what was going on in the world, being a touch simple, let it out that they had received word from the Red Cross that their Albert was a prisoner-of-war and in a military hospital somewhere in France, but she did not know where.

'After that there did not seem very much I could do. I mooched around the army camp at Richmond Park and in the pubs in Kingston but it seemed that everybody was getting fed up with me and Lorna Smith. We were being a nuisance. Nobody seemed to care but me. My superiors even told me straight out to drop the case until after the war. And, in addition, it was very difficult to go asking questions around anywhere that particular summer, especially at military establishments. Twice I was arrested by the army police on suspicion of espionage.

'Then came one of those twists of fate which change people's lives. In July 1940 there was a conference being held at the Military Staff College at Camberley in Surrey and all sorts of high-ups were there. Every day we expected the Germans to invade, although I personally did not, and this conference was to discuss resistance operations to be carried out if the enemy occupied Southern England. It seemed funny to think of the Germans taking over Kent and Surrey, although in the odd way I was thinking about things just then, it did cross my mind that if they did occupy this country then at least France and Britain would be under the same umbrella, so to speak, and it might well be easier to get Smales. I know it seems amazing now that I should have thought like that, but I certainly did, I remember clearly. Naturally I kept it to myself. If I'd have mentioned it to anybody I'm sure they would have put me in the Tower of London for treason.

'Anyway, at this Staff College conference there was naturally a lot of security and I was given the job of keeping an eye on a man called Brigadier Elvin Clark during the off-duty time. He stayed at the Staff College but he went out to Virginia Water to dinner in a hotel a couple of times and once he got off early in the afternoon to have a game of golf. I can't say I was looking forward to this a lot because it was my job to stay with him all the time and I didn't fancy traipsing around a golf course. But there was nothing for it so I set out with him and the caddy. There was nobody else playing and he said he did not mind because he quite enjoyed going around by himself. I made a bit of a joke about it, I remember, telling him that at least in that way you didn't get beaten. He asked me if I had played golf and I said I hadn't although I had played football for the Metropolitan Police team before the war.

'It was a warm July evening and it was strange out there on the green fairways to think that the Germans had been sending over bombers all day and the sky had been full of dog fights. Even now the vapour trails of the Spitfires and Hurricanes were drifting in the blue sky and a Nazi Dornier had crashed that afternoon only half a mile from where we were. The Brigadier never talked about the war at all (I suppose he was tired of it already) but only about golf and his home and his family in Scotland.

'After a while he began to ask me about my police work and, almost by accident it seemed (although in my state of mind it was more or less bound to come out, I suppose), I started to tell him about Lorna Smith and my efforts to get the man Smales. The Brigadier was a man who listened intently, I could see that, even when he was playing golf shots, which he did pretty well as far as I could see with an inexpert eye. Then, like the intelligence officer he was, he began to ask me questions about the case and my feelings towards it. It was like a cross-examination in the witness box and I had to think very carefully about my replies.

'"Where is this man in hospital?" he asked.

'"I don't know," I said. "All I know is he's a prisoner and he's in hospital in France. He's safe for a while anyway."

'For a quarter of an hour he did not speak. Even I could see he knew how to play the game well and he did not take many strokes over the par. "And you'd still like to get at this man, would you?" he went on eventually, as if we had never interrupted the conversation. It was a statement, quietly put, more than a question. I thought it was just something to say.

'"I'd say I would," I answered.

'"Why is that?" he asked shrewdly.

'I was a bit shaken. "Well ... well to start with, I'm sure he killed that girl," I began. "I want to get him for that. I want him brought to court."

' "But surely there are one or two murderers, maybe even more, running around loose today," he said to me. "And they're get-at-able, here in this country. Why not go after one of them?"

'I was not sure how to answer. "This is my case, sir." I hesitated. "And I don't like to be beaten. I think crime should be punished. I'm a bit of a puritan like that."

' "What about after the war?" he said, putting the ball right into the hole from all of twenty feet. He hardly paused in his talking. "Don't you think that with things as they are you ought to get your mind off it? After all the Germans could be playing this hole in a month's time." He paused again, then decided to go on. "Do you think it's a sort of frustration because you're not serving in the army?"

' "A sort of guilt you mean?" I said, knowing he did mean that. "Well it might look like that, I admit."

'He had played the last hole. He scratched his nose with his putter. "I mean," he said turning away, "how do you feel about the war? Does it worry you?"

'The questions were confusing me. "Yes sir," I answered. "Of course I worry like everybody else. I read the papers and I hear the news. I mean, I wouldn't like us to lose."

' "But you're not actually taking much part." It was funny, I thought, he was so persistent. We were walking towards the club house and he asked me to go in with him for a drink. "Who *is* taking part at the moment?" I asked, probably a bit rudely because he had touched a tender spot. "As far as I can see we're all sitting here, just waiting."

' "Right," he agreed sportingly. "You've got a point Ormerod. Not many of us are fighting just now. Except the chaps up there in the Spitfires. But don't mind my saying so please – it just seems from what you've been telling me that the war itself is a trifle ... well ... remote ... yes, remote, from you."

' "You could say that," I agreed moodily in the end. Then I thought I might as well say it. "Albert Smales is my war." '

Two weeks after his conversation with Brigadier Elvin Clark, Superintendent Lowe of Wandsworth police station called Ormerod into his office and amazed him by telling him that a confidential message had been sent to the division requesting that Detective-Sergeant George Ormerod should report to a department at the War Office on the following day.

'What have you been up to?' the Superintendent said, eyeing him cagily from the desk. 'All this top secret stuff. You've got to see this Brigadier Clark. He was the one you kept an eye on during the Staff College conference wasn't it?'

Ormerod shrugged. 'That's him, sir,' he said. 'Can't think what he wants. Probably thinks I'll make a good batman or caddy. I traipsed around the golf course with him. He'll have another think coming if that's what he's after. God, I could hardly walk for a week after that.'

'Well, he wants to see you, so you'd better go,' Lowe laughed. 'This could be one of those things when we don't see you until after the war George. You'd better pay the tea club and empty your locker.'

'The tea club's paid and there's nothing in my locker except a spare pair of shoes. I don't keep a lot there. After all, you never know when you might not return from Battersea Park in this job.'

The Superintendent frowned. 'Oh come on, George. We're doing as much as we can. It's not very spectacular, I know, police work, but people still steal, kids still go missing, and the peace, such as we have, has got to be maintained.' He stood and thrust his head towards Ormerod, like a bull. 'Most of the manpower of this country is now sitting on its arse waiting to see if the Germans make the next move. Personally I'd strike back now, while they're taking a breather. Invade in the Brittany area, around Brest. Get around the back of the bastards. Strike first.'

Lowe was one of those who really believed it, despite the fact that at that moment elderly men in quiet hamlets where there had been no violence since the Conqueror were sharpening pitchforks and seriously hoping to annihilate a Panzer division. Ormerod had no inclination to argue, indeed he was not sure he did not agree. He went out and took his spare shoes from his locker, just in case, and then went home.

On the following morning he took the underground to Westminster. He was early so he walked through the park to the War Office. The bombing of London had not started in earnest for the Luftwaffe were attacking Biggin Hill and other airfields from which the British fighter planes were taking off to intercept the bombers. It was a promising summer morning with the trees and flower beds shining with sun and freshness. There were pyramids of sandbags all around. The pelicans squatted ponderously on the lake. Around the park were anti-aircraft guns and people walked about, their gasmasks either in oblong cases like picnic boxes or in tubular tins. Policemen wore their newly-issued, cumbersome revolvers a little selfconsciously.

Although he was a Metropolitan policeman, Ormerod never felt at home in Central London. He was never sure where anything was for a start. He produced his warrant card, asked a policeman the whereabouts of the War Office and was treated to a supercilious grin for not knowing. If he had asked at random, and without showing his authority, he might very well have been taken for one of the mythical German parachutists the entire nation was hunting.

There appeared to be a complete regiment guarding the War Office and it was some time before he could persuade anyone to let him in, although a cheerful milkman breezed right through the defences while Ormerod stood waiting; soldiers and policemen kept coming to have a look at him while he stood awkwardly in a waiting room, bare of any decoration except for a poster warning against careless talk which announced: 'Walls Have Ears.' He pursed his lips as though to stop himself divulging a thousand secrets.

A frowning corporal of military police came in. The man had a bright red face as if he were always shouting and a small moustache like gold wire.

'Department Four BX,' recited the corporal. 'That's where you're heading. Part of MIR, see. Military Intelligence Research. Got your authority, have you?'

The man knew full well that he had both his warrant card and the authorizing letter because he had already asked for them, and seen them, twice. Ormerod had also displayed them to numerous other security guards and officials, so faceless they could have been phantoms. 'It's getting worn out,' he observed to the corporal, handing the authority across. 'The paper's not all that thick.'

The military policeman had no concealed channel of humour. 'It should last,' he grunted. 'These sort of things are done on thin paper, you understand, in case they have to be destroyed. There might come a day when every bit in this building might have to be. Follow me.'

Ormerod went after him, conjuring a mental picture of the entire staff of the War Office frantically chewing thin secret paper in the face of an advancing German army. They went through many corridors hung with signs and arrows and across two large chambers where senior military men were talking in whispers, their voices hissing up to the tall ceilings.

They arrived at a lift which was not working because of the war and they had to walk up twelve flights of stone steps to reach the fourth floor. 'I'll come and fetch you to take you out again,' said the corporal stiffly as they walked by doors marked with titles like algebra problems. 'We don't like visitors memorizing their way around.'

'No, well you wouldn't, would you,' agreed Ormerod, puffing after the exertion of the stairs.

His escort gave a stiff sniff which hissed along the vacant corridor like the lash of a whip. They reached the second of two doors marked 'Four BX. Strictly No Entry' and the corporal knocked with what Ormerod thought might be a secret signal. The 'No Entry' sign was obviously another clever ruse to fool the enemy because the door opened quite easily and they went in.

Ormerod was relieved to see that, after the frigid aspect of the outer corridors and their denizens, this office was comfortingly untidy with two desks not quite in line or order, piles of paper and haphazard trays, one of which was loaded crazily with dirty tea cups. A cheerful girl clerk, with a pneumatic bosom almost rending the buttons of her uniform tunic, got up from the floor where she had been collecting the spilled contents of a box of paper clips. Ormerod took her in appreciatively as she got to her feet, red-faced and slightly out of breath. The escorting corporal said: 'This is Detective-

Sergeant Ormerod.' He hovered, apparently undecided whether he ought, after all, to leave Ormerod there. The girl decided him. 'Thank you, corporal,' she said sweetly. 'You can leave him with me. He'll be quite safe.'

'Oh yes,' blinked the corporal. He cast a last suspicious glance at Ormerod and then withdrew with military movements. Ormerod grinned sheepishly. 'I thought he might ask you to sign for me,' he said.

'Don't put ideas into their heads,' the girl pleaded. She looked around the polished floor. 'Now are there any more of these blessed clips down there? I'm always doing it. Knocking them down.'

'Put in for a magnet,' suggested Ormerod, bending and picking up two clips from behind the leg of the desk. 'Pick them all up more or less at once then. And you won't lose so many.'

The girl looked at him with some admiration. 'You know, I never thought of that,' she beamed. 'I will. I'll indent for a magnet. I expect they'll ask why, but it's going to save hundreds of man-hours, well woman-hours, during the whole war, isn't it? You're not a sort of boffin are you? One of those people they have in the special department? Not everyone would think of getting a magnet. I wouldn't for one. And this is supposed to be Intelligence, Four BX.'

'So I hear,' nodded Ormerod. 'But I'm not a boffin, whatever that might be. I'm a policeman.

'That's right. Of course you are. Well, in your job, you obviously have to think logically as well, don't you?' She wrote down the word 'Magnet' on a pad. 'Brigadier Clark will see you in a minute. He's got a Frenchman in there at the moment. You should see all his medals. Acres of them. You wouldn't think they'd lost. Would you like some tea?'

Ormerod eyed the cups and she saw him doing it. 'You'll get a clean cup,' she promised. 'Don't take any notice of those.'

'Oh, all right. Thanks,' said Ormerod. 'What are they there for then? Those cups? Another booby trap for the Germans?' She grinned at him. He said: 'They come in here, dying for a cup of tea, drink out of one of the poisoned cups and urgh! Another Hun dead.'

'You know that's not a bad idea,' she said, busying herself

with a teapot. She took two clean cups from a cupboard and held them up so he could see. 'Perhaps we could extend it. Open all the cafes along the south coast and fill them with dirty cups. The Germans land, rush for a cup of tea at the Bognor Esplanade Tea Rooms, and they're wiped out to a man. Not bad.'

'Make sure all the pubs open when they land,' contributed Ormerod. 'The beer's like poison now, anyway. That should take care of the ones that don't drink tea.'

The inner door opened to destroy the fantasy. A tall man in the uniform of the Free French Forces came out of the room followed by Brigadier Clark. Both men put their caps on and saluted each other, shook hands and then saluted each other again, a performance which, for some reason, acutely embarrassed Ormerod. He had uncertainly risen to his feet at the first salute, in the same way as he would have done had the National Anthem been played, half sat down at the handshake and then stood up again at the second salue. The Frenchman, only glancing at him, went out briskly and Brigadier Clark took off his cap and shook hands with the bewildered Ormerod who had thought that because he had put his cap on he was leaving the room. The officer saw the reason for his expression. 'Had to salute,' he said, motioning Ormerod into his office. 'So had to put the damned cap on. Can't salute without a cap you see.'

'Oh, that's right,' recalled Ormerod. 'I seem to remember now.'

'You didn't really have enough time in the army to get any rank did you?' said Brigadier Clark indicating a chair. He opened a folder and glanced inside. Ormerod stared at the folder as he sat down. The Brigadier balanced on the corner of his desk. He was a tall man and his feet were comfortably on the floor.

'Rank? Me? Oh, I rose to lance-bombardier,' said Ormerod.

Clark laughed good-humouredly. 'At least in the police force you've done a bit better than that,' he said. Then immediately, 'Are you sorry you're out of the army, Ormerod?'

Ormerod said : 'Well, to be honest, no sir.' Then he slowed and looked at the officer carefully. 'And anyway, I feel I'm doing a worthwhile job as I am. I mean we're all here together now, if you understand my meaning, sir. All besieged. If the Germans come we'll all be in the army won't we? They've given the police guns and that's not to direct the traffic is it?'

The answer obviously amused and satisfied Clark. He nodded and smiled and went around to the chair behind the desk. 'You won't have to worry,' he said. 'I'm not giving you your calling-up papers. Would you like some tea?'

Ormerod said yes for the second time in ten minutes. As if she had been eavesdropping the busty girl came in with a tray and poured two cups for them. They had sugar too, Ormerod observed, obviously part of the emergency rations in case of a siege. For the first time in months he took two lumps. He looked up guiltily but nobody seemed to mind. The Brigadier refused and Ormerod thought it was strange that the girl should have offered it to him. If she worked there she must have known that he did not take sugar. Then it occurred to him that he had taken the officer's lump as well. He felt embarrassed and even thought of fishing it out again. But it was already well dissolved.

There followed a difficult silence, the staff officer and the detective drinking tea from thick WD cups. It was an occupation that required complete attention at least until the heavy brown tea was lower than danger level. Once it was they could look at each other again. Embarrassed, they both looked up at the same moment. Clark seemed too shy to say something he wanted to say.

'Er ... played at all recently, sir?' Ormerod asked to fill the void.

'Played? Oh, golf. No. Well, not much. The war seems to be getting in the way. Just get a decent fourball arranged and dammit if there's not a red emergency from the coast or something. I'll wager if Jerry does turn up I shall be somewhere out on the fourteenth and by the time I get back the whole bloody show will be over.' He seemed relieved that Ormerod had given him a start. 'Ormerod,' he said. 'I've found out where your murderer chum is holed up. Wasn't all that difficult, actually.'

The policeman felt his eyebrows rise and his jaw drop. 'You have, sir?' he managed to say. 'Where would that be?'

Brigadier Clark pulled down a map of Europe on the wall

behind his desk. 'Right there,' he said pointing to the middle of Normandy. 'Bagnoles de l'Orne.'

He turned from the map to see, as he expected, Ormerod's astonishment. It appeared to embarrass him and he went back to the map again.

'Nice spot,' he mumbled. Then, more firmly, 'Was before the war anyway. Played golf there. Very genteel and so on, full of old ladies with bad legs and chaps with sticks, but that's what you get at a watering hole don't you? The water comes from the spring at a steady eighty-one degrees. Supposed to work miracles with various afflictions and aches. Story goes that years ago some farmer chap had a very old horse and rather than have it put down he sent it to die in the forest. Blow me if the brute didn't come back looking twenty years younger. He'd found the magic spring. The farmer followed him and bathed in the well with miraculous results. I took the waters there myself once, although I can't say it made me feel any younger. Very good for the feet though.' At once he looked directly at Ormerod across the desk. He said deliberately: 'You really ought to try it sometime.'

Baffled, Ormerod stared from his chair. The Brigadier saw his expression and looked sorry. 'Look Ormerod,' he said, rushing to the point. 'The real reason I invited you here today was to ask you if you'd like to take a trip off to Bagnoles de l'Orne to find your murderer.'

Now Ormerod was transfixed. He was certain the man had gone mad. 'Very nice idea, sir,' he said nervously. 'But ... the Germans. What about them?'

'We won't tell them,' smiled the Brigadier triumphantly. He saw the policeman's look of overwhelming consternation and held up a reassuring hand. 'No, no, I've not gone off my rocker. It's a serious plan. You would be doing something you have quite urgently wanted to do and also rendering a service to this country and to France – in fact to the world.'

Ormerod thought of the French officer going out. He remembered his sideways glance. Realization arrived coldly in his stomach. 'You want me to ... er go to France?' he said incredulously. 'Me?'

'Not alone,' said Clark. 'You'd be accompanied by a trained operator.'

'But *me*? I'm a London copper sir. Don't you have experienced agents and that sort of thing?'

'Trained, yes. A few. Experienced, no. There's not been much scope for experience has there? Europe's not been occupied up until now. The basic idea is that you are landed in France, Normandy or Brittany, and that you make your way to Paris by a prescribed route, contacting resistance groups, or potential groups, *if any*, and at the same time tracking down this man you so desperately want to apprehend.' He attempted an encouraging smile as though it were all simple. 'Your function would be almost one of bodyguard because the agent going with you is a young woman, a former schoolteacher from Normandy, who is a trained operator but needs some er ... well muscle ... she needs a man to go with her, although she won't admit that. We're trying to cobble together some sort of organization to operate in Europe, but frankly in the state we are in at the moment we cannot spare another trained man to go with her. It only needs one experienced person. You simply go to ... well, to be *with* her.'

'I see,' said Ormerod slowly. The wonder of it was still stunning him. 'You don't want to risk anyone *good*. But it's all right if it's me.'

'You're what they call "expendable",' Clarke nodded with sad honesty. 'This idea has been buzzing around in the trade for some time, ever since Dunkirk, but nobody wanted to sacrifice ... well, spare, two agents. And the girl is absolutely ideal. She comes from Normandy and she's fanatically French. She hates the Hun. Come to think of it she's not all that keen on us either. But she's a woman for all that. She needs a travelling companion.' He tried to beam encouragingly. 'And you wanted to go to France. Now's your chance.'

Clark took a file from the drawer of his desk. 'You're a good pistol shot, I see,' he said, looking at a sheet of paper from the file. 'You impressed the small arms instructor at Woolwich when you did your army training. And physically you seem to be in excellent condition. You have a policeman's mind, training and outlook. And your record with the force is quite out-standing. All plusses, Ormerod, all plusses. How's your French?'

Ormerod was now regarding him with new horror. The whole business seemed to be cut and dried, running out of control. 'French? Well ... not very good. *Merci, bonjour*, 'allo Mademoiselle. That's about the extent of it.'

The Brigadier smiled encouragingly. 'Well that's all right. After all the French are on *our* side. They'll be the only ones who'll notice. It's the Germans we must worry about and most of them won't speak French. Not the ordinary private soldier anyway. And if you ever get to officer level then the game's up with you anyway, so it won't matter either way. You don't speak German, I suppose?'

As though he was walking through a dream Ormerod said: 'I played football for the Metropolitan Police against the Berlin Police before the war and we had a return match in Germany. I tried to learn a bit of German for that. But it's mostly football like "goal" and "off-side" and "foul" ...'

'It might just come in useful, said Clark with frankly bogus optimism. 'Anyway we've settled that you're going, Ormerod.' It was not even a half question.

'Have we?' mumbled Ormerod. 'Well I suppose that's it then, isn't it. Right now I can't say I'm looking forward to it. I just wanted to catch a bloke that's done a crime, not take on the Master Race.'

Clark regarded him with professional seriousness. 'I want to tell you that you will be doing your country a great service. Churchill himself is right behind this, you'll be glad to hear.'

'Oh I am,' said Ormerod flatly. 'Ever so glad.'

'He has said that he wants to "set Europe alight". You could be the first match.'

Ormerod sighed woefully. 'Well it looks as though I'm going,' he said. 'When is it?'

'Can't tell you. Sorry, it's a secret. Anyway we don't know. But within a few weeks. You'll have a concentrated training course, small arms, explosives, all the usual stuff, and of course we'll have you taken off police duties right away.'

'Right,' nodded Ormerod. 'I'm glad I don't have to do it in my spare time. What can I tell my wife?'

'Ah yes, your wife. Well I'm afraid you can't tell her the truth. Now what can we do? Can you go on some sort of police training course? We could arrange for everybody to be told that.'

'Yes, I could go on a police course,' said Ormerod dully. 'That should be all right.'

'You haven't any children have you?' said Clark looking at the file. 'It says "no" here.'

'It's right,' answered Ormerod. 'I've only been married a year. No time yet.'

'And you are ... er thirty-five.'

'Yes.'

Clark took a celluloid card from the desk and ran his finger down a column of figures. 'If anything happens to you, your wife will get quite a decent pension.' He looked up brightly.

'Oh good. That's a relief anyway,' said Ormerod. 'I'm really pleased about that.'

'Right,' said Clark holding out his hand. 'You're a great chap Ormerod. This war will be won by men like you. Within days you will receive further orders. You'll have to go down to Ash Vale in Hampshire for your training and detailed briefing. After that it could happen any time.'

Shaking the outstretched military hand, Ormerod said: 'I won't have to parachute, will I sir? I don't fancy parachuting.'

'Oh no. It will be a sea landing, I imagine.'

'I get seasick,' said Ormerod. 'But I'd rather the sea than the sky. The sky always seems so empty.'

'Yes it does a bit,' said the Brigadier as though it had never occurred to him before. He looked out of the window and examined the sky. 'Jolly empty,' he agreed. 'A long drop.'

He led Ormerod to the door. The busty girl had again knocked the paper clips on the floor and had just finished gathering them. 'I must get that magnet,' she smiled at Ormerod. 'It was a very good idea.'

'I'm full of them,' said Ormerod flatly.

'Did you like the tea?'

'Delicious,' said Ormerod. 'Best thing that's happened to me all day.'

The girl went into the inner office to collect the cups. Clark leaned confidingly towards Ormerod's ear. 'The junket hasn't got a classified codename yet,' he said. 'Purely privately, I'm calling it Ormerod's Landing.'

'Oh, you've named it after *me*,' said Ormerod, trying to sound pleased.

'But it's only for the present. It will get a proper code later and you will have a codename. It won't do to use your real name. If you die on this sort of jaunt, it's better that you die anonymously.'

three

After a week in the special camp at Ash Vale, near Aldershot, Ormerod could still scarcely credit what was happening to him. At night he would lie staring at the ceiling of the small room which had been allocated to him at the remote end of the empty army hut, wondering, and not the first man to do so, whatever was to become of him in the following weeks. For him, with his personal sense of isolation from the war, it was an accentuated doubt. It was as if he was being thrown into a serious conflict that was nothing whatever to do with him. Even the thought that he was to be given the chance to seek out the shameful Albert Smales had lost a proportion of its previous attraction. He looked at the map of France and realized how many miles it was overland from the Normandy coast to Paris. Somehow he had to get *back* as well. *With Smales.* He groaned in the darkness, slept fitfully, and woke to bare daylight with the English birds singing beyond the cold-eyed window.

A cheerfully grubby private in an ill-defined regiment brought him a mug of tea every morning, whether from friendship or duty Ormerod never discovered. He drank half the tea and used the rest as shaving water, as advised by the soldier, because there was no hot water in the taps of the elderly latrines of his empty billet. At the end of the week he had a brown chin from the tannin.

'Everything all right then?' the private would say ritually every morning. 'Treating you okay, are they?'

'Great,' nodded Ormerod grimly. 'Wonderful.'

'What will you be doing today then?'

'Deserting.'

'Can't do that, mate. They'll only catch you. I kept hopping off and I'm more or less on permanent jankers. The only chance I've got of getting out of this bloody hole is if the Germans come and get me.'

'Just like me,' agreed Ormerod. 'It's a rotten choice.'

'Cheer up. It'll be all over when we're dead.'

'Thanks. You make it seem all worth while. Now sod off.'

Wearing an anonymous army battledress he spent his days in the study of maps and photographs and films of Normandy from the Manche *département* on the coast to the Perche country inland, half the way to Paris. He sat solitary, in a lecture hut like a dull and lonely child kept after school, while two instructors took it in turn to teach him the geography, topography, history, industry and humanity of the region.

He was taken to a small arms range and further instructed in the use and care of a variety of pistols and automatic weapons and, for some reason he could not fathom, except that it was part of the set syllabus, how to charge fiercely with a bayonet. Despite his solid policeman's outlook, Ormerod was a sensitive man and, as many sensitive men have discovered, the shouting charge with a bayonet to stab a sack supposed to be an enemy was the most sickening experience. 'Do I *have* to shout?' he pleaded with the instructor, a fat, jolly fellow from Cornwall. 'I mean I thought the whole operation was supposed to be done on the quiet. It's *secret*. I can't see I'm going to have to *shout* under any circumstances. And where do I get the rifle and bayonet in the first place? I can't march through Occupied Europe with a rifle and bayonet now can I?'

'I don' know anythin' about your business, my old darlin',' said the instructor with a wide western smile. 'All I know is that the use of the bayonet is in the course, so that's why we be a-doin' it, see? Now get the fuckin' thing stuck in that sack.'

He was better with more stationary training, especially marksmanship. He had always enjoyed the special skill that went with drawing a line on a distant target, steadying the hand, the eye, the gut, the breath, and drawing the trigger. His marks were high. 'Keep it like that,' advised the pistol instructor grudgingly. 'It's the difference between life and death.' He paused and added: 'Yours.'

One afternoon a week was devoted to camouflage and concealment, a subject, Ormerod suspected, which again had to be included simply because it was in the manual, and the army stuck by the manual. He was taken to a path beside a Hampshire field, scarred and muddy with the tracks of training tanks. It was as void and open as any field he had ever seen and after a lecture by two young officer instructors he was told to go anywhere within two hundred yards and lie low. They would then spot him and tell him where he had gone wrong.

They had driven to the field in an army fifteen hundredweight platoon truck, which was standing a few yards away on the track, and while the instructors turned their backs and, in a curiously juvenile way, hid their eyes in their hands and counted to a hundred, Ormerod quietly climbed into the back of the truck and lay there. The counting completed, the instructors turned and, searching with their binoculars, went over every yard of the landscape of mud and coarse grass. They failed to find him. Eventually one said: 'That's bloody well impossible, Justin. No one could lie *that* flat. I think he may have buggered off.'

'Let's see, Archie,' said Justin. He cupped his hands to his mouth. 'Righty-ho you can come out now!'

Grinning, Ormerod rose from the truck only two yards in front of them. They stared at him in disbelief as if he were a spoilsport. 'Bang,' he said quietly. 'Bang.'

He was given training in the use and maintenance of the portable wireless receiver and transmitter and spent an idyllic afternoon lying in a meadow of thyme and buttercups, relaying practice messages, gazing up at the enormous sky and listening to the lyrical larks.

There was an hour's physical training every morning, orchestrated by a man with the leanings of a sadist, supplemented by a fierce course in unarmed combat under the charge of a blond boy whom Ormerod regarded with the gravest suspicion.

'Do you know Mrs Sweetman?' smiled the instructor as the opening line of their first session.

'No, can't say I do,' replied the mildly surprised Ormerod.

'Well, I'm her son Charles.'

'Oh, I see.'

The young man almost simpered. 'I'm going to teach you silent killing.'

Ormerod found the youth's scented hair almost too much for him in their close-in fighting and the instructor grabbed his testicles rather more times than he would have thought necessary during the course of the training, but there was no doubt that Staff-Sergeant Sweetman knew his business. Ormerod's natural revulsion at tearing apart the nose of another human being with his outstretched fingers, enemy or not, was tempered by the immediate need to protect himself against the assaults of the slight young man. Eventually they were throwing each other around like the best of enemies.

During the entire time of his training, a total of five weeks, he was virtually in solitary confinement, for he saw no one close but his instructors and the grubby private who delivered the tea. On a couple of occasions he saw three men, mysteriously wearing snow suits in the bright sun, undergoing some sort of ritual at the distant end of the camp, but he was told he could not contact them because they were on secret training also, and in any case they were Norwegian. He ate his meals alone in a yawning army mess-hall and in the evening he swotted up his geography and listened to the BBC Forces Programme in the threadbare room. Every weekend he telephoned his wife and told her how his police course was going.

Three days before his time at Ash Vale was finished, although he did not know that at the time, he was called to a briefing given by a major and a captain. He had spent the morning brushing up his facts on Normandy and making his will (advised in that order by the grubby private who apparently knew more of what he was doing and where he was going than anyone else).

'When these two blokes come to see you then it's a racing certainty that you'll be disappearing soon,' the perpetual jankerwallah forecast cheerfully. 'They won't have you hanging around here for the duration. It goes without saying.' He nodded at the Michelin Guide, *Country Walks In Normandy*, *The Normans*, *A History of Normandy* and the maps on Ormerod's bed. 'Mind you,' he said eagerly. 'After reading all that guff you'll probably find they shoot you off to Norway with those other poor buggers.'

It would not have surprised Ormerod either. But when he reported at two in the afternoon to the briefing room he saw there was a reassuring map of France spread across the wall. The briefing officers, the major and the captain, were a strange pair, like a music hall turn, Ormerod thought. The major short and young and the captain tall and almost elderly. They sat behind twin desks and the moment that Ormerod went in the major asked: 'Have they taught you burial yet?'

'Burial?' said the horrified Ormerod. 'Er ... no. They haven't got to that yet.'

'Very important, burial,' said the captain. His voice was squeaky and insistent while the major's was slow and sleepy. Ormerod wondered if they had spent a long time rehearsing.

'Secret burial, that is,' enlarged the major. 'Essential. Must give you a crash course before you actually take off. It's not any use hiding out yourself if you leave your dead pals lying around. It's bound to give you away. I mean, I suppose they've taught you to bury your parachute haven't they? I jolly well hope so.'

Ormerod's heart appropriately dropped. 'Parachute? They said I wouldn't have to go by parachute. Brigadier Clark promised.'

'Promises in wartime,' shrugged the captain, 'are promises in wartime. They are hardly ever kept, you know.'

'But ... I can't even ...'

'Don't worry, as it happens,' put in the major. 'We've actually discounted the parachute notion in case you missed the damned island because it's no size at all. You have to go by submarine.'

'Island?' asked the bemused Ormerod. 'There's an island?'

'Chausey Island. Oh for God's sake, they've crammed you with the geography haven't they? You're supposed to have covered all of Normandy.'

'Yes sir, I have,' said Ormerod carefully. 'Except Chausey Island. They seem to have overlooked that. I don't even know where it is.'

'Wouldn't they *just*,' sighed the captain. 'It's typical.' As if propelled by the force of the sigh he stood and went to the map of France. He picked up his officer's cane as he went and used it to point.

'France,' he said dramatically.

Ormerod's eyebrows ascended. 'Yes sir,' was all he could say.

'Normandy,' said the captain knocking the cane on the map again. He moved it north a few inches. 'Chausey Island,' he added with theatrical patience. 'Seven miles, give or take a bit, off the Cherbourg Peninsular . . .'

'Ah, the Cotentin Peninsular,' Ormerod put in quickly to show that he knew. The captain looked at the major, not at Ormerod, and raised his face in a shrug. 'Chausey,' he continued sternly, 'is one main island, two kilometres long and about seven hundred metres at its widest, and a number of small uninhabited islands and a few hundred rocks. It's the only one of the Channel Islands that belongs to the French.'

Ormerod, thinking he was expected to contribute, nodded and said brightly: 'They all belong to the Germans now.'

Both officers regarded him with expressions they apparently reserved for dolts. 'That,' said the major stiffly, 'is why we're going in there.' He smiled an almost sinister smile. 'Well . . . you are.'

The captain continued, tapping the map impatiently with his cane. 'The island is normally inhabited by fishermen, that type of fellow. We don't know how many Germans there are because the only contact we've had since the occupation is someone signalling with torches at overflying aircraft. God only knows what they're trying to say.' He smiled. 'Unless it's "help!"'

'How's your French?' asked the major abruptly.

'It doesn't exist, according to this,' said the captain looking at a sheet in his hand.

'Good God. No French?'

Ormerod shook his head feebly. 'I told Brigadier Clark that,' he pointed out. 'But he didn't seem to think it mattered. He said the ordinary German soldier wouldn't understand a lot of French anyway. And if I got to officer level, then it would be too late. I've got to try and avoid talking to the Germans.'

'Not a bad idea,' intoned the captain. 'My advice to you Ormerod is if you get into a situation – you know, a *situation* – where you can't avoid it, you should try to make out you're drunk, insane or a deaf mute. Then they'll probably just kick you up the arse and let you go. So do you think you could impersonate a deaf mute? That's the favourite I'd say.'

'I could practise,' promised Ormerod.

The captain suddenly became very friendly and, advancing on Ormerod, put his arm about the policeman's shoulder. 'Listen, old chap, I expect you'll handle the whole thing very well.' He glanced at the major for confirmation.

'Oh, very well indeed,' said the major. 'Very well.'

'Now you'll be getting a detailed briefing before you're actually off on this outing,' said the captain returning to the map. He pointed at the island again. 'But anyway – Chausey. Landing by submarine. Then you've just got to make your local arrangements to get onto the mainland. We can't risk a submarine too near the French coast. Valuable things apparently, submarines.'

Ormerod, doubt from forehead to chin, looked at the map. 'On Chausey,' he asked tentatively, 'there won't be ... there won't be anyone to meet us?'

Both officers looked blank, then astonished. 'Meet you?' said the elder captain. 'Good God old chap, it's not Paddington station. We haven't got a clue as to who or what is on Chausey. People from Mars for all we know, old boy. That's the object of the exercise, to contact resistance groups, or potential resistance groups. I mean for all we know there's a bloody tank regiment on Chausey, although that, I must admit, is a bit unlikely.' He spread his hands. 'We simply don't know, Ormerod. There hasn't been a lot of to-ing and fro-ing lately. Not since Dunkirk.'

The major sniffed approval of the sarcasm and glanced at the captain. The captain nodded as if agreeing to tell. 'You know it's a woman,' he said, 'going with you.'

'I was told that,' said Ormerod, glad there was something he knew.

The captain said breezily. 'Nothing wrong with women. I mean, they don't scare you or anything, do they?'

'No,' said Ormerod, shaking his head. 'Not at all. I've recently got married to one. But I'm just ... well, surprised, that's all. I thought it would be a man naturally. A trained agent. I mean, using a gun and all that.'

The major did not look directly at Ormerod. 'She's trained but not *experienced*. There's a difference you understand. But she can use a gun all right, from what I hear,' he muttered. 'Better than most. And she's not going to be squeamish about it either. She'll look after you.'

'Thanks,' said Ormerod. 'Thanks very much.'

'You'll be meeting her tomorrow, or the day after I expect,' said the captain. 'You'll be called for detailed briefing and then, at the magic hour, you're off.'

'Any more questions?' asked the major, unnecessarily adding: 'Ormerod.'

'Well yes, there is as a matter of fact. You know about me going to France to find a wanted man, don't you? He's wanted for murder. Brigadier Clark knows all about it.'

The captain looked surprised but the major tapped his teeth with a pencil. 'Ah yes. Now you remind me, there *was* something like that. Very odd business, I must say. Anyway that's all right, Ormerod. It's something you'll more or less have to do in your spare time.'

A dull despair rolled along Ormerod's stomach. 'I see, sir,' he said bitterly. 'In case I get bored.'

The major laughed unpleasantly. 'That's it! You're *all right* Ormerod! Absolutely *all right*! I like your sense of humour. You'll make out fine in France. I don't think we could have picked a better chap.' He looked at the captain. 'What do you think?'

'No,' said the captain with a sly smile. 'I think he'll have great fun. Off to France with a woman – and a beautiful woman at that. Sounds like everybody's dream.'

Ormerod had had enough of them. Another five minutes and he thought he might have tried out the silent killing which the unarmed combat instructor had shown him. He said nothing.

'Righty-ho,' said the major cheerfully. 'Detailed briefing to-morrow. A car will come to you at ten hundred hours. At Ashbridge, Herts or Bucks, whatever it is. Decent little day out if the weather keeps up. Then, pretty quickly I would think – it depends if the navy can rustle up a submarine – off you go. And any further questions? Made your will and all that rubbish?'

'Yes,' said Ormerod. The two officers advanced on him and extravagantly shook his hand. He could have sworn the captain's eyes were glistening. 'Cheerio then,' said the major. 'See you when you get your medal.'

'I hope I'm there to get it in person,' said Ormerod evenly. 'Is it possible to ask how I am supposed to get back?'

'Arrangements,' said the major, as though that covered it. 'They'll be made. You'll know in time.'

'Thanks,' said Ormerod hollowly. 'I just thought I would ask. I'm glad it's all taken care of.'

He went out of the hut. The two officers sat down side by side and stared at the map of Normandy. 'Buggered if I'd ever heard of Chausey Island either,' said the major reflectively. 'Not until last week.'

'Nor me,' sighed the captain. 'We'd better allocate this fairy tale a codename hadn't we? What's the next letter in the book?'

'We'll have to use D,' said the major. 'A, B and C were all used in Norway. The Jerries know all about them because they nabbed the agents if you recall.'

'Yes, I remember that,' said the captain as if it were only with difficulty. 'Right, D it is then.'

The major opened a file. 'Letter D,' he said. 'Here we are. Ah, just the thing.'

'What is it?'

'Dodo. Operation Dodo,' said the major. 'And we can give him the name Dodo too.'

The captain nodded. 'Right,' he agreed. 'He's as good as dead.'

At ten the following morning an army car arrived at the Ash Vale camp to take Ormerod to the final briefing. He was told to leave his anonymous battledress behind and to make the journey in his civilian blue suit. Ormerod sat in the back of the car, the taciturn military driver never turning his head, and they drove from Hampshire into Surrey and then into Berkshire and Hertfordshire. Because he was a town man, used to living in streets, Ormerod had never noticed much of the country. Now he saw it lying brilliantly all about him, the most vivid autumn after a hot summer, miles of yellow trees, copper trees, vermilion trees, unrolling as they journeyed.

'Nice time of the year this,' ventured Ormerod to the driver.

'Lovely,' said the man, a Cockney. 'Does a treat, don't it sir.' He nodded out of the window. 'Just like miles of wall-paper.'

'What's this place Ashridge, anyway?' asked Ormerod, now he knew the man was allowed to talk.

'Ashridge Park, sir?' said the driver. They were going through Windsor with the Thames blue with the deep reflection of the sky. Ormerod gave a nod of acknowledgement towards the castle. 'Well, sir, they've got the Public Records Office at Ashridge. Brought it from London, tons and tons of books and papers, like a blinking salvage drive. They had to get it out in case it got bombed. Make a very nasty fire all them papers.'

Ormerod wondered why his briefing was being held at the Public Records Office, but did not press the matter. They arrived after just over an hour's drive, turning into parkland so full of bright leaves it hurt the eyes. In the centre of the park was a fine, grave house, and adjacent to the house, under covering trees, rows of prefabricated, asbestos buildings, an affront to the surroundings. The car stopped at one of these and an ATS girl came out and showed Ormerod into a stark waiting room. He sat down, the melancholy of the place settling quickly on him. After a while the oldest man he had ever seen, wearing the oldest clothes he had ever seen, striped trousers and black jacket almost grey with age and dust, came in and began intently to sharpen a white quill with a miniature penknife. He looked up at Ormerod and smiled beatifically. 'Lovely, isn't it?' he said, nodding at the autumn extravagance outside the imprisoning window. 'The sun on all the trees. Part of nature's war effort, I suppose. She's trying to make up for some of the discomforts.'

'She's probably doing it for the Germans as well,' pointed out Ormerod. The old man considered both Ormerod's point and that of the quill; he nodded philosophically. 'Very true, I imagine,' he agreed. He dropped his voice conspiratorially. 'I don't believe this rubbish about God only being on our side, you know. It's propaganda, sheer government propaganda.'

He was trimming his quill with a great art. Ormerod watched him carefully for he had never seen anyone who used a quill before. A serene smile touched the man's face at his interest. 'Great shortage, of course,' he said, holding up the feather. 'The war again. Although why we can't get goose feathers is beyond me. Surely the geese still grow them.'

Ormerod could not believe that the ancient man was anything to do with his own presence there. 'Public Records Office are you?' he asked.

'Indeed, indeed,' nodded the man benignly. 'All transported from London. Quite a miracle, I suppose, although our working conditions are hardly in keeping, as you might judge.' He looked around caustically at the almost derelict waiting room. 'You'd think a jam-jar of flowers would not be too much to ask for wouldn't you?' he said. 'And perhaps a few decent pictures on the walls.'

Ormerod nodded. 'Certainly make it look less ... formal,' he said. The man had finished sharpening his quill but he was not in a hurry to depart. 'We have the entire history of our great country in this building, you know,' he said. 'Even Magna Carta. We *had* to bring that of course. It's quite priceless. And if the Germans do come and conquer us it will be reassuring to be able to read it and know what we fought for, even if we lost.' He paused as if wondering whether to impart some secret information. 'I myself,' he said eventually, 'am working on documents appertaining to the battles of 1899 in South Africa.'

'You're a couple of wars behind then,' said Ormerod.

'For the rest of the world, yes,' acknowledged the man. 'But for us, no. Here we never like to hurry these things.' He turned to go but paused at the door. 'If you would like to see Magna Carta this afternoon, I can arrange it,' he offered. 'It's something everybody should see.'

Omerod was touched at the real generosity. 'Thank you,' he said. 'If I've got time, I will.'

The man nodded and continued nodding as if he were unable to stop. 'I'm the first room along the corridor,' he said before leaving the room. 'Just knock quietly. I'll hear you. We don't make a lot of din here.'

Bemused, Ormerod watched him shuffle and nod away. He felt a kind of envy. How peaceful it must be sorting out the Boer War. He stood up and looked through the grubby window at the extravagant trees. The driver was right. It was just like wallpaper. Someone came into the room behind him and he turned unhurriedly. It was the ATS girl. He could see at once that she knew why he was there because she was regarding him with a sympathetic sort of hero-worship. No one had ever looked at him like that before. 'Penny for your thoughts,' she said after she had smiled.

'Hardly worth that much,' he smiled back. 'I was just thinking that somebody is going to have a job clearing up all the leaves around here.'

'You're right,' she said. 'But it's a quiet job isn't it? You wouldn't know there was a war on. Not here.' She paused, then said, almost with embarrassment: 'They're waiting for you now. Will you follow me?'

He went after her, watching her tight, khaki-clad backside moving two yards ahead. A brief thought of his wife made him momentarily homesick. He would have to forget that. He had telephoned her several times from Ash Vale but she was always formal to the point of stiffness on the telephone. How was the police course going? Would he be getting extra allowance for being away? Could he fix the kettle when he got home because it had gone wrong again, please? It was hardly a romantic marriage.

The girl showed him into yet another grubby chamber where

49

two men in neat suits, like bank clerks, stood staring at a wide map of Normandy on the wall. As he came in one brushed his hand across the map. 'Couldn't tell whether that was a small town or a house fly,' he smiled weakly at his colleague. They seemed surprised to see Ormerod standing behind them and both came forward with bogus diffidence to shake his hand.

'Jolly glad to meet you,' said the first clerky man. He wore a grey suit with some sort of significantly striped tie and had the kind of pale wispy hair that is almost as good as being bald. The other man was wearing a pin-striped suit with another kind of significantly striped tie and his dark hair had been sleeked down as if it had been painted to his head. 'Sit down, please,' said the second man. 'Might as well get some rest while you can, eh?'

Ormerod was getting familiar with the type. He sat down heavily. The first man took some kind of form and showed it to the second. 'AF G 146,' he intoned. 'That's right, isn't it Charles?'

'Think so, Gerry. Probably do anyway.'

Even in that moment they seemed to have forgotten Ormerod was sitting there, and that he was the subject of the interview and a great deal of what was to come after it. They looked up and smiled, almost surprised smiles as thought they had just noticed him. 'Interesting name, Ormerod,' said the grey-suited Gerry. 'O-R-M-E-R-O-D,' he spelt it out and then recited, 'Ormer – a mollusc, tough shell-fish adhering to rocks, makes good eating. Rod – as in the Rod of Aaron or rod, pole or perch, or a fishing rod.'

'Rod, pole or perch,' said the striped Charles reflectively. 'Fishing rod ... There's a good *Times* crossword clue there somewhere.'

'Damned difficult to compile, crosswords,' said Gerry. Once more they seemed to have completely forgotten Ormerod. He sat looking spiritually shattered while they gossiped like fifth formers at their desks. 'Much easier to solve them.'

They looked up together as if their heads were interlocked and saw Ormerod's distraught expression. 'Don't fret about us,' said Charles jovially. 'Our department is full of odd-bods like us. Some of them worse, hey Gerry?'

'Damned sight worse,' agreed Gerry. 'Infinitely. Still we need to be ... different.' He pulled his shoulders together and leaned his elbows on the desk as if as a sign he was getting down to business. 'I'm navy,' he said. 'Intelligence of course. Charles here is one of those brown jobs.'

'Brown jobs?' asked Ormerod. He was wondering who was madder, them or him for allowing them to send him on a perilous mission.

'Yes, brown jobs,' confirmed Gerry. 'You know, army.'

'We've got to fill you in with a few last details before we see you off,' said Charles. 'One thing we don't want you to do is to *worry*.'

'Worry? Oh, I won't worry,' muttered Ormerod still staring at them unbelievingly. 'I've got nothing to worry about have I? It's all being done for me.'

Charles and Gerry looked at each other as if unsure how to take this. They decided he was serious. 'We do our best,' said Charles smugly. 'It's all we can do. Now – here we have some rather jolly aerial photographs of Chausey Island which we might as well confess neither of us had ever heard of until this little bit of fun.' He took half a dozen misty prints out of a folder. 'Early morning stuff,' he said, 'so they have a bit of fog here and there, but you can get a general idea of the place. Looks very cosy, I must say. Few fishermen's cottages, light-house, church, all mod cons. No sign of the Boche, although these were taken a couple of weeks ago. He may have moved in a Panzer division by now.'

'Everyone says that,' nodded Ormerod.

'These jokes go around,' shrugged Gerry, taking up the thread. 'Point is we can't get the submarine too close to the island itself. See here ...' He drew his finger along a narrow neck of water. 'That's called The Sund, it's the main anchorage. But any submarine sticking her nose in there would be really asking for it. So what we intend to do ...' His elegant finger swept the photograph, '... is to drop you off here. It looks from the picture as if you'll be in the middle of the hoggin, as the chaps say on the lower deck. That's the sea ...' He glanced at Ormerod to make sure he understood. Ormerod nodded.

'Yes, the hoggin,' continued Charles. 'But in fact it's an illusion. On a low tide – and the autumn tides are really amazing – a drop of forty feet and more so they say, anyway on the low tide all sorts of jolly little islands appear. Most of them are not much more than rocks. But if we get you ashore on one of these at the right time, you'll more or less be able to walk across to the channel of the main island. It's something over a mile but you'll be able to do it. Bit hard on the feet I expect.' He flicked up a few pages of his notes as though checking the fact.

'Well, there'll be plenty of rock pools,' chimed in Gerry cheerfully. 'Treat them to a paddle. Nothing like a drop of brine for feet.'

'Frankly,' said Charles, glaring at Ormerod with sudden drama, 'we can't guarantee what's going to happen when you get ashore. We take it that the fishermen will help. After all they're bloody French and they're still more or less on our side. You may run into all sorts of trouble or it may be a piece of cake. Simply cannot tell. We've had no time to find out either. We've hardly had time to get ourselves sorted out since Dunkirk. You might not guess it, Ormerod, but we're pretty new to this ourselves. We haven't even got a proper decent office yet, have we Gerry?'

'No fear,' confirmed Gerry. 'That's why we have to use this funny little place.'

'I hope you get somewhere decent soon,' said Ormerod heavily. 'One thing I haven't asked. How do we get from the submarine to the shore?'

'Collapsible boat,' said Charles firmly as if he had been waiting for the question. 'No trouble at all. Sub half surfaces, over the side, into the canvas boat. Any more for the skylark! Well, almost. Row ashore. If something goes wrong you may have to swim.'

'I *can't* swim, said Ormerod stonily.

'Oh God,' said Gerry, concern wrapped around his face. 'They always overlook something. Do you remember that chap who went to Norway, Charles, suffered from snow-blindness.'

'Black chaps often do,' said Charles.

'Black?' said Ormerod with slowly realized horror. 'You sent a black man to Norway?'

'Bad planning,' agreed Gerry. 'Bloody bad. But, as I said, we've hardly got ourselves organized properly yet.'

'Anyway,' said Charles firmly, wanting to get away from that aspect, 'there's no time to teach you to swim now. Not unless you're a damn quick learner. You'll be on your way in twenty-four hours.'

Ormerod felt a stone turn in his stomach. 'That soon?' he said.

'That soon,' confirmed Gerry. 'Time and tide and all that nonsense, you know.'

'What about the other agent, the lady?' asked Ormerod. 'I thought I was going to meet her today.'

'Stood you up, I shouldn't wonder,' laughed Charles.

'She'll be with you later, don't fret,' said Gerry. 'She'll join you at Portsmouth. That's where you get the sub. I gather she's really something. Wouldn't mind toddling off with her myself.'

They sat looking at him in a special sort of silence after that for what seemed like several cold minutes. Then Charles said apologetically, 'I wish we could tell you more about what will happen, Ormerod. But to tell you the blessed truth we don't know. Somehow you've got to get from Chausey Island to the mainland. We must hope the natives are friendly.' He got up and went to the map and scribbled his finger across it. 'Obviously they'll have to land you somewhere quiet on the mainland. But there are lots of small beaches and such like and the Germans can't be properly organized in Normandy. I mean, they've hardly had time to move in. There *must* be lots of loopholes. In a way, I suppose, it's just as well you're the early bird, one of the first back. Catch them before they've got their flies done up, as it were.' He saw something on the map. 'See, here's an appropriate beach, and ha! Look at this, Gerry, what a name! St Jean le Thomas! St John Thomas, dammit!'

Gerry bounced up and laughed youthfully. Ormerod accepted their invitation to see the place was genuine, that it was no joke. He smiled woodenly. Another half an hour of this, he thought, and I'll kill these two bastards before I've ever laid a finger on the Germans.

There was another twenty minutes of it. At the end they said they couldn't help him any further. He was on his own. He thanked them without enthusiasm. 'Get a good night's sleep,' advised Charles. 'No sloping off down the pub.' They laughed again heartily but when Ormerod did not join in they lapsed into hurt silence. 'The car will be along in a minute,' said Charles huffily. They shook hands stiffly with him and he went out.

He knocked on the door of the old man from the Public Records Office. 'I'd like to see the Magna Carta,' he said. 'If it's convenient.'

'If I'm going to die,' he thought, 'I might as well see what I'm dying for.'

It rained the next day, the variety of rain peculiar to dockyard towns like Portsmouth, a lean sea-hung drizzle across the grim wartime streets and the grey and crowded naval tenements in the port. Seagulls croaked in the wet. Ormerod was taken to a naval barracks and there, as if it were part of a well-oiled and minutely rehearsed operation, he was once again given lunch in a deserted room. He ate moodily, although he had been eating alone for weeks, reflecting that this was how he had felt when he was in quarantine with chicken pox as a boy. Every now and then someone came and stared through the window at him, patently knowing that he was something of a curiosity, and then went away. He found himself becoming bad-tempered at this, unusually so, but he put it down to the proxi-mity of the dangerous mission. As he was eating his Royal Navy rhubarb and custard he poked his tongue out at two pale young officers who had come to look at him. They retreated abruptly.

A short, spongy sailor who had served the meal came in with a mug of tea and a smile. He was the naval counterpart of the grubby private at Ash Vale. 'Off to France then?' he said, conversationally. Ormerod choked over the last spoonful of rhubarb. 'How did you know?' he demanded. 'How the hell .. ?'

'Don't get shirty,' said the sailor. 'Every bugger knows. But we promise we won't tell the Germans. God's honour.'

'I should bloody well hope not,' said Ormerod sourly, taking the tea. 'I've got a short enough life expectancy as it is. Everybody knows do they? Anybody thought to ring the local Nazi spy and tell him?'

The sailor hunched his shoulders. 'It's the submarine, see,' he explained, leaning confidingly. 'She's sailing tonight and she'll be back tomorrow. That much we know, see, because there's a football match and the crew have been promised faithfully they'll be back for that. Well, where can you go in less than twenty-four hours? Not far. So the guess is right?'

'I'm not saying,' grunted Ormerod bitterly. 'I don't care. I'm only relieved they're getting back for their precious bloody football match, that's all. I wouldn't have liked them to be late for the kick-off.'

The sailor laughed jovially. 'Don't you worry your head about that, mate,' he promised. 'They'll be back all right. Even if it means dumping you anywhere convenient and making a dash for it. Oh, they'll be back.' He regarded the miserable face of Ormerod below him. 'And you'll get back all right too,' he said in a poor attempt at reassurance. 'Don't you fret. How did you get into this anyway?'

Ignoring the question Ormerod said: 'Can you get seasick in a submarine?'

'Ever so,' nodded the sailor. 'Oh blimey, sick! They reckon it can be worse under the hoggin than on top of the hoggin. I wouldn't know because I've never been on it or under it. I'm having my war right here.'

'Convenient,' nodded Ormerod. 'Nice for you. I was hoping that the submarine, anyway, would be on the steady side.'

'They roll,' the sailor said, demonstrating by moving the empty tea mug from side to side. 'Like my mum's mangle, I'm told. Never mind. It can't be for long, can it?'

A naval lieutenant put his head around the door and whistled shrilly. 'I say old boy,' he called to Ormerod. 'You're the special chap, aren't you?'

'So I'm told,' said Ormerod.

'Right-ho. Just toddle across to the other side of the parade ground will you. Go through the door marked "No Admittance", down the corridor and into the last room on the left. Final briefing I think.'

'Christ, not another final briefing,' said Ormerod getting up heavily. 'Not another.'

'I know,' nodded the young officer sympathetically. 'They will keep having them, won't they? We usually find they give you eight final briefings then cancel the whole show anyway. Probably forget what it was all about in the first place. Anyway, pop over there will you?'

Ormerod sighed and walked out of the building. The September rain was flying enthusiastically across Portsmouth harbour driven by a growling wind. In the dock beyond the bleak barracks and the parade ground a submarine wallowed in the oily water. Ormerod closed his eyes and began to walk.

He had gone twenty paces across the square towards a formation of marching marines when the sergeant drilling them turned and spotted him. The man shuddered, swung as if he were on some mechanically operated spring, and stumped towards Ormerod. 'You!' he bawled. 'You!'

Ormerod stopped and looked up through the rain to his front. The marine sergeant was bristling, twenty-five yards away. 'You!' he bellowed again.

Ormerod had now had enough. 'Me?' he bawled back. 'Me?'

The marine NCO looked astounded. Disbelief burst on his face. He drew himself up on his toes like an ignited rocket just before taking off. 'You,' he howled hysterically.

'Me?' Ormerod shouted back. 'Me?'

'Yes – you! Come here! And quick!'

Ormerod stood his ground. The rain was licking his forehead. His very soul felt damp. 'No,' he challenged. 'You come here.'

The marine sergeant could not credit it. He had gone purple in the dark afternoon. Then an internal brake seemed to be suddenly released and he strutted at Ormerod like a puff-chested bird. As the two men seemed about to collide the drill sergeant came to a stamping stop two feet away. He was the same height as Ormerod and he glared vividly into the policeman's tired eyes.

'You are walking across our parade ground!' snarled the NCO. 'You realize that? On the parade ground!'

'Fuck off,' suggested Ormerod quietly. He thought: God I hope they do put me in a cell, then I won't have to go. 'Go on, fuck off,' he repeated walking past the NCO. He continued his slow amble across the square until he came to the door marked 'No Admittance' and he went in.

He could hear the expected commotion on the barrack square behind him but nothing worried him now. He felt as if his body had entered a tight capsule, that his existence, and the things he did, had no bearing on the real and normal world, even if there were any longer such a thing. He entered into the last room along the corridor, knocked and went in without waiting for an answer. He did not feel in the mood for waiting for answers.

There was a girl in an ATS tunic sitting at a desk writing on various sheets of paper. She looked up briefly. Ormerod said: 'My name's Ormerod. I've been told to come here.'

'Yes,' she said succinctly. 'Will you please wait. In a few moments you will be attended to.'

Attended to! Christ, it sounded like a dog being brought into a vet's for doctoring! They were *attending* to him all right. All of them. Here he was going off to risk his life – no, more than that, probably *give* his life – on some dreamlike mission and they gave him rhubarb and fucking custard and a mouthful of abuse. There was a knock at the door. The girl did not look up from the desk so Ormerod defiantly said: 'Come in.' He had a feeling it was for him. He was right.

The parade ground sergeant was there stiff and puce in the face like a piece of frozen fruit, and with him was the young officer, now obviously embarrassed, who had called him after lunch.

'Been telling tales?' Ormerod mocked the drill sergeant. He mimicked. 'Sir, that naughty man walked right across our nice clean parade ground.' He glared at the sergeant as a rebellious boy might regard the school sneak. Both the officer and the NCO opened their mouths but Ormerod got in first again. 'Listen chaps,' he said with deep disdain. 'Since I'm just about to be pushed off to trespass on enemy-occupied-bloody-Europe, I'm not all that worried about trespassing on your manky parade ground.'

With that he closed the door in their rigid and astonished faces. To his surprise the uniformed girl at the desk suddenly jumped up, called him a fool and opened the door again. She went outside with the two complainants and Ormerod sat down, deflated and sick. Who was she to call him a fool?

Within two minutes she was back, giving the impression that she had given the military pair short shrift. She was small and neat with dark tidy hair and notable eyes. 'How in God's name could you do that?' she demanded.

'What? Walk across their parade ground?'

'No. You shouted about going to Europe. Are you mad or something?'

'Everybody else knows,' he shrugged. 'The submarine crew know for a start. I wouldn't be surprised if Hitler himself didn't know by now. And, if you don't mind, don't call me a fool. I may be one – in fact I think I am one – but I don't like being called one. Who am I waiting for anyway? Nobody tells me anything.'

'Mr Ormerod, you are waiting for me,' she said briskly, returning to the desk and sitting down. 'I am Marie-Thérèse Velin. We are in this together.'

His jaw slackened. He half rose from the chair. 'You ...' he began. 'You're the girl? The agent?'

'I am,' she said almost primly. 'But please do not tell the world.'

He stood up the rest of the way. 'I suppose we better shake hands,' he ventured, holding his out. 'Since, as you say, we are in this together.'

'Of course,' she said, offering her hand but remaining stiffly behind the desk. 'How do you do? Are you looking forward to this?'

Ormerod sat down again. He couldn't believe they would send someone so small. She looked as if she should be behind a drapery counter. 'I can't say I am,' he answered eventually. 'Not one bit.'

'You are frightened?'

'About average frightened,' he nodded. 'But the whole thing seems such a mess, such a hotch-potch. It's all so bloody amateur, if you'll excuse my language. Does *anybody* know what they are really doing?'

'I doubt if they do,' she said, suddenly smiling. Her teeth

were small and perfect. 'But once we are there in France, we will be on our own. *We* will know what we are doing. We will not have all this hotch-botch, as you say.'

'Hotch-potch,' he corrected. She repeated it. Her English was touched only with the minutest of accents and the occasional rearrangement of words. Her eyes were grey and her hands now flickering through the papers on her desk were finely formed. They did not look substantial enough to hold a gun.

'In any case,' she said, 'I understand you are very excited about going there because there is a criminal you wish to catch in France.'

'Yes,' he said. 'I was. Albert Smales. He's a murderer.'

'France is full of murderers right now,' she said grimly. 'If we are successful, within a short time you and I, Mr Ormerod, will be numbered among them.'

'I wish Smales had hopped it to Birmingham or somewhere a bit easier like that,' said Ormerod moodily.

She laughed briskly. 'We will make an epic, don't you worry. We will make a trail across France. The Boche will know that Dodo and Dove have passed that way.'

'Who?' he asked, half hoping that it might be someone else. 'Dodo and Dove? Who are they when they're at home?'

'You are Dodo and I am Dove,' she said in a pleased voice as if they had both been given citations.

He considered the implications. 'Somebody's got a sense of humour, anyway,' he grunted. 'Even if it is at my expense. It's the first time I've heard it. Still, there's a lot I haven't been told.'

She shrugged. 'There is little to tell,' she said. 'We will be the first true agents to enter Occupied France, which is an honour in itself. We are to see what the prospects are for the formation of underground resistance groups in Normandy continuing down to Paris and, where it is possible, we are to help in the organization of these groups, Mr Ormerod. My countrymen are waiting to fight the Germans who have fouled France.'

'You think so?' said Ormerod. 'I'd have thought they were fed up with the whole business by now.'

Marie-Thérèse regarded him caustically. 'It was the British who ran away, if I may remind you,' she said. 'Three months ago at Dunkirk.'

'And the French stayed and surrendered,' shrugged Ormerod. 'So?'

'Betrayed,' she said bitterly. 'Betrayed by the British, betrayed by their own leaders. But they will fight again. They will see the banner unfurled.'

'You sound like Joan of Arc,' smiled Ormerod quietly.

'She was too flamboyant,' she replied. 'I think my way will be better.'

Ormerod leaned forward. 'What do you know that I don't know?' he inquired. 'I didn't come here to argue. I'd like to know what the exact plan is.'

'All right,' she smiled tightly. She riffled through the papers on the desk and selected an inked map. 'There *is* no exact plan.'

'You surprise me,' he groaned.

'From the moment we are off the submarine we are on our own,' she said. Her finger traced the outline of the map. 'Chausey Island,' she said. 'We cannot land in the place marked The Sund, right here, because the submarine cannot risk entering there. So we land over here.' Her finger ran across the forms of outlying islands and rocks. 'The submarine will come a little to the surface and we will take a canvas boat to get to the shore. Afterwards we must sink it without trace. No one will find it. We then make our path across these rocks and little isles which are out of the sea at low tide, until we reach the eastern side of The Sund. Then we must get across to the main island and wait there for the opportunity to get to the mainland.'

'Always accepting the natives are friendly,' pointed out Ormerod.

Her eyebrows went up and she projected her lips impatiently. 'They are Normans,' she said as if no further explanation were necessary.

'What about the Germans? Surely there are bound to be Germans on the island.'

'That is logical I suppose. But signals have been seen by planes flying over Chausey – and they are seen regularly. So, if there are Germans they are not very much awake. But if they are there, and they get in the way of our plans, we must eliminate them.'

'Of course, of course,' nodded Ormerod as though he eliminated Germans every day.

She glanced at him and smiled. 'It will be all right,' she said. 'You will learn.'

'You know I don't speak any French,' he said, looking directly at her.

'So I believe.'

'The best way for me to get across France is as a deaf mute.'

'At first,' she told him, 'I thought it was ridiculous, crazy, sending somebody like you. But they said there was no trained agent they could send. And you wanted to go, to get this man – what is his name?'

'Smales. I should have kept my mouth shut.'

'But later,' she continued, ignoring the remark, 'I thought that an amateur would be just as good, it could be even better. As long as you can look after yourself. Sometimes trained people become too ... how can I say it? ... too involved, too sophisticated. Because of this they might be caught. They seek perfection. You will not do that. And if they catch you, the Germans, then a trained agent has not been wasted. This is only a kind of ... exploration, yes exploration, anyway.'

'Everybody's so nice about me being expendable,' grumbled Ormerod.

She laughed genuinely. 'I'm sorry for you,' she said. 'We are all expendable, but it's more difficult to replace some than others.'

'Well I'll have to keep my mouth shut in France,' he said solemnly. 'Deaf, dumb, drunk or doolally, that's me.'

'Doolally, what is that?'

'Mad,' he said. 'Batty. That probably fits better than any of them.'

'It will not be so difficult moving about,' she continued. 'I am certain of this. I have your forged identity papers and ration book here for you. Many men are still returning to their homes from the French army, after the surrender. Those permitted by the Boche. Some of them are walking across the country. Also there are many people who work in Normandy at this time of the year on the gathering of the apples for cider. They travel also from place to place.'

'Cider. You have cider in Normandy?'

'Of course. It is the Norman's wine. You have this in England also?'

'Cider? Yes, they make it in the West Country.'

'The Normans probably brought it over with William the Conqueror,' she said airily. 'But to return to the point, there are many workers who will be moving around the countryside from farm to farm.'

'Won't the Germans be checking on them?' said Ormerod.

'They will, I expect. But our papers are as good as anybody else's. The Boche knows that the farming must go on, life must go on, even if he is the boss for the moment. People must eat and drink.'

Ormerod said: 'I'm partial to a glass of cider myself.'

'This western part of Normandy,' she continued, ignoring the observation, 'was not damaged by the battles. The country-side is peaceful as it was before. And the Germans, they are not organized yet. They have only been there for a few weeks. Also their security services are not good. They fight all the time between each other, themselves, I mean. There are many things in our favour.'

There was a sharp knock on the office door. Marie-Thérèse nodded and Ormerod opened it. A petty officer and two ratings stood outside. 'Captain Peterson's compliments, sir,' he said to Ormerod. 'We've come to take you to the ship.'

Ormerod stood aside and let the girl go first. To his surprise he saw some hesitation in her expression. She glanced at him as she moved forward.

'It is this submarine I do not like,' she whispered. 'I do not like it one bit.'

Ormerod attempted a grin. He touched her arm. 'Don't worry dear,' he said. 'It can only sink.'

four

On September 20th, 1940, the highest tide of the year occurred along the Channel coast of Normandy and Brittany, giving a rise and fall of no less than forty-one feet. If the sea was powerful, however, the air was still. The night was moonless and without stars. At four o'clock in the morning HM submarine *Trenchant* was in position off the eastern rocks of Chausey Island.

The submarine partially surfaced just after dawn which was at 6.22 a.m. and two minutes later the conning tower hatch opened and a petty officer looked out at the island. 'Found it,' he said with satisfaction. He and two ratings led Ormerod and Marie-Thérèse Velin along the deck and assisted them in the launching of the collapsible canvas boat. Both Ormerod and the girl were armed with pistols. They were each in possession of a full set of forged identification documents and the girl had a reduced-scale Admiralty chart of the locality. Both were dressed in blue Breton fishermen's trousers and jerseys. Ormerod also carried a prayer sheet issued by the Missions to Seamen which had been discreetly and decently given to him by a religious rating aboard the submarine. Marie-Thérèse had five hundred thousand francs in one thousand franc notes.

Ormerod was first, climbing clumsily into the jerky canvas boat. He wobbled and all but capsized it while Marie-Thérèse regarded him doubtfully through the insipid light. He returned the look apologetically and the ratings helped her into the boat. The petty officer saluted with some sense of drama and then leaned over confidingly. 'Bugger off quick,' he advised. He nodded towards the submarine's conning tower. 'Before this can of beans goes down again, or she'll take you under with us.'

'All right,' said Ormerod. One of the other things they had not taught him in training was to row a boat at sea. Possibly because there were no facilities at Ash Vale, in the middle of Hampshire. 'Have a good football match,' he whispered laconically to the petty officer who nodded as though he appreciated the thought and jogged thankfully back along the wet deck towards the conning tower. Ormerod began to pull at the oars.

'Haven't done this for years,' he puffed at Marie-Thérèse as the canvas boat moved sluggishly in the uneven water. 'Southend before the war.'

The girl smiled wanly and at about the moment of the smile two German soldiers innocently night fishing off the outer rocks of Chausey turned their small boat around an islet and saw the British submarine lying on the surface half a mile away. While the astonishment was still on their faces they saw the vessel begin to drop into the engulfing sea and within a minute there was only foam to mark the place where she had been.

The two men simultaneously spotted the small canvas boat moving clumsily towards the shore. One of the soldiers was a corporal, who hoped to be a sergeant, and the other was a private. The corporal nodded and they quietly manoeuvred their dinghy around the headland and pulled it into a sharp pebble beach. Their rifles were in the bottom boards of the fishing boat and they took them and went carefully along the shingle to the place where they estimated the canvas boat would come ashore.

The rocks were wet, sharp with shellfish and slippery with weed. When the soldiers reached the highest point of the small island on which they had landed they saw that they had made an error. The canvas boat and its two passengers had come to shore across a channel of water on another outcrop of low-tide rocks three hundred yards away. The two Germans, dropping behind a stony parapet, immediately and prematurely opened fire with their rifles. The first shots cracked through the still early air, the bullets shrieking as they ricocheted from the stone outcrops above Ormerod and Marie-Thérèse.

'Christ – already!' exclaimed Ormerod, pulling the girl out of the boat. 'Get down for God's sake!' They crouched behind the rocks. The girl began swearing in French. Ormerod poked his head out to have a look. 'The Germany army,' he muttered as he saw the soldiers running down the shingle and plunging up to their waists as they crossed the small channel, their rifles held above their heads. 'Well, two of them.'

'We will have to kill them,' she said, as though it were merely an inconvenience. 'So soon. It is very bad luck for us.'

'And them,' mentioned Ormerod more surely than he felt. 'How are we going to do it?'

The girl put her head out of their cover so she could see the Germans. They were still struggling to cross the channel, half-way over with the water up to their armpits. 'We will move,' she said decisively. 'Towards the main island. Perhaps we can make an ambush for them. Come.'

It was the first time that Ormerod had fully appreciated that she was actually in charge. He grunted but before he had finished she was climbing away from their hiding place and moving quickly over the rocks, going west. Ormerod followed her heavily, puffing a few yards in her wake. They climbed outcrops, slid down the other side and squelched across flat leads of seaweed-hung water. At the top of one of the small heights Ormerod saw the white cottages and the lighthouse on Chausey a mile away. He wondered if they would ever get there.

It was not difficult to hear the Germans coming in pursuit. They clattered clumsily over the resounding surface, slithering and cursing as they went. They knew that the two people in front had spotted them but they were not worried. Sooner or later they would come to The Sund, the deep trough between the islets and rocks and the main island. That had to be crossed. It could not be avoided for when the tide came back all the outlying surface rocks would be completely covered again.

The corporal was quite a clever young man. Had he lived he might have gone far in the Wehrmacht. He motioned his companion to move to the north while he went southwards, making a model pincer movement, that manoeuvre so beloved of the German army. They moved carefully now, making sure each step was secure and without making a noise. The corporal eventually raised his head and was delighted to see his quarry crouching in a shell-strewn bay looking in the other direction. He glanced up and saw that his compatriot had succeeded in coming around the rear from the other flank. The plan had worked well. Where the two people crouched he could see a lobster pot, filled with a catch, wallowing a few yards off shore. That ought to have told him there were others around but he failed to register the clue. He motioned his comrade to move in. Now he had decided he did not want to shoot the invaders. They would be of much more value as captives. He moved inwards towards the other German soldier. Then, when they were only five yards apart he rose casually above the rocks and shouted to Ormerod and the girl to raise their hands.

They looked up and knew they had to obey. Standing helplessly they put their hands above their heads. The German corporal said something to his companion and at that moment an amazing thing occurred. Something pushed them from behind and, shouting in fright, they both stumbled and came flying over the top of the parapet of rock.

Slack-jawed, Ormerod watched them, spread-eagled as they flew, their faces disfigured with horror and astonishment. It was only a drop of twenty-five feet or so but both Germans struck outstanding rocks and bounced flamboyantly before hitting the shingle and the sand and lying grotesquely still.

The eyes of Marie-Thérèse and Ormerod travelled up from the recumbent grey figures to the ledge where they had been standing. Like a comic actor coming forward on cue to take his bow a young man appeared. He was wearing a Breton blue jersey the arms of which were spread out as if acknowledging applause. He was leering strangely. 'Moi,' he said briefly. 'C'est moi.'

A group of other men, all fishermen, appeared on the surrounding outcrops of rocks, and silently looked down on the scene. They began clambering down to the group. The oldest of them, once square, now rotund, looked at the youth who had done the damage and then to Ormerod and the girl.

'You must understand he is mad,' he said. 'His head is mad.'

'Thank God for mad people,' answered Marie-Thérèse.

'There will be trouble,' said the fisherman. He stared at the youth who smiled weakly and performed a pushing movement to demonstrate what he had done. The others said nothing. Marie-Thérèse moved forward and turned both Germans on their backs.

'They are not dead,' she said in her businesslike way. 'It is no use shooting them. It will show. We must drown them.'

She had spoken to the fishermen and they regarded her with horrified amazement. She turned to Ormerod. 'I think we must persuade them.' She produced her pistol and, after hesitating, Ormerod did likewise. 'We must drown them,' repeated Marie-Thérèse in French in the direction of the fishermen.

'Put your weapons away,' replied the old man calmly. 'Because of what the boy has done we are in this matter just as much as you. He may be mad but he is still one of us. We will do as you say.'

Dumbly the fishermen picked up the Germans and carried them along the gulleys. They reached a point poised about twenty feet above the sea. The girl, her face hard as a pebble, said something else, almost barking at the fishermen. They hesitated, then obeyed. They scrambled over the shingle and returned with a large seine fishing net. The two soldiers were wrapped in this and then, while Ormerod stood as in a stupor, two large boulders were attached as weights and the Germans rolled down the short cliff and into the sea. They sank horribly.

'Thank you,' said Marie-Thérèse to her countrymen. 'You did a great service for France.'

'Jesus help me,' muttered Ormerod. 'That was terrible.'

'Terrible?' asked the girl practically. She looked at Ormerod gazing at the place where the net and the bodies had gone below the green surface of the early morning sea. 'Have you never seen men die before?' she asked.

'Yes. But I've never *watched* them die,' he said. 'There's a difference.'

Marie-Thérèse shrugged. 'The way anybody dies makes no difference to them,' she said. 'To them it was no different to being shot. In fact better. Water is soft. Bullets are hard.' Now she turned and spoke to the French fishermen, explaining who she and Ormerod were, and instructing them what to do next. She again went back to Ormerod. 'Killing is what war is all about, Dodo,' she said almost happily, using the codename for the first time. 'I have told these men to make a hole in the Germans' boat so that it seems it may have struck a rock and sunk. Also to sink our boat. They say that the two Germans came from the mainland to fish. We are lucky. There are no Boche on the island.'

'That's good news anyway,' said Ormerod. 'For them as well.'

She laughed at him outright. 'It is much easier to kill when they do not look like other men. If they had taken your country as they have taken mine then perhaps you would have found it easier.'

He nodded and said: 'Yes, I suppose I would. Why do you think there aren't any Germans on Chausey?' They had begun to walk down to a small beach where, Ormerod now saw, a long fishing boat was drawn up. Two of the Frenchmen, who had scarcely spoken a word during the whole episode, had gone to find the two boats at the far side of the rocks. Two of the others carried the German rifles. These they now took to a blunt piece of rock overlooking the place where they had dropped the enmeshed bodies and, simultaneously, they threw the rifles into the sea. Marie-Thérèse tried to stop them by shouting but they took no notice. The rifles sank and she berated the men in French. Their reply was in a sulky monotone. She turned away and bit her lip.

'They don't want to know, do they?' guessed Ormerod. He was surprised to hear the satisfaction in his own voice.

'They are crazy,' muttered the girl. 'Already they have killed two German soldiers, so why not keep the rifles? They will need them to kill more.'

'I think that you're probably going to find that a lot of your countrymen have had enough,' he forecast. 'They don't want to go on with the war. After all that's why they surrendered.'

She looked at him angrily. 'They are already involved in it. They will always be at war until the last German is dead or out of France. And these men are now deep in it – whether or not they like the idea.'

They began to walk along the shingle towards the fishing boat. The sun was rising with its customary assurance, flooding the sea and the islands with a fine green light. The water lapped along the shingle and Ormerod had a feeling that it would be nice to paddle his feet. 'How did these people know?' he asked, nodding at the fishermen.

'They spotted the submarine,' she said. 'There is not much they do not see. They saw us come ashore and they knew the Germans were fishing in the area. The Germans went to the island last night for food and drink. They come from the garrison at Granville. The fishermen came over to their lobster pots and perhaps to warn us.'

'And they end up resistance fighters,' smiled Omerod grimly. 'I expect that is how a good many heroes are made. Just by poking their noses in. Still, if this lot had not got to us, we'd now be in irons, I expect.'

'Rubbish,' said Marie-Thérèse vehemently. 'I would have killed those fools anyway. As it was the job was done for me.'

Ormerod's eyebrows went up. 'You're a really violent lady, aren't you?' he said.

'If they had needed a woman who was good at sewing they would have sent her,' she answered sullenly.

They climbed into the fishing boat. The September day was growing confidently all around them. Ormerod unhappily studied the five fishermen. Apart from the man who had done the talking, two were middle-aged, grey and with silent faces. Another was a younger man with an injured arm, probably one of those returned from the war. The fourth was the simpleton, a puzzled smiler, strongly made, but with the helpless look of one who is never sure of anything. They all wore the thick Breton jerseys and hard blue trousers.

They waited for ten minutes after getting into the boat, nobody speaking, until the other two men, both in their twenties and with more eagerness about them, returned around the rocks. 'It is done,' they said to Marie-Thérèse. 'The boats are now also under the sea.' They climbed aboard and the slim vessel started across the two hundred yards or so of deep water that was called The Sund.

'These men say that the Germans have not put any men on Chausey,' said Marie-Thérèse to Ormerod. 'They only come over from the mainland to fish or to buy some lobster.'

'Buy some?' said Ormerod. 'I thought that conquerors always took what they wanted. Food, women, everything.'

She made a face as if sniffing the salt morning air. 'They will,' she said. 'When the time comes. At the moment they do not want to make trouble for themselves. They are not sure of their feet. Once they are sure they will begin to take what they wish to have. You will see.'

Ormerod did not argue with her. 'It beats me why they haven't got troops on the island though,' he grunted. 'An anti-aircraft gun at least.'

'They will come, too I expect. But the men here say it is because the Germans are in great strength in Jersey and Guernsey in the English Channel Islands. They are making them fortified. So Chausey is of no importance yet. Later it may be. It seems we are lucky, Dodo. Very lucky.'

The boat turned into an enclosed anchorage. Ormerod looked out on the most peaceful of scenes, a row of serene stone cottages with boats pulled up almost to their doors, a larger house, like a farm, standing back, creepers on its walls and dogs about its wide archway. There was a small church on the promontory, some further houses in the distance and a lighthouse standing like a daytime ghost at the southern extreme. In the middle of the island, where the land dipped into a sheltered meadow, some full trees were growing, and at the northern end he could see the shoulders of a substantial house.

Marie Thérèse spoke to the fishermen. No one answered for a moment, then the older man, apparently having made some decision himself, replied. She smiled at Ormerod. 'We are going into prison,' she said.

'So soon?'

'It is not like that. There is an old fortress on the island, from the last century. I have seen it marked on the maps. It has eight sides and it is sunk into the ground. They will keep us there.'

'They've agreed to hide us then?'

'Not with a good heart. They are telling me the Germans will be over soon to look for their missing friends. Our comrades here do not want to hide us too carefully because, in the first place, they say there are not many places to hide. I don't believe that. But if we are caught hiding then it would be bad for the population. They would have reprisals on them.'

Ormerod nodded. The small boat was at the anchorage now

and they were able to step out into the translucent water only inches deep and then on to the soft beach. A woman with a cooking pot in her hands and some sunburned children appeared at the low cottages and watched. 'I can't say I blame them,' said Ormerod. 'They look as if they are having a nice peaceful sort of life. You can't blame them for wanting to keep it that way.'

She sniffed. 'They are in it,' she said practically. 'They are in the war. Deep with us. They will have to learn that.'

Ormerod politely helped her from the boat, taking the petite hand and holding her small elbow. 'You're not going to make yourself very popular, lady,' he thought, looking at her.

She seemed to read the thought. 'They will not like me,' she sniffed. 'There are few who will. But they must be taught to fight, to resist. The French must make up for the past.'

'But they won't hide us.' He was beginning to walk up the beach.

'No. They say we can keep out of sight. But that is not the same as hiding us. We can take shelter in one of the cells at the old fortress.'

They were at the top of the shingle now. The morning air was unstirring, full of warmth and promise. Chickens stalked about and a man in a wide white hat rode a bicycle on the single track road with not a glance in their direction. On the other side of the island a dog began to howl. The woman with the cooking pot had been joined by two others. They looked rough and simple. Children dangled around them. They all backed away as the two strangers and the fishermen reached the top of the beach. One of the woman said to the oldest man: 'We heard shooting.'

'It was nothing,' he said. 'Nothing to worry about.'

The woman looked suspiciously at Marie-Thérèse but hardly gave a second glance at Ormerod. Ormerod thought how odd it was that women so rarely trusted women. For the first time Marie Thérèse seemed uncomfortable. She turned to Ormerod as if she had to say something to get away from their glances. 'This place has been the same since the days of William of Normandy, the Conqueror,' she joked. 'And some of these women look as though they've been here since then.'

The oldest man began to plod along in the direction of the large house and he indicated that they should follow him. 'They are being difficult,' said Marie-Thérèse. 'Cowards. Keep your gun ready. We may need to persuade them to do things our way.'

'You're not choosy who you shoot, are you?' observed Ormerod. They seemed accidentally to be walking like prisoners, with the Frenchmen grouped around them.

'I cannot afford to be,' she shrugged. 'One day it may be necessary for me to shoot *you*, Dodo.'

'Let me know in advance, will you?' he grunted.

'It may not be possible.'

They had reached the top of a small incline that had begun with the beach. Now a man came from the courtyard preparing to mount a bicycle and with two dogs at his feet. He was obviously some sort of leader because the men treated him with deference. Marie-Thérèse was not prepared to let them tell the story, however, and she pushed her way forward. Speaking quickly, she soon covered the circumstances and, turning the advantage with an ease that made Ormerod nod with admiration, began to ask questions in her turn. Her words came out quickly and forcefully. The man, reluctantly at first as his position was usurped, began to answer. Eventually he turned to the others and spoke volubly. The old fisherman answered him, shaking his large, teddy-bear head. The others mumbled agreement. The man returned to Marie-Thérèse. He spoke slowly now, but it was clear to Ormerod that they had decided on their position and they were not going to move from it. Eventually the girl turned to him.

'They have no guts,' she said briefly. 'Not even for France. They will not hide us. They say we can hide ourselves, but they will not hide us. They will leave a boat for us to get to the mainland but they will not take us.'

'Can't blame them,' sighed Ormerod. 'I wouldn't in their position either. Have they got a cup of tea?'

The leader of the men understood. 'Please come with me,' he said in English. 'We have some Liptons. The quicker you leave this place the happier we will be.'

*

Three hours later Ormerod awoke in the dry dimness of a nineteenth-century room in the fortress. It was piled with nets, lobster pots and other tarry equipment. The happenings of the night and the early morning had drained him and as soon as the Chausey fishermen had shown them their refuge, he had stretched out on some dry nets and fallen into the deepest sleep. At first he was conscious of Marie-Thérèse moving about, but only vaguely, and then not at all. When he awoke she was not there. A fan of sunlight was coming through the ill-fitting doors. He looked at his watch. It was half past eleven. As he stretched he felt a dozen aches. He stumbled to his feet and disturbed three mice who were gnawing at some tallow in one corner. They startled him as much as he startled them. He had reached for his pistol, only to put it away with relief when he saw what had caused the noise. He scratched himself and made for the narrow sunlight.

The rough door opened easily and the warmth of the strange enclosure outside the cell came to him. It was like a symmetrical crater, a hundred feet across, with octagonal stone walls piled up around and the close atmosphere of the September day trapped in its confines. What had been soldiers' quarters and cells all around were now small storehouses for fishing and agricultural equipment. There was a decrepit dinghy lying in the centre of the space, weeds and wild flowers climbing enthusiastically over it, pushing their tendrils through its split boards. Alongside the boat was a group of small sheltered trees between which fishing nets were slung to dry. Outsized bees and flapping butterflies moved around the walls and the flowers. Ormerod sniffed appreciatively and looked up to an octagon of cloudless sky. It was a lovely day to be an invader.

He felt his pistol, a mixture of comfort and anxiety to him, in the holster below his armpit, stepped out into the trapped sunlight and saw immediately the movement of a man, a fisherman, who was sitting on the top of the wall where the garrison guards had once been stationed. The man looked startled at Ormerod's appearance, but then waved in a relaxed manner and sat down again.

There was a flight of pocked stone steps leading from the

floor of the small fortress to the parapet on the walls. He walked solidly up them, hesitating near the summit before he exposed his head to the skyline, then cautiously rose until he was standing on the wall. It was a thick embankment like the fortifications found in a stronghold of the Middle Ages. There was a sturdy carpet of grass decorated with small and vivid wild flowers. The smell came back to him, the sweet dryness of summer, something from childhood he had almost forgotten. He had lived a long time in the city.

Ormerod had a good view from up there. He could see almost the entire length of the island. The lighthouse was upright on the cliff almost at his back and before him the slim land stretched, shaped like a veal cutlet, narrowing and then running to fat. He could see the church with its small tower and below him a smaller steeple which he guessed was a navigational seamark. There was a schoolhouse with children in its enclosure and scattered houses in the varying dells and alongside the bay where they had landed that morning. In the anchorage were several small boats and in The Sund, the channel between the main island and the other rocks and islets, several more were riding on the thickening tide. The rocks over which they had been pursued by the two German soldiers that morning were now as submerged as the Germans themselves.

Now he was there he felt better, relieved that all the waiting and the idiocy of his preparations were over. But it was something of an anti-climax, even taking into account the excitement of the action that morning, for here the war seemed further away than ever. Seagulls mewed impatiently over the water, a donkey brayed back; the air was full of scents and humming and a thin web of smoke came from one of the bay cottages and hung in the still air. Ormerod descended from the wall and began to pick blackberries.

They were plump and luscious, just as he remembered them from youth but had never come across since. He selected them ambitiously, always reaching for a bigger and better berry a few inches deeper into the catching thorns. He had been occupied like this for five minutes and his mouth was stained blue-black when he noticed a half-concealed path that had come into view with his progress around the flanks of the bushes.

With his newly-acquired carefulness he dropped down into the trench-like track and began to follow it with no great object other than to see where it went. It smelled beautifully rotten, bursting with late summery odours, and with small birds whistling in its green banks and wiry hawthorns. Eventually it curved and, to his pleasure, opened out on to a cupped beach, some two hundred yards away, without a footprint defacing the sand. Towards the centre of the beach were two tough rocks which seagulls sat on and shouted. The sea, a fine shade of green, eased itself without fuss on to the sand.

Ormerod in his summery mood was about to tread the beach, thinking perhaps that he might paddle in the sea, when he saw a movement only a few yards away to his left. His view was almost obscured by some tussocks of heavy marram grass so he eased himself up a minor sand-dune and, to his utter astonishment, saw Marie-Thérèse sitting naked in a good-sized oval rock pool. He felt himself blush for his involuntary voyeurism and pulled his head back below the grass again. He waited, his conscience hovering, then had another look.

She was sitting in the pool washing herself like some model Aphrodite. He was surprised at her smallness. She was not much bigger than a young girl, her body and her breasts well shaped, her hair lying carelessly across her forehead and shoulder, her face concerned with something between her toes. Ormerod withdrew his head and his gaze and lay against the warm sand.

Gently he allowed himself to fall down the slope of the sand and then, picking his steps, he withdrew towards the sunken path by which he had reached the place. He returned to the blackberry bushes near the old fort and sat eating the berries in the sun until, after ten minutes, Marie-Thérèse returned, also along the path.

'You look like a boy,' she said, but with a smile. 'You will have an ache in your belly.' She sat down on the same bank and he handed her some blackberries. She took them and throwing them up like a juggler caught them in her mouth.

'You seem happy,' he observed. He could not help but look at her breasts beneath the blue woollen jersey, guiltily thinking how he had seen them a few minutes before. He had never been a very sexual man and he had not seen many pairs of breasts.

'It is still summer,' she said, answering his remark. 'And I am back in France. That makes me happy. How do you feel?'

'Better after that shut-eye,' he said. 'I didn't realize how exhausting this invasion business can be.' He put some more berries in his mouth. 'There's a lot of these aren't there? Nobody seems to have been collecting them.'

'These people are lazy,' she said at once, nodding inland. 'Always they have had a good life here – as long as they did not ask for too much. Now they want to go on in that way, as if the war was nothing to do with them. As if France was still free.'

'You can't blame them really,' said Ormerod shaking his head. 'I wish nobody had thought of bothering me.'

'Fishermen make good spies,' she said regretfully, her face dropping. 'They move about and see many things. And they can make contact when they are out in the fishing grounds. They could be so useful.' She looked up again at him. 'And everyone is bothered, as you call it, in the end. Everybody. Nobody can keep away from the war.' She smiled wryly. 'Even when they run away from it, like the British.'

'You're not all that fond of us, are you?' said Ormerod.

She did not look at him. She threw another blackberry into her mouth. She turned towards him for further supply but he nodded at the bush. 'Pick your own if you're so independent,' he said.

She smiled at him. 'You, Dodo, have a heart. Whatever else you do not have, you have a heart. All I say is that unless your countrymen fight a little better and with more heart than in the past, then the Germans will be in London just as sure as they are in Paris.'

'I'd have nowhere to go home to then would I?' he sniffed. 'I wouldn't even be able to take friend Smales back.'

'*Back*? You're not thinking of taking him back, are you?' She looked astounded.

'Well, that was my general idea. Yes. He has to be charged and appear in court and everything. The proper way. Other than getting him back I don't see how justice will be done. It's not going to be easy, I'll grant you that.'

Marie-Thérèse lay back on the spiky grass and laughed. Her face was bright in the sun and her breasts moved below the wool. 'My God!' she giggled. 'They all think *I'm* mad, but you're madder than me!'

As the evening thickened into night they sat in the old barrack cell, a low oil lamp projecting their crouching shadows on to the wall like the forms of some ancient cave dwellers. They had talked little in an hour. Two men had come from the houses with some food and a bottle of cider for them. Now it was finished. They sat in idleness yet with a tautness about them that made them start at every quiet scurry of a mouse or a moth in the enclosed air. They had both cleaned their pistols. Now there was nothing else.

'One thing we forgot,' mentioned Ormerod. 'We should have brought some cards. We might be here days.'

'We cannot leave the island yet,' agreed the girl sullenly. 'The Germans are bound to send a boat out to see what has happened to the two soldiers we drowned.' Ormerod momentarily reacted to the word 'we' but she did not seem to notice and continued: 'If we try to get to the mainland too soon they will certainly see us in the sea and that would be the end of the matter. We will wait until they have come and gone away again.'

Ormerod sniffed like a dog in the shadows. 'I can't see our friends here being all that keen on landing us on the mainland,' he observed. 'So far they haven't shown the sort of bulldog spirit to say the least. The only one who's gone out of the way to be friendly is the village idiot. And he thinks we're the British invasion. He's asked me three times when the rest of the troops are arriving.'

The girl laughed, a dry laugh that made for a sharp echo in the confined place. 'Perhaps all fools should stay together,' she said. 'We are the only ones who seem to understand. They *must* take us to the mainland. If I have to make them at the end of a gun they will take us.' She stood up and walked the length of the old cell, her shadow thin like an insect on the wall. 'In truth, Dodo, I don't like the way we are here.'

'In this hole?' he said. 'Well, I'll second that.'

'I think that it would be better if we were with the islanders. Here they tell us we are hiding, but we have very conveniently made ourselves prisoners. We are in a *souricière* – a mousetrap. When the Boche arrive these men could quite easily lead them to us.'

Ormerod looked at her in surprise. 'But they're still French,' he said. 'They wouldn't do that.'

She shook her head. 'I would like to think that also. But I think it is foolish to be here, shut up like this. Perhaps the Germans may search the island and it would not take them long to find us in this place.' Her eyes regarded him brightly in the dimness. 'No, I think we are sitting like chickens in this mousetrap. Come, we will go and join my countrymen.'

They went out into the early night. It was balmy, with fresh stars looking down on the island and the scent of the sea coming clearly to them. The lighthouse sent its beam over the dark channel. Ormerod nodded that way. 'They'll have a radio there,' he said. 'Do you think they will have sneaked on us?'

Marie-Thérèse was trudging beside him down the stony path that led to the village houses. She shook her head vigorously. 'I don't think they would *betray* us by sending a message,' she said firmly. 'They would never do that. But if the Germans were here, on Chausey, and the people here considered it was dangerous for them to conceal us, I think then we would soon be discovered.'

The houses had observed only nondescript blackout, and cracks of light could be seen in windows as they appeared. For the first time Ormerod noticed a larger building almost on The Sund from which two men came. They opened a door and warm light and a whirr of voices came out. Marie-Thérèse touched Ormerod's shoulder and they sank into some bushes, a painful interlude for Ormerod because his bush was one of the many blackberry thorns. They waited until the men disappeared, talking deeply, in the direction of the landing place, and then, rising cautiously and in Ormerod's case gratefully, they moved towards the building and spied through the cracks in the ill-fitting blinds. It was obviously the island inn. There were rough tables and benches, with oil lamps burning, and with perhaps fifteen men sitting around holding mugs of cider. Two women moved about replenishing the glasses. The youth who was the island idiot was in a corner plucking haphazardly at a ukelele. Marie-Thérèse moved to the door, touched the latch and pushed it open with her foot.

They walked in together. Ormerod saw that the girl had her pistol in her small, pale hand. If the Gestapo had entered the effect could not have been heightened. The men stared at them in the lamplight and one of the young girls dropped a flagon of cider onto the floor and ran weeping to get a cloth to wipe it up. The simple boy produced a dramatic strumming chord on the ukelele.

'Bonsoir, mes amis,' smiled Marie-Thérèse, closing the door behind her.

'Evening all,' said Ormerod, nodding around.

'We were lonely,' the girl said, sitting down on a bench. She eyed Ormerod and he sat on another at the other side of the room. It would not do to be too close together. A mangy mongrel came and sniffed around his boots as if it smelled a foreigner. 'Do you offer your guests a drink?' asked Marie-Thérèse.

The older man who had been with them in the morning on the outer rocks nodded and called to the second girl, who was standing stupefied, and she brought a flagon and two glasses. Ormerod was glad of the drink. The cider was dark and powerful. Drunk in England it had never failed to give him a bad stomach, but he needed a drink. The girl raised her glass and looked through the dark liquid. 'To France,' she said to the islanders, 'our country.'

With an astonishing sullenness they raised their glasses and repeated the toast. She added another. 'To victory.' They answered this with a mumble.

She drank once and then fixed them with her hard gaze. 'Don't you want victory? Don't you love France?'

They looked shamefaced into their glasses. It was the old man who replied. 'Here,' he said, 'on this little island, we want only peace. We want no trouble. The Germans have left us alone. They come here sometimes to buy lobster – and they pay a fair price. Sometimes they come to take some wine from the château in the north of the island. We do not care. There is no one in the château now. The wine is not ours. In any case if they want to take the wine there is nothing we can do. They have guns. You must understand that the only trouble we have experienced here so far has occurred today – you, madame. And your English friend.'

Ormerod hardly understood a word. But the apologetic tone was obvious. 'They've had someone signalling aircraft,' he reminded Marie-Thérèse. She put it to the old man. He shrugged and pointed to the youth with the ukelele. 'It was the fool in the corner,' he shrugged. The youth, who was trying to fit his fingers over the strings, looked up and acknowledged the reference as if it were a compliment. 'We have taken the torch from him now. He is a poor idiot but we still want him to live.'

Marie-Thérèse said: 'Well, you may not like us here, but we are here. So that is that. The quicker we get to the mainland – and that means that you must get us there – the better it will be for us all.' She looked at them scornfully. 'I have no wish to stay in this place with you.'

The mangy mongrel, having smelled Ormerod's feet in detail, lifted its scrawny leg and urinated down his trousers. Ormerod felt the warm wetness soak through. He pushed the dog away violently. Nobody smiled. The old man drank a glass of cider with one lift. 'The Germans will be coming very soon,' he said quietly when he had put the empty glass on the table. 'They will be looking for the two men you ... er ... killed today. If we try to get to the mainland and they are coming across in their boats they will stop us. Then we will all be shot. You will have to wait until they come here.'

'Then we must wait with you,' said Marie-Thérèse pointedly. Her pistol was only an inch from her hand on the table. Some of the men could hardly take their gaze from it. 'We are not holing up in that place you call a fort. They will find us easily there. We must be part of this island.'

'You will never be that,' said one of the men suddenly. 'Here we keep peace.'

'While your country is in slavery!' she replied angrily. 'Have you no guts, no fight?'

'The time for guts and fighting is over,' said the man facing her with solid fatalism. 'You have come too late.'

That night, at the insistence of Marie-Thérèse, Ormerod went to sleep at the house of the island idiot. She went to the home of the older man. If the Germans came in the middle of the night it would appear better that way.

The idiot, whose name was Clément, was patently delighted that Ormerod was to stay at his mother's cottage and they went home across the sand, under a bursting moon, with the young man playing wildly and tunelessly on his ukelele and Ormerod blithely joining in the ragged song. As they went an aero-engine sound came from the north and a solitary RAF Blenheim flew across the island at about two hundred feet. Clément, now relieved of his torch, gesticulated excitedly and Ormerod, feeling he had to do something, performed a forlorn wave. 'One of ours,' he nodded knowingly at the boy. The plane crossed against the stars. It made him feel homesick for Putney.

Clément's mother was sane but insanitary and she welcomed him to their cottage, sitting him down and giving him a large lump of bread like a stone and some cold fish followed by some of the foulest coffee he had ever consumed. She was glad to have him to stay, she assured him, for there were many little jobs about the house he could do. She was a fat, wobbling woman with hair that had defended itself against any comb for the past thirty years. She kept smiling at Ormerod and jabbering at the boy who eventually wished Ormerod a mad goodnight and went up the short flight of stairs to his bed.

Ormerod fell to wondering how many bedrooms there were in the cottage. He had an uneasy feeling there could hardly be more than two. The suspicion increased when the woman began making pointing movements towards the staircase, and he eventually mounted it, bending his head as he reached the low landing.

To his relief the steamy woman remained downstairs, looking at herself in a stained mirror. In the room a wide and lumpy double bed took up most of the available space, covered by a patchwork quilt that gave it the appearance of undulating countryside. There was an oil lamp on a table jammed in one corner. Ormerod felt excessively weary. He reached down his back and pulled the bulky jersey over his head. Then he took off his trousers and got into the bed.

Three minutes later Clément's awful mother clumped up the stairs, came into the room and unceremoniously got into the bed on the other side.

'Wait a minute! Hang on!' protested Ormerod, waking and sitting abruptly upright. 'What are you doing, madame?'

'*Mon lit,*' the lady said gummily. She had taken her teeth out and donned a voluminous flannel nightdress. Her eyes glittered blackly. She let off a great soft grin. Ormerod glared at her, horrified.

'*Mon lit,*' she insisted. '*Mon grand lit.*' She leaned over and punched his pillow. '*Pour vous, monsieur.*' Then she repeated the punch on her own side of the bed. '*Pour moi.*' With that she flung herself under the quilt and discharged a tremendous rush of wind. Ormerod, further horrified, remained sitting and staring.

But Clément's mother went quickly to sleep, snoring profusely and scratching herself frenetically at intervals. Ormerod felt the tiredness gripping him throughout his body. His head lolled and he dropped back against the brass headrail. His own weight made him descend into the bed and eventually he too pulled the quilt around him and slept dreamlessly.

In the morning the sun came like fire into the room. He stirred and realized where he was. To his relief his bed partner had gone and eventually the idiot son appeared balancing a cup of coffee which he promptly dropped just inside the door and had to go back for replenishment. Ormerod drank the coffee, washed in a bowl of water on the dressing table and went down the tight, crooked stairs.

On the lowest step he was confronted by the old woman brandishing a chopper. She appeared belligerent but she merely thrust it into his hand and pointed irrevocably to the back of the cottage. Ormerod walked, obedient but puzzled, opened the door and was faced by an eight-foot pile of logs. He turned and looked askance at the woman. She uttered a shriek like an old raven and made a chopping movement. Clément appeared and pointed clownishly at the logs. Ormerod began chopping.

He could hardly have foreseen that his first full day as a secret agent would begin with a session of chopping wood. He sweated in the early sunshine and wondered where Marie-Thérèse was. Even as he thought of her she appeared at the small gate at the end of the back garden of the house. Seeing him she stopped and, for the first time since they had been together, he saw her laugh without restraint. She laughed like a young girl, her hands trying to cover her mouth. 'Oh my God, Dodo,' she mocked. 'You are a wood-chopper!'

'Go on, enjoy yourself,' he said bitterly. 'This is not the worst of it. I had to sleep in the same bed as that old hag last night. I'm having a bloody marvellous time, believe me. I think I'll surrender to the Germans.'

The very mention of the word seemed enough to bring her seriousness back. She advanced up the path. She looked fresh and pink, her hair just curling over the blue jersey. 'It is good that you look like one of the islanders,' she said. 'We must be part of the landscape.'

'Any sign of the Boche?' he said. He realized that he had used her word. She noticed it.

'They have radioed to the lighthouse asking if the two soldiers have been seen,' she shrugged. 'But it seems their fishing trip was not official. Their officers did not know.'

'Taken French leave, eh?' he said. 'That's if Germans can take French leave.'

'Their comrades are trying to find them – also unofficially,' she went on. 'They do not want to make too much stir because they will make trouble with their own officers. The men are not permitted to come this far out to sea.'

Ormerod put the chopper down. He bawled towards the house: 'Is this enough missus?' The woman came to the door, saw Marie-Thérèse and with no change of expression went into the shadows again. Clément came out and, seeing the girl, beamed like a child and went forward to shake her hand.

'Can we expect them out here with a boat soon?' asked Ormerod. 'They won't leave it too long.'

'By tonight,' she said. 'They can ask their questions and once they have gone we can go to the mainland and begin work.'

'They'll have to report their pals missing – officially – sooner or later,' pointed out Ormerod. 'Then they'll be back to search for the boat. I hope to God the bodies don't float to the surface.'

She shook her head. 'The rocks in the net weighed them down. Also there is a lot of weed in the place where we drowned them. The weather is changing too. They may find the boat but they won't find the men. They will think they have just gone missing on a fishing trip. Many people have.'

He split a log with a single blow of the chopper. Clément was impressed and clapped. Marie-Thérèse said: 'I think it would be a good thing if we walked right around this island. It will give us some idea of how the land is. Just in case we need to move at night. In case they start looking for their friends. Has madame given you some breakfast?'

'No, but I think I'll skip it. She's more dangerous than the Jerries. If it's anything like the coffee, I'll never finish this assignment on two feet. I'll come with you now.' He handed the chopper to Clément. 'Here son,' he said. 'You have a bash.'

Doubtfully the youth took the implement and Ormerod quietly went towards the back gate with Marie-Thérèse. They let themselves out and began to walk over the filmy morning grass towards the north of Chausey. Behind them they heard the blows of the chopper as Clément attacked the wood.

five

They walked, at first unhurriedly, to the top of as much of a hill as the island could boast. The grass was springy beneath their feet and the undergrowth gave off a ferny smell. Once Marie-Thérèse slipped and Ormerod put out his hand to assist her, but she waved it away as if ashamed that she had lost her footing.

From the top of the hill, which was not much more than a knoll, they could see the entire island and all the satin sea around them. The tide was running away and the off-shore islands and rocks were humped like cattle. The autumn morning sun was increasing in strength and the sky was without clouds. Below them they could view the everyday domestic life of the settlement going on like a ritual dance. Some of the men were loading an obese boat with lobster kreels, two women did their washing in tin tubs outside their cottages and carried the cleansed clothes to hang on long poles in the breeze. Dogs sat and watched and cats slouched on walls. From the schoolhouse the sound of high reciting voices drifted to them.

At every inlet and cape of the island the sea eased itself against sand and rocks without hurry, in the manner of a besieging army that knows it will never break a fortress. The small fields of the island were easy green and cattle moved as if every step were carefully considered. To the south the lighthouse stood in its daytime doze and to the north the house called the château stood on the end cliff like a solitary man looking hopefully towards England. And France, a low but distant horseshoe of land, curved around the eastern horizon. Ormerod sat down heavily and took it all in.

'Bit peaceful for a war, isn't it?' he observed to Marie-Thérèse.

She stood beside him for a moment, as if she were guarding him, then she dropped with a sigh to the turf and sat down a yard away. 'Everything is too peaceful,' she said unhappily. 'Nobody seems to realize that there *is* a war.'

'Don't you know there's a war on?' He mimicked the slogan he had heard bandied about so much in England. She remembered it too. She laughed wryly.

'Anyway,' he said. 'At least you can *see* France.'

'Yes, I see it,' she replied quietly.

'How long have you been away?'

'Almost a year,' she said to his surprise. 'I went to London in November. I returned for a few days at Christmas and then I went back again to England.'

'I didn't realize that,' he said. 'I thought you'd probably gone over about the time of Dunkirk with all the others who got away.'

85

She shook her head. 'No, I was training for this,' she replied. Her chin dropped sadly. 'I never thought France would surrender. I did not imagine it could happen. I thought I would be training to go to Austria or Poland. But not France. Not my own country.'

Just off-shore the gulls had found some fish debris floating on the surface and whirled about it like pieces of paper caught in a wind spout. The men below them had finished landing the boat and were sitting on the stones around the beach drinking coffee. One of the washing women was singing tunelessly, plaintively and the thin song came to them on their hillock.

'Where's this place St Jean le Thomas?' asked Ormerod, looking at the vague horizon. He said it more to bring her from her chagrin than anything.

'It is about that point,' she said, pointing to the south-east. 'Perhaps we will land there. It has a long beach and it is quiet. The Germans must watch it but there is very much to watch. Perhaps we will get so far by boat and swim the rest.'

'I can't swim,' Ormerod told her. 'Didn't they tell you that?'

She sighed. 'I thought perhaps you could not,' she said, shaking her head. 'You get better and better.'

'If I'm not satisfactory, send me home,' he suggested. 'Please.'

She apologized suddenly. 'I am unreasonable,' she said. 'But you must realize how I feel. I have been training all this time and then they send me with ... well ... you.'

'I'm sorry,' he said. 'Take it from me, it wasn't my idea.'

'Of course not. But for God's sake the matter could have been planned better by that mad boy who lives down there.'

Ormerod nodded. 'From what I saw of the briefing officers in England that lad would be a colonel in no time,' he agreed. 'Where's Granville?'

'It is above St Jean le Thomas. So it would be about there.' She pointed to the left of the lighthouse dome. 'I hope we will be able to begin our work in Granville. There must be the opportunity to form a resistance group, if one is not begun already.'

'You certainly haven't had a lot of luck here with this bunch,' observed Ormerod, looking down at the miniature men still idling on the shores of the beach. Brightly coloured children came out into the school playground with a sound like seagulls.

'They are soft,' she said with only a touch of disgust. 'They have hardly seen a German yet. If the Boche came over here with some anti-aircraft guns, which is what I suppose they will do in time, they will soon realize what it means to be conquered.'

'You can't make them fight if they don't know what they're fighting,' agreed Ormerod. 'I'm still not convinced that they will not hand us over to the first Jerry that appears.'

She had lit a cigarette. She drew on it fiercely, her mouth like a beak. 'They will not do that. I have already made an arrangement with Marcel, the old man, in the house last night.'

'An arrangement? What?'

'I have told him I will shoot him and his son if the Germans are told,' she said coolly. 'And any other person from this island who is there while I still have my gun. I think he understands me.'

'Jesus wept,' murmured Ormerod. 'And well he might. You would too, wouldn't you?'

'If it meant they had betrayed us then I would,' she said. 'I have plenty of bullets for traitors.'

Ormerod leaned back on the placid grass. He closed his eyes and let the increasing warmth of the day across his face. 'God this feels like having a day off and lying in our local park,' he said. 'If it wasn't for the gulls screeching, and the smell of the salt, and you talking about shooting people.'

'Are you happy in your marriage?' she asked in her sudden way.

He was surprised by the inquiry but he did not open his eyes. 'I don't know yet. I've only been married a year. I expect I'll find out in time,' he mumbled.

Her voice seemed quite distant. 'Yes, I suppose you are right about that,' she said. She paused for more than a minute. 'When I am in Normandy I will go for a short visit to my village,' she continued. 'To see my children.'

For some reason he was amazed. He released one eye, then the other, and then got up onto his elbows. 'You've got kids?' he said. 'Somehow that never occurred to me. You, married.'

'I am not certain I am married,' she corrected. 'My husband

was taken away by the Nazis, so I have been told, so I expect he is now dead. They do not keep people as guests, you know.'

He looked at her sympathetically. Her expression had not changed. 'I see,' he said. 'That's one of your reasons, is it?'

'One of them,' she nodded. She had turned her head and was now looking towards the jumping children in the school yard. 'I have two like that. Clovis and Suzanne.'

'Boy and a girl, eh?' Ormerod said conventionally. 'Nice. Haven't thought much about kids myself. Not yet. Not with the war and everything.'

'What do you think about?' she asked. 'In your life?'

'Crime,' he said decisively. 'Nabbing people who've done it. It's my interest in life, I suppose. Sometimes it gets to be an obsession with me. That's why I want to get our chummy Smales.'

'Ah, Monsieur Smales,' she half smiled. 'Well he will not be the only criminal you will find over the water. You will have the chance to be – how do you say? – nabbing more than one man.'

'We *are* going to Bagnoles, aren't we?' he said, leaning towards her. 'For sure I mean. That's where he was last heard of. In hospital.'

Her eyebrows went up a little mockingly. 'You would arrest a wounded man?' she asked.

'Even if I have to carry the bastard over my shoulder,' he grunted. 'I *really* want to get my hands on him.'

'This girl he murdered, did you love her?' she asked. He looked at her again in astonishment.

'You wouldn't be French would you?' he protested grumpily. 'It's not all romance and tragedy you know. Of course I didn't love her. God, she was only eighteen. I know her parents, but it was nothing personal. It's just a young life chucked away because some man got drunk and couldn't control his randiness.'

'You make it sound as if it is personal,' she shrugged. 'Perhaps you fell in love with her after she was dead.'

In the evening the Germans arrived. There were twenty villagers in the room of the inn, drinking cider in the smoke, with Ormerod sitting among them and Marie-Thérèse standing behind the bar handing the tankards of drink to the two young girls to place on the tables. At nine o'clock there was a brisk knock on the door and it seemed that twenty cooperative voices called '*Entrez!*' Marcel, the old man, suddenly bent and picked the ragged mongrel of the bar up and threw it in the surprised Ormerod's lap. Ormerod glanced at Marie-Thérèse and saw her dart a look at the old man. His eyes were calm. Ormerod felt his pistol under his armpit like a small crutch. The dog settled in his lap. The door opened and a decent-faced German sergeant came in, followed by four apprehensive soldiers. They held their rifles as though they would drop them and run at the first indication of trouble. It was the second time that Ormerod had seen German soldiers and once again he thought that soldiers were the same everywhere. Afraid.

They clumbered into the room and shut the door politely behind them. The sergeant saw the old man Marcel, and recognized him. He sat down beside him. The fisherman nodded towards Marie-Thérèse and, tight-lipped, she poured five glasses of cider and gave them to the girls to give to the soldiers.

In difficult French the sergeant asked the old man if they had seen two of their comrades who had gone fishing and not returned. With relief Ormerod saw that the fisherman was shaking his head before the question was finished. 'Not today at all,' Marcel said. 'We heard from the lighthouse that they were missing. Two days ago they were in their boat close inshore to the island. They came to land for some bread and fish and cider. But they went over to the east somewhere.'

The sergeant sighed. 'It is terrible,' he said. 'They are good boys. But they are not supposed to come out here. It is against the rule of the army, you see. So far we have kept it a secret. Nobody knows officially. That is why we have come over at this time of night. We ourselves are not supposed to be here, you understand.'

The elder fisherman nodded. The sergeant said: 'One is a boy from my home town. If anything has happened to him I will be the one to have to tell his mother.' He seemed close to tears. 'In the war you can be killed,' he said. 'That is understood. But fishing . . .'

Ormerod sat with the dog curled untidily on his lap and his anxiety sitting on his shoulder. But even in that condition he felt a certain sorrow for the German sergeant who now sat down and wiped his good-natured eyes. Ormerod thought he saw Marie-Thérèse curl her lip.

Apart from the sergeant, the other soldiers were very young. One of them, his pint of cider held nervously beneath his nose, moved over towards Ormerod and sat down, putting his hand out to pat the mongrel. As though afraid of the German, the animal made a small wet on the Englishman's lap.

'Wie heisst er?' asked the young soldier. 'Quel est son nom?'

Ormerod looked down at the dog as if wondering whether to ask it. It was a mean, mangy mongrel, with watery eyes, a dirty white, brown and grey coat and bad breath.

'Formidable,' Ormerod replied in what he hoped sounded like a French voice. All the fishermen began to laugh and the eyes of Marie-Thérèse darkened. Nothing must seem strange or come as a surprise. But the Germans laughed too and it seemed to cheer the sergeant up. He winked at the older man. 'While we are on Chausey,' he said, 'we will take back a little wine from the château. Nobody will miss a few bottles.'

Marcel shrugged. 'You are the bosses,' he said. 'There is much wine there. By the end of the war it will be sour anyway. Go and help yourselves.'

'And,' said the sergeant, now seriously, looking more like a German soldier, 'we must return tonight. As I told you, our journey is not official, although I think we must now report the two boys missing. But we need someone to pilot us to Granville. It is difficult in the dark. Who will it be?'

The old man would have made a good spy or an actor. Not a flicker of expression crossed his face. 'I will take you,' he answered with a heavy nod. 'I know every rock and current. And you can do a service for us, mein Herr.'

'What is that?' asked the sergeant. His men were moving out of the door into the moonless night. One of them began to sing softly.

'This man,' said Marcel pointing to Ormerod. Ormerod stiffened. 'And this woman,' he nodded at Marie-Thérèse. 'They have to visit a woman at Julioville, the lady's grandmother. She is sick. Could we take them also?'

Ormerod marvelled at the simplicity of it. He thought he detected a quick touch of amusement in the girl's straight mouth. The sergeant looked at them and nodded immediately. 'Yes, yes, that will be all right,' he said in his French. 'There is plenty of room in the boat.' He went to the door. 'Be ready in twenty minutes,' he said. 'We will be back with the wine then.'

For a long interval after he had gone there was silence in the room. They could hear the sergeant calling through the night after his men. His shouts diminished and the grins spread around the faces. Only the old man remained serious. 'Is that satisfactory?' he said to Marie-Thérèse.

'Very poetic, monsieur,' she replied politely. 'You get the Germans themselves to deliver us.'

'We will be rid of you,' he said without a smile. 'They are doing us a service.' He turned to Ormerod and for some reason his expression eased. 'You must take the dog with you, monsieur,' he said. 'Your *Formidable*.' He saw a protest about to break from Marie-Thérèse and he put his hand up to hush her. 'A man with a dog, especially a poor dog like that, will never cause suspicion,' he said. 'That is why I placed the animal on his lap. People always think that a man with a dog comes from the district where he is seen with the dog – that he cannot be a stranger. So take him. We will be rid of him also.'

Ormerod glanced at Marie-Thérèse. She knew a good idea when she heard one. She nodded. 'Yes. That is right,' she said grudgingly. 'We will take him. I am glad we have found *something* at least in this place.'

The old man looked at her sourly but merely shrugged. 'You have yet to see the rest of Normandy,' he said. 'You may be disappointed.'

'I think I will find some *fight* in Normandy,' said the girl bitterly. 'Some men with guts.'

'I think you will find they are busy gathering the corn and the apples,' Marcel replied evenly. 'Just as they have always done at this time, as you well know. The countryside between this part of the coast and Paris has not been touched by the war, there is no destruction, and many French soldiers, those that survived, are back in their homes. Just ask them if they want to fight. You may find you are mistaken. The time when they could fight, when they had the heart to fight, is gone, my dear.'

He stood carefully. 'I must get my coat for it looks like rain,' he said, still looking at the girl. 'When I get back I expect the soldiers will be here, so now I would like to wish you luck – at least the luck to survive.' He turned to Ormerod, whom he seemed to regard, rightly, as a victim of circumstances. He shook his hand. 'I hope that you see England again, monsieur,' he said more gently. 'Try and stay away from trouble if you can.'

'Thank you, I shall,' said Ormerod, struggling for something to say. He stood up and the dog dropped from his lap leaving a wet patch on the front of his trousers. The fishermen all grinned boyishly. 'Incidentally, what's the dog's real name?' he asked. 'I mean, if I need to call him, it's no good calling him *Formidable*, because he won't answer. And that will certainly look suspicious.'

'He has never had a name,' said the old fisherman. 'Not that I know. *Formidable* suits him very well. He will soon get used to it.' He grinned with broken teeth like a fallen stone wall. 'Perhaps you are his destiny.'

Granville stands almost at the base of the upraised finger of the Cotentin Peninsula, twenty-six kilometres north-east of Avranches, and above the right angle where Brittany and Normandy join. On a fine day the pile of Mont St Michel can be seen from the pont across the enormous bay.

It is an old rock town, with a dominant cape carrying the *haute ville* high over the sea and with a complete view of the safe and enclosed harbour. On the high ground is a solid granite church with a dome and almost beside it a quadrangle of stone barracks dating from the nineteenth century, which in the autumn of 1940 housed the German garrison of the town. The place smells of salt fish and oil. It is the home of the family of Christian Dior.

The boat carrying the five Germans and their modestly looted wine and with Marcel, Ormerod and Marie-Thérèse approached the outer harbour at ten minutes to midnight on September 21st. Ormerod, sitting on a cross bench, with *Formidable* sleeping damply under his arm, felt tension and alarm as he watched the ramparts of the town grow around them in the dark. It was like going into a large and gloomy prison. The girl sat moodily beside him, trying to smile when one of the young soldiers attempted conversation in fragmented French. Fortunately the sergeant, the only German whose French was adequate, was in the wheelhouse, so talking with him was unnecessary.

The unaccustomed gun under Ormerod's armpit was rubbing and hurting. It would have been a relief to have taken it out. He wondered how the soldiers, since their trip was unofficial, would get beyond the eyes of the guards at the harbour entrance, but apparently this had been arranged. The old fisherman had taken the wheel to enter the harbour and the German sergeant picked up a signal lamp and flashed three long beams in the direction of the stone mole. A single flash returned. Someone shouted from there and the sergeant waved his arm.

The boat chugged through the watery shadows of the harbour and eventually curled in easily alongside a wooden quay where Marcel eased back the engine and then stopped it completely.

'Good, good,' said the German sergeant. 'Thank you, my friend. Now where will you stay? And how will these people get to Julioville? It is five kilometres. We would give you a lift in our truck, but the military police do not approve.'

'It does not matter,' said Marcel. 'I have many friends here in Granville. I will get a bed. These people also. Tomorrow they can go to Julioville. It would be no good waking a sick woman at this hour anyway.'

'Fine,' said the sergeant. 'Come on boys.' He motioned the young soldiers up the weedy wooden ladder and onto the pier. They tramped up, each carrying two bottles of wine. Then he nodded to the Chausey fisherman and then to the girl and Ormerod. Marie-Thérèse went up the ladder first and then Ormerod and then the old man. The sergeant said to the latter as he was leaving the boat: 'It is a pity that one does not smile. She would be very pretty.'

'She is nervous of soldiers,' said the fisherman. 'And of your soldiers especially.'

'I see. Well, that is to be expected. Invaders, monsieur, can hardly be expected to be loved. *Auf wiedersehen*.'

'*Au revoir*,' said the Frenchman.

'*Au revoir*,' repeated Ormerod and the girl almost together. They had reached the top of the wooden ladder. He set the dog down on the cobbles where it cocked its leg against a pile of cable. Ormerod looked towards the dark town. It was ten minutes past midnight. Ormerod was in Occupied France. He had made his landing.

'Where are we going?' asked Marie-Thérèse. The landing in France seemed, for the moment anyway, to have reduced her aggression. She looked about her as if she were in a foreign country.

'There is a house not far from here,' replied the old man. 'It is owned by a man called Paul Le Fèvre. He is somebody who has some sympathy with your cause.'

Ormerod saw how quickly the sharp lights came into the eyes of the woman. 'It is your cause also,' she said to Marcel. 'Remember that.'

He shrugged. 'I am too old for causes, madame,' he said. 'I have seen too many of them.' He obviously considered that was answer enough because he began to move along the cobbles of the harbour. They had only gone a short distance, Ormerod and Marie-Thérèse following the fisherman, when the sergeant and the soldiers returned in their small truck.

'*Heil Hitler*,' recited Marie-Thérèse quietly as it pulled to a stop.

The sergeant leaned out of the cab. 'We'd better give you a lift after all,' he whispered. 'There's some sort of emergency happening. God knows what we've got to fear from the English, but we do. You'll be picked up in no time – there's a patrol just along the road. Jump in.'

All three clambered in and the German soldiers dutifully surrounded them. 'If you're in trouble – we're in trouble,' the

94

sergeant called back as he started the engine. 'Where shall I drop you?'

'By the bar on the corner of the hill,' instructed the old man.

'*La Belle Hélène*,' said the sergeant immediately. 'I know it.'

Standing among the young German soldiers in the back of the truck, Marie-Thérèse shot a glance at the fisherman. His face was expressionless. His eyes were dull. The truck started forward and in less than two minutes the soldiers were calling joking remarks to their comrades on a patrol line marching along the harbour.

They drew up shortly after and the two men, the girl and the dog jumped to the road. The sergeant's arm came from the cab in farewell.

'Wave,' said Marie-Thérèse bleakly. 'Show how friendly we are.'

'Well *he* was,' said Ormerod reasonably. 'Couldn't have found a nicer chap.'

'We are not fighting one sergeant,' she returned. 'At least I am not.'

'It was still very obliging of them to deliver us,' said Ormerod quietly. 'Christ, he'd get shot too if we were caught.' The fisherman had pushed a bell and now a window opened and a head emerged.

'Who is it? What's going on?' it demanded.

'Paul,' said the fisherman, 'it is Marcel from Chausey.'

'My God, what are you doing in Granville at this time of night?'

'I have brought some ... people.'

'I see ... wait a minute.'

A thin light appeared behind the door of the bar and it was unlocked and unbolted. They slid in through the half-door. The bar was shabby, tables and chairs and a counter, all in need of renovation, with a parrot in a cage over the counter. There was a cloth over the parrot but Ormerod could hear it clucking in annoyance at being disturbed.

Paul Le Fèvre was an ugly, balding man with a grin like a monkey. He set the lamp down on the table and pulled out chairs for them. 'I will get you some cognac,' he said, going towards the bar. 'It gets cold now.' He busied himself in the shadowy bar. His body was short and round and his arms long. His shadow looked like that of a well-fed spider. 'I closed early tonight,' he said over his shoulder. 'The Germans have some make-believe emergency, so the customers stayed away.'

'They prefer to stay in their houses when the Boche are around,' said Marie-Thérèse confidently.

'No, but the Germans couldn't come either. They like to come in here. They have taken to cider. It makes them sing.'

'Is nobody serious about the war?' the girl suddenly demanded angrily. 'You make it sound as if the Germans are liberators. You're all the same.'

Paul Le Fèvre turned in the dimness, the glasses in his hand. 'I wondered why you called them the Boche,' he said. 'If you lived here, you would know that you have to exist with them. We are their prisoners but in some ways they are *our* prisoners too. And I have to earn a living in my bar. They pay for their drinks like any other man.' He returned to the table almost stealthily and looked carefully at the girl. 'That is not to say I love them or what they have done to France. I would kill them for that. But for the moment I serve them drinks.'

The girl said: 'I am called Dove.' This was a surprise to Ormerod because she had not used the name before. Then he realized that on Chausey they had told no one their names. 'And I'm Dodo,' he added hastily, following her French. He pointed to the dog sitting tiredly by his chair. '*Formidable,*' he said.

At the sound of Ormerod's accent some sort of eagerness came into the man's face. He handed out the drinks and now he sat down and leaned anxiously towards them. 'So, you have come,' he said. 'From England?'

Marcel, the Chausey fisherman, stood up slowly and drained his cognac. 'I must leave,' he said, as if not wanting to hear more. 'I will wake my daughter. She lives near here. *Au revoir.*'

They watched him as he walked towards the door. Paul rose and went with him to unlock it. When it was open he looked into the street first and then let the old man out. Marcel went with a tired wave of his hand but without looking back.

The girl said: 'We need shelter and help.'

'You have both,' said Paul coming back to the table. 'What

are you going to do? Can you tell me?' Then with new eagerness: 'There is a goods train at the station. We could blow it
up!'

Marie-Thérèse closed her eyes briefly but tiredly. 'I think we
must not run too fast,' she said. 'I want to know how many
men in Granville we could trust to help. It is necessary to form
a resistance group. That is my task here.'

'He brought you from Chausey?' he said.

'The Germans did,' said Marie-Thérèse, smiling for once.
'They can be obliging. They are also stupid. But never mind,
we need somewhere safe.'

'Here,' said Le Fèvre. 'This is safe.'

'You said the Germans come here to drink.'

'So they do. Where can you be better concealed than in
among the enemy?'

'But he does not speak French,' she said, nodding rudely to
Ormerod.

'Nor do the Germans,' he shrugged. 'They get so drunk on a
few glasses of cider that they would not take any notice anyway. As you say, they are stupid. He can hide upstairs if there
is an officer around, or somebody who might suspect. But they
are not on the alert. They think they have won the war.'

Marie-Thérèse nodded approvingly. 'They will know different,' she said. She looked at him with a hard challenge. 'How
many men in Granville love France? Enough to die for
her?'

Two hours later, Ormerod, who had just been a spectator
during the long conversation, most of which he did not understand, went up the stairs at the back of the bar to the toilet.
The door would not shut so he stood peeing with the voices
from the room below drifting up to him. A sudden wider beam
of light showed that the door down there was opened more
widely. He did up his buttons and went onto the landing. Le
Fèvre was coming up the stairs followed by the girl.

'Is there any question you want to ask?' Marie-Thérèse asked
Ormerod as though all at once remembering that he existed.
Le Fèvre looked intensely ugly in the light of the lamp he
carried, like a dwarf in a coalmine. He looked at Ormerod.

'Questions? Me? No, not really,' said Ormerod. 'I expect you've covered everything.'

She shook her head at Le Fèvre. He nodded to a bedroom door just along the landing and then, shaking hands with them both, turned the corner of the stairs and went up a further flight, the lamp diminishing as he went.

'What's happening now?' asked Ormerod. Weariness was hanging on him.

'We sleep. Tomorrow I can begin to organize matters. Here I feel we have a good beginning.' She pushed the bedroom door open and shone her torch into the void. Standing on bare floorboards was a large undulating double bed with a deep white quilt covering it.

Ormerod looked into the room. 'Where's mine?' he inquired.

'It is for both,' she said practically. 'They have no other room.'

She pushed him firmly before her like a mother shoving a reluctant child. Ormerod stepped forward. 'I'll sleep on the floor then,' he said. 'I expect those bare boards could be made comfortable.'

She walked in after him and closed the door. 'There is no necessity,' she said briskly. 'The bed is for both. You need to be rested as well as me.'

He looked at her carefully but she waved an impatient hand at him. 'In our situation we can have no time for modesty,' she said. 'You are so obvious, you English.'

'All right ... but ...' he stumbled. 'Don't blame me ..'

'There will be nothing to blame you for,' she replied firmly. '*I* am going to sleep. We will often sleep together. We will have to. Surely you realize that.'

'Maybe we ought to have announced our engagement,' muttered Ormerod in the dark.

'Do not worry, monsieur,' she said, taking her shoes off and pulling her jersey over her head. She had put out the torch and she moved in the dark like a shadow. 'If we have any danger here it will not be to your virtue. If you wish to know ... I do not have time or thought for sexual matters. They are nothing to me now. Not even a necessity, like eating. So you are safe. In any case, I prefer small, elegant men.'

With that she dropped her trousers and rolled into the bed. Ormerod began to undress more slowly. 'All I hope is that I don't forget myself in the night,' he muttered as he got tentatively into the other side of the bed, wearing his shirt and underpants.

She had almost disappeared under the blankets. He eased himself down into the soft luxury. 'Do not worry Dodo,' she said as she yawned. 'If you do forget I will kick you or poke my fingers in your eye. Then you will know I am not your wife.'

'Don't count on it,' he said. 'That's the sort of thing she does.'

Seagulls woke him the following morning. He stirred and turned towards a stick of sunlight that was poking between the window shutters. Marie-Thérèse had gone out with Paul Le Fèvre leaving a message with Madame Le Fèvre that he must stay in the house until her return.

Ormerod was grateful for the sleep. He eased himself from the bed and took his time over his ablutions and dressing. Madame Le Fèvre, a surprisingly pretty wife for such an ugly husband, brought him some coffee, bread and *confiture*, apologizing for the lack of butter. Apparently the Germans had used all the butter. 'They eat it without bread,' she said in disgust. 'Like ice cream.'

He remained in the room, cleaning his pistol, and then lying back on the bed and wondering, not for the first time, what he was doing there. Marie-Thérèse returned before midday.

'Dodo, I have a radio contact,' she said with restrained eagerness. He could see the enthusiasm in her eyes. 'And three men already who are waiting to help. There are others also. This is much better Dodo.'

'You're very keen aren't you,' he said quietly. 'You can't wait to start some trouble here.'

'Of course not,' she replied. 'I want to give the Boche trouble.'

He sighed. 'I know you're right. But logically, logically I'm saying, not emotionally or anything, this place seems to me pretty much like it was before the war. I'm only guessing, because I wasn't here. But it looks peaceful enough and no-body's been shot. There's a shortage of butter I understand, but that's not disastrous, is it? We don't have much on the ration in England . . .'

She interrupted him. Not angrily as she had before but with a surprising sort of pleading. He was sitting on the side of the bumpy bed and she stood before him and said: 'Look, you have no idea. These people in this town are ruled by a foreign soldier. Don't you understand what that means? They are at his disposal. They could be taken away and shot or put into concentration camps. Anything. And – in any case – please realize this – the Boche have no *right* to be here. No right!' She turned away abruptly and went towards the window. It looked out on the old backs of some other houses with a small segment of sea showing pale blue between two slate roofs. 'God,' she said. 'How could I be sent with a coward?'

Ormerod bridled at that. 'I'm not a coward,' he pointed out carefully. 'Although I'll run away with the next man. All I can see is a peaceful town – occupied though it is – and what I can see in the future is trouble. If you start something here, start blowing up something or shooting Germans, they're going to come down on the ordinary people here like a bloody ton of bricks. They might not catch us, we'll be away by then . . .'

His voice trailed. She had turned and was staring at him. He nodded. 'Okay, okay,' he said. 'You win. You're right. It's war. You have to do these things in war. I remember seeing a film like that not all that long ago.'

'If you want to quit you can quit,' she said, her voice sulky. 'I can manage on my own. I think that you will be a liability thinking like you do. A pacifist can be a dangerous man.'

He stood up and walked the two paces towards her and put his large hands on her arms. It was the first time there had been any intentional physical contact between them. She looked at him, still hurt and annoyed. 'I'm no pacifist,' he said. 'Maybe you're right. Maybe I'm a coward. But I'm not just a coward for myself. I'm a coward for a lot of other people as well.'

'I understand what you are saying,' she said quietly. 'But you cannot think like that and also fight.'

'I'll fight, don't worry,' he said with half a grin. 'I'll be there with you.'

'You promise?' she said doubtfully. 'I would prefer it if you ran away now instead of at some time when I needed you urgently.'

'Don't worry, I'll stay,' he said. 'The next ferry to England won't be for another ten years or so, unless the Germans start one. I'm with you, Dove.'

It was the first time he had used the name. It seemed to reassure her and she smiled tightly and for some reason they shook hands. 'Right,' she said in a businesslike way. 'Now I tell you. I have found a man willing to keep radio contact with England. He has a transmitter which he kept after the surrender, although to do that is risking his life. When the resistance group is formed here he will be of great value, and of even more value when the invasion to liberate France comes. I will take you there now.'

They went from the room. Le Fèvre's little daughter, who had been playing on the stairs, curtseyed shyly as they went by, part of some private game then occupying her. Ormerod bowed gravely and the child put her finger in her mouth.

Outside it was an airy day. *Formidable* was on a length of string and he found the smelly pavements full of delight after the familiar grass and rock of Chausey. Two German soldiers on bicycles came wobbling by along the street and one of them whistled at the dog as they went by. Marie-Thérèse and Ormerod smiled at the soldiers.

'I think our dog is going to be useful,' said Ormerod.

'It is a good cover,' she agreed. 'It is something to remember for the future. It's a pity he smells.'

They turned a corner and another, catching a view of the fishing boats in the harbour, and then went down into the basement by some crumbling steps. There were some unkempt potted plants on the steps and an old bicycle against the wall. The girl knocked with three short and one long knock – the morse V-sign – and the door was cautiously opened. Standing there was a man wearing small rimless glasses perched on a nose as blue as a badly bruised thumb.

'I have brought him,' she said, nodding at Ormerod. The

man nodded and let them in. 'I speak English,' he said to Ormerod enthusiastically. 'My name is Pierre Dubois.'

The room was crowded with unwieldy pieces of furniture and smelled of leather and sawdust. A door at the back was half open and as he moved Ormerod saw it was an upholsterer's workshop. Dubois went immediately into the workshop and fumbled in the guts of a large sofa which looked as if it had exploded on the floor. He pulled out a wooden case and brought it with some pride into the room. 'My secret,' he said to Ormerod. 'I took it from beneath the pigs of the Boche. I mean the *snouts* of the Boche.'

Ormerod nodded with what he hoped looked like appreciation. The man set the box on the floor, then, with a quick thought, went to the door and pedantically locked it. 'Nobody can see through the window,' he said. 'We are too deep here.'

Dubois began to turn the knobs and the dials, a pair of earphones held ready to pull over his head. 'Also I listen to the BBC,' he said proudly. 'I know all the news from my other radio set. I like Workers' Playtime too. Have you heard that? And all the national songs of the Allies – the anthems. They play those on Sundays. They last a long time, you know monsieur, it takes twenty minutes to play them all. It is very encouraging to know so many countries are on our side.'

'Very,' said Ormerod caustically. 'Especially as most of them are occupied. It's a long time to stand to attention though, isn't it, twenty minutes? If we didn't have so many allies it would be easier on the feet.'

Dubois smiled uncertainly. 'It is good to joke in bad times,' he said eventually. His head gave a small jerk. 'Ah, now.' He had one earphone to his ear and now he slipped the other on. He looked like a face in a frame. He began to tap a call sign on the morse key. 'Already today I have contacted them,' he said. 'It was someone with the name of Percy. Every day I speak to them but so far, until today, I have not had anything important to say. Now I can tell them you have arrived at Granville.'

An answering series of bleeps came from the set and Dubois began tapping eagerly. 'Dove and Dodo, that is correct is it not?' he queried.

'It is correct,' nodded Marie-Thérèse.

Monsieur Dubois looked concerned. He tapped a little harder as if that might make some difference. 'They do not seem to know who you are,' he muttered. 'They are making inquiries.' His cheek had gone white.

'That's great,' said Ormerod in a disgusted tone. 'Just bloody great that is. Forgotten us already. Typical . . .'

'Hush,' said Marie-Thérèse. It was obvious by her expression that she was disconcerted. Then the morse began to return more surely and Dubois's visage cleared. 'Ah, it is all right. They have found you in the files.' His blue nose turned towards them. 'It is good for me also. I thought for a moment, maybe you were the Nazis.'

'I could see we'd put the wind up you,' mentioned Ormerod.

Marie-Thérèse handed the man a piece of paper on which she had written a message. She saw Ormerod straining his neck to look. 'It is just to say that we have arrived here and I am establishing my contacts,' she said. 'There is not much more to report at the moment. Later it will be different. Ah, yes . . .' She took the page back from the operator's hand. 'There is something. We have cut the size of the German army by two. I must tell them that.'

Ormerod shrugged. 'Hardly the turning point of the war,' he said. 'But if it makes you feel better, tell them.'

She scowled. 'It does make me feel better. I am sorry it does not do the same thing for you. Here.' She returned the message to the listening Dubois. He began to tap it out. When he had finished he waited and within two minutes the morse began to bleep from the other side. When it had finished he took the earphones from his head and turned his bruised nose. He handed the transcript back to Marie-Thérèse. She read it. 'It says "Carry On",' she said flatly.

'Just that? Not a lot to cheer about in that,' said Ormerod. 'But at least they remember now who we are. That's comforting.' The girl's face had fallen to disappointment like a failed pupil who had expected to do well. 'They will remember us in *future*,' she said sullenly. 'Many people will.'

When it became dark that evening Marie-Thérèse went out

103

from the Bar *Belle Hélène*, leaving Ormerod and *Formidable* in the room. The Englishman lay on the large bed and stared at the crazed ceiling. He began to wish he had brought a book with him. He wondered, without conviction, if the Germans permitted the sale of French–English dictionaries in Granville.

After an hour or so he heard the conversation in the bar below thicken and he realized the Germans were coming in for the evening. He sat up on the bed, anxiety nailed to his face. The talk grew in volume. It was like sitting above an engine room. Another hour went by before the laughter became raucous and the singing began. There were German and French songs and the solitary, recumbent Ormerod, to pass the time, began to sing too where he could pick up the words of the repeated choruses. Then *Formidable*, who had begun dozing beneath the bed, got up and loped across to the door where he began whining against the crack. Ormerod could hear someone outside. He had half risen from the bed, intending to get hold of the dog, when the door was opened. Paul Le Fèvre had said that locked doors created suspicion.

A German soldier who had just been to the toilet stood on the landing in the half light. Ormerod's breath stopped. The German looked at him and he looked at the German. *'Bonsoir,'* said Ormerod thinly.

'Ach so, gute Nacht,' replied the soldier, amiably enough. *'Bonsoir, gute Nacht.'* *Formidable* had gone onto the landing and now proceeded to descend the stairs. Ormerod, making anxious noises, followed him. The German laughed at him chasing the mongrel and came down behind.

Ormerod got into the room. It was crowded with German soldiers and a few French civilians. Paul's wife was working behind the bar. Their little girl was sitting in the corner watching the revelry. There was hanging smoke and the sharp odour of Normandy cider everywhere. Cécile Le Fèvre quickly handed Ormerod a large tankard across the counter. That was as good a concealment as any. The German soldier who had discovered him had returned to a group of his comrades in one corner and was joining in their bellows of laughter at some joke. Ormerod was hugely relieved at this and picked up *Formidable*, went to a corner and sat next to an old and stoic French couple who were watching the scene with heavily passive eyes. He put the dog on his lap.

He drank the cider and enjoyed it. Suddenly the German who had come upstairs appeared and handed him another tankard. *'Merci, danke schön,'* said Ormerod anxiously. The German grinned and drank his large tankard clean in one long swallow. He nodded at Ormerod inviting him to attempt the same. There was nothing for it but to try. Several of the soldier's comrades gathered to watch. Ormerod took a deep breath and with a skill born of considerable practice on British ale drank his way through the glass also. He began to feel he was entering into the spirit of the thing. The Germans cheered and clapped and another two tankards appeared. The soldier took one and handed the second to Ormerod. The Englishman caught the troubled eye of Cécile from the other side of the bar. He winked at her confidentially. This time the German and he had a race. They drained their tankards and Ormerod felt the cider bubbling inside him. He had not had such a feeling of well-being for a long time. Another one? *Ah, oui. Danke schön!* Two more tankards appeared.

The company was getting rowdy now, with a song started in one corner progressing across the room and finally engulfing everyone. To Ormerod's own amazement he found himself trying to sing along with his enemies. They did not seem to be a bad bunch of enemies at all. Then *Formidable*, sitting on his lap, began to howl dismally with the tune, delighting friend and foe. Soon, and without realizing, Ormerod was on his feet and oo joined with half a dozen field-grey soldiers, singing 'We March Against England' at the utmost of his voice. Arms about each other, they swayed drunkenly across the bar room, while those on the fringe, including the silent old French couple with whom Ormerod had sat, clapped and joined in. Their faces remained set but they mouthed the words, making the best of a bad job.

At the height of the song and dance, with Ormerod's arms encompassing a tall, blond private and a fat, sweating corporal, Marie-Thérèse came through the back of the bar.

Two hours later, when only the stale smell downstairs remained of the evening's conviviality, Marie-Thérèse confronted him in the bedroom with all her pent up anger exploding.

'Fuck!' she shouted at him. She bent close to his contrite face. 'Fuck!' she shouted again.

Ormerod regarded her dizzily. He felt weary after so much cider. It seemed to have drained him. 'What do you mean by that?' he inquired with difficulty. His head was bad too. Her face seemed a long distance away. Then it zoomed close.

'You know what it means,' she almost snarled. 'It is a good English word.'

'Yes, yes,' argued Ormerod with the patience of a drunk. 'I know what it *means*. I was just inquiring why you said it.'

'Because it is the only word. Fuck! Fuck! Fuck!'

'Don't go on so,' pleaded Ormerod. 'You'll have everyone awake. And my head's feeling horrible.'

He sat heavily on the bed. 'Are you coming to bed, dear,' he inquired domestically. She stood back and hit him across the head with her hand. Angrily, she did it again and again.

The amazement he felt at the blows was doubled when he looked up and saw she was crying. 'Here, hang on a minute,' he said, catching hold of her hands firmly. They felt like soft branches. 'What's all this caper about?'

She stumbled to her knees on the floor. Her crying was real and angry. 'You... you *clown*!' she sobbed. '*You* dancing with the fucking Boche. How do you think it was for me to come in and see that? Dancing and singing German songs?'

'What did you expect? "The White Cliffs of Dover"?' he said. He patted her softly. 'Come on, Dove. I'm sorry. I couldn't help it. One of them blokes came up the stairs and found me. I had to go down. And they kept pouring that cider of yours down my throat. I couldn't refuse could I? They might have got difficult.'

'Dancing and singing German songs,' she repeated in a hurt whisper. She wiped her eyes with the back of her hand. She had recovered from her brief emotion. 'One day, monsieur,' she said solemnly, 'you are going to have to kill men like that. Perhaps those same men you are so friendly with. I hope that when the time comes you can do it.'

*

Twenty-four hours later she came into the darkened room and prodded him, making him jump startled from sleep. 'Oh, it's you,' he said, discontinuing his frantic feel for his gun under the pillow. 'Home late again.' Even in the dimness he could sense there was something eager about her.

'Dodo,' she said, 'we're ready to strike our first blow. Tonight. In one hour.'

Alarmed he sat up. 'What are you going to do?' he inquired suspiciously.

'We have six men,' she whispered. 'All to be trusted. We have explosives. Dodo, we are going to blow up a train!'

An immediate heavy weight settled on his stomach. He stumbled from the bed. Impulsively, like an excited child, she held his large hand. He tried to pull his trousers on with the other. 'Now you're sure now, aren't you?' he said. 'You don't want the first thing you do to be buggered up.'

'It will not be, as you say, buggered up,' she assured him firmly. She released his hand as though disappointed that she had not communicated her enthusiasm to him. 'Everybody is ready.' She leaned, again eagerly, towards him. 'Do you know what the working man's shoe is called in France?'

Surprised, he shook his head.

'*Le sabot*,' she replied. 'And that is where the word *sabotage* came from. It was invented by the French worker.'

'Let's hope they haven't forgotten then,' he said. Then cautiously: 'These men will know what they're up to, won't they? The Germans are not fools you know. Who's the explosives expert for a start?' He stood up and scratched himself violently in the dark.

'The man with the radio,' she said, trying to sound convincing. 'He knows. The man we went to see.'

'Monsieur Dubious?' sighed Ormerod.

'Monsieur Dubois,' she corrected. 'It is *Dubois*.'

'I prefer it my way,' said Ormerod. 'That man knows about explosives?'

'He was an expert in the French army,' she said. 'And he is brave, monsieur. We need bravery as much as we need knowledge.'

He thought it might be a dig at him. He pulled his jersey over his face. 'Who else?' he asked when he emerged from the neck. 'Le Fèvre?'

'Naturally Le Fèvre. He wants to do something for France.'

'If he keeps pouring cider down the Jerries he gets in the bar downstairs, he'll kill them with that,' he said. 'All right. Who else?'

'We have three others,' she said. Then, almost apologetically: 'And you.' He could see her eyes in the dark. 'There is some difficulty about one man,' she admitted unhappily. 'He goes to a chess club and then to drink with the other players. So he may not be with us.' He could sense the words clouding with doubt. 'You see if he did not go to the chess club they would notice.'

'Now we're back to me dancing with the Germans,' he pointed out. 'If you don't, then it arouses suspicion. All right. What's the plan?'

He was sitting on the bed and she squatted down in the strange manner she had. 'At midnight there is a goods train arriving at the station in Granville. We blow it up. It is simple.'

'What's it carrying?' he asked.

'Supplies for the Boche,' she said stoutly. 'Of course.'

'Not explosives? We don't want the whole bleeding town going through the sky do we?'

'It is not explosives,' she confirmed. 'But other things. What it carries is not so important, Dodo. It is a *gesture*. It will show them that we do not sleep.'

'Why blow it up in the station? This is the end of the line. It is not even going to block the railway because it stops here.'

'It has to be here,' she said. 'The men are Granville men. And we must wait until the driver of the train and the fireman have got safely away. They are Frenchmen too.'

'Couldn't you start off with something a bit less ambitious,' he suggested, touching her small shoulder. 'Cutting telephone wires or painting some rude words on walls.'

'The telephone wires have already been cut once,' she said reluctantly. 'A month ago. Dubois and Le Fèvre did it. And some citizens of Granville complained. They said it was an inconvenience. It interrupted their business. Some people would open a shop in hell.'

Ormerod sighed. 'Even our friend Le Fèvre admits that he's got to earn a living, no matter who's in the driving seat,' he said.

'Are you ready?' she asked, unwilling to talk further with him. 'It is getting towards the time.'

'Ready as I'll ever be,' he said. 'Where's Le Fèvre?'

'Paul is down the stairs. The last of the drunken Boche have gone. He will come with us. The others are coming here to rendezvous. Then we will go in pairs to the station. The train is due in fifteen minutes. We will give the driver and the other Frenchman time to go home – then bang, Dodo – bang!'

'Bang, bang,' he repeated, regarding her almost sorrowfully. He strapped the gun under his arm. 'All right, I'm ready. Let's go and get it over with.'

He led the way down the shadowed stairs. The girl followed him lightly, touching his back in her eagerness. Le Fèvre was solemnly wiping his glasses behind the bar, his short, ugly form reflected in the ornate mirror at his back. He looked up with hooded eyes. From upstairs they heard his child call out and Ormerod thought the man swore under his breath. He went to the stairs and called up to his wife to keep the girl quiet. His wife answered sharply. There was a lot of tension in the place.

There came a V-sign knock on the street door of the bar and Le Fèvre went quickly to it and pulled the bolt. Dubois came in with exaggerated stealth, followed immediately by another, puzzled looking man and a youth of about seventeen. Ormerod's heart fell further as he saw them.

Dubois, his bruised nose almost black, produced a small suitcase and patted it reassuringly. He looked, Ormerod thought, like a back-street abortionist. The other man and the youth, who were never named, looked at the suitcase with distrust and fascination. 'The explosives,' explained Marie-Thérèse proudly. 'Dubois knows all about explosives.'

'Christ almighty,' thought Ormerod glumly. He wouldn't have trusted Dubois with a firework. Even Marie-Thérèse was looking at the collection of misfits with a late misgiving. She shrugged and said to Ormerod, who had said nothing: 'Armies are not always perfect.'

'In the dark all cats are black,' answered Ormerod dully.

'Let's hope they can run. What's the lad doing here?'

'He is a brave boy. He wants to kill some Germans.'

'As long as he's back in time for school,' muttered Ormerod. 'As for the other bloke, why does he keep shifting his eyes back and forward? He looks like he's trying to cross the road.'

'Are you ready?' Marie-Thérèse said, annoyed. 'Or are you going to criticize all night. Just make sure, Dodo, that you're not the first to run.'

'I'll wait for the others,' he promised. *Formidable* began scratching himself with a noise like a machine in a corner of the bar room. 'What about the dog?' said Ormerod.

Marie-Thérèse sighed impatiently. 'Leave it here,' she said. 'It's served its purpose.'

'Just as we were becoming friends,' said Ormerod. 'All right. Let's get on with it. Goodbye *Formidable*.' He gave the dog a quiet push with his foot. 'I don't think we'll be coming back this way.'

Two by two, with Le Fèvre and the girl leading, at one minute intervals they left the bar and went through the void streets and shadows of the town towards the station.

It turned out to be the most terrible and bloody night of Ormerod's life. At least up to then. When they arrived at the railway embankment, some two hundred yards east of the station, the midnight goods train had arrived and was standing exhaling ghostly steam into the placid gloom. The odd sabotage group waited, lying close to the dampening railway grass. Ormerod tried to control a shiver. In the starlight he could see the eyes of Marie-Thérèse as she lay close to him, and heard her breathing as he had heard it at night in their chaste communal bed.

From up the line, magnified in the dark still air, they heard the calling voices of the train driver and the fireman. Eventually the steam settled like an apparition going to sleep and the men could be seen moving along the line towards the obscure roofs of the station. Everything there quietened. Night noises could be heard from far away. At a signal from Marie-Thérèse the group moved forward.

A hundred yards short of the train they crouched and solidified. A German soldier was ambling along the line, presumably to look at the engine. Marie-Thérèse loked vexed. 'A sentry,' whispered Ormerod caustically. 'The devils think of everything'. Her anger was transmitted to him without words. The guard seemed to take an overlong interest in the locomotive. Ormerod thought perhaps he was a railway enthusiast. He even climbed into the cab. Marie-Thérèse half turned her head and nodded to Paul Le Fèvre. To Ormerod's amazed and unexplained horror, the bar keeper produced a dull, long knife, and with a set expression on his ugly face moved like a hunchback along the embankment.

He did it with no noise, reappearing in five minutes at the side of the engine and lifting his bent arm like a spider might lift a claw. Marie-Thérèse let out a short gasp of excitement and relief. They moved quickly down the line.

The German soldier was lying dead in the engine cab, an expression of bemusement on his face. They all took a look at him. The young boy went back twice. Marie-Thérèse nodded firmly to Le Fèvre and to Dubois and then to the others. She and the puzzled man with the shifting eyes moved down the line to keep watch and guard, and Ormerod and the dull boy went in the other direction. They crept to within a few feet of the station and crouched below the concrete parapet at the end of the platform. There was no movement along the platform except the arch of a prowling cat. At the end of the station there was a light showing through the door left ajar. Ormerod guessed that was the guardroom. The dead German's comrades would be there. For the first time he was conscious of the comfort of the gun in his hand.

The boy squatted beside Ormerod and the Englishman was saddened to see a pale, silly grin on his face as if he were involved in some juvenile prank. But his skinny hand trembled as he held the gun he had been given. Impatiently Ormerod looked over his shoulder to where Le Fèvre and Dubois were crouched beside the undercarriage of the locomotive. He saw one of the shadows move away quickly from the train, the other remaining. Then, as Ormerod was turning back to keep his eyes on the station platform, there was a small explosion from behind. It was followed at once by an enormous bang and a flash and both he and the boy whirled around to see the engine shudder on the track and fall back engulfed in a fan of fire.

'Too bloody soon,' swore Ormerod. The boy looked at him in alarm. At the end of the platform the door of the guardroom was flung open and two German soldiers, both in stockinged feet, padded clumsily towards them. Ormerod felt the boy shiver although he was two feet away. He released the safety catch on his gun, and then, calmer than he ever thought he would be, he half rose above the level of the platform and shot his first man. He hit the German in the chest and the soldier fell down with a resounding thud, a clatter of equipment and a look of sheer disbelief on his mouth. It was an expression shared with his live comrade. He stood stockinged, still staring at Ormerod. The movement to bring his rifle into position was almost slow motion, so slow that it occurred to Ormerod that the whole thing was unsporting. Then he heard the gun go off in the youth's hand and the little whine of triumph issuing from the gaping mouth of the thin boy as the big soldier stumbled, fell spectacularly and slid towards them along the platform as if he had slipped on an icy patch.

'What marksmanship,' muttered Ormerod, filled with a strange disgust for himself. He looked at the two heavily encumbered corpses, then turned as the voice of Marie-Thérèse called them through the smoke from the engine.

The youth seemed almost as transfixed as the man he had shot. He stood admiring his handiwork, the gun trembling eagerly in his hand. He looked as if he might fire another bullet for luck. Ormerod tugged at him and they moved back towards where the locomotive was steaming like a cooking pot.

'I got one! I got one!' exclaimed the youth as they hurried through the vapour.

'Shut up!' snapped Ormerod. 'You haven't scored a fucking goal.'

The youth did not comprehend. He stared at Ormerod with a kind of surprised malevolence but he stopped shouting and they hurried back to the others.

Dubois was lying beside the track, dead and covered with blood. Le Fèvre was standing shaking a few yards away. The man with the shifting eyes had controlled them sufficiently to stare down at the corpse. Marie-Thérèse said simply: 'It went wrong.'

'I can see it did,' said Ormerod. He looked at her and she returned the expression angrily. 'Don't stare,' she snapped. 'We must get him away. We must try and hide him or the Germans will find the transmitter in his house.'

'Not to mention his family,' said Ormerod. He suddenly recalled the supercilious voice of the briefing officer at Ash Vale. 'Have you done emergency burial yet?' This was it.

'It's no use trying to pick him up in that state,' said Ormerod, with bitter commonsense. 'Bits will be falling off him all over the place.' He looked along the track. 'Get that tarpaulin and get him in that. And then let's piss off a bit sharpish. The rest of the German army will be here soon.'

Le Fèvre saw what he meant. He pulled himself out of his shocked state and scrambled along the track to pull the tarpaulin away from a stack of railway equipment. The shifty man suddenly ran to assist him. 'Get him to the cemetery,' said Ormerod to the girl. She translated to the others. They looked at her askance. The youth began to cry. She urged them on. They picked up the tarpaulin. 'The cemetery?' she said to Ormerod as they hurried down the embankment.

'It's the only place when you're dead,' recommended Ormerod. He was as frightened as the other men. Whistles were shrieking in the night. They could hear cars and motorcycles coming towards them through the town. A fire engine sounded.

They got across the road from the railway just before the first German troops arrived. There was a covered lane, lined with sooty trees and old rubbish. Along this they went as quickly as they could, the pallbearers jogging uncomfortably with their burden. 'When we get there,' puffed Ormerod, 'we put him in one of the vaults. It does have vaults?'

'Of course.'

'We break into one and set him down there. If we're lucky they won't look there.'

She nodded, apparently reluctant to acknowledge his decisiveness, his taking the initiative from her. She rasped something in French to the boy who was still blubbing and getting under their feet. She pushed him up ahead of the tarpaulin. The commotion behind them at the station grew. Whistles were blowing frantically as if it were a rough football match. Some French people had come from their houses and were looking in the direction of the noise. No one saw the group in the deep lane. The smoky glow from the locomotive could be seen discolouring the housetops.

Then Ormerod saw the ghostly outline of the town cemetery ahead, the roofs of the many vaults lining the boundary wall like those of some miniature town. The two men with the body unceremoniously heaved it over the wall and turned and looked at Marie-Thérèse. They were clearly waiting to get away. 'Tell them to go,' said Ormerod. 'Get rid of them.'

The girl made the decision quickly. She ordered them away and the expressions of relief could be seen in the night. They went quickly, only the idiotic boy turning around and giving the victory sign. Ormerod reversed his fingers and made the sign back. Then, without more delay, he turned and picking the girl up, bodily lifted her to the top of the cemetery wall. She controlled her surprise and dropped onto the other side. Ormerod climbed up heavily after her.

The body was lying disgustingly, having half fallen out of the tarpaulin. Ormerod half closed his eyes and heaved it back. Marie-Thérèse was already moving quickly along the line of pointed-roofed vaults in the manner of someone looking for an address. 'Here,' she called quietly. She hurried back to help him with the body. It was fortunately only a few yards. A number of the vaults had fallen into disrepair and the doors fitted crookedly. The girl pushed at the one she had chosen and it opened with a haunting creak. She glanced up at Ormerod.

'Throw him in,' he said. 'There's no time for a bloody service.'

Together they heaved the sagging sheet into the dim void of the vault. They heard it fall with heavy softness and Ormerod grimaced. 'Let's get out of here,' he said. 'It gives me the creeps.'

They moved across the dark open country at the rear of the cemetery away from the town to the east, going cautiously but with no interruptions. The Germans, inexperienced in the techniques of counter-espionage, threw a delayed cordon about Granville later that night but by that time they were clear.

Keeping to lanes and the edges of fields they had gone several miles before the sky began to curl at the edges of a new September day that opened across Normandy. Ormerod's feet began to hurt.

They said little as they hurried through the darkness, the girl moving easily like a stoat across the open country while the big Englishman progressed less certainly. At dawn they came to a brief valley buttoned with cider apple trees and with a house and barn at its elbow. They went towards the barn.

Even as they approached they scented the sharp sweetness of the apples in the building. There was a small door in the stonework at the rear and they prudently chose that in preference to the large entrance at the front. It was still barely past dawn and even the calling of cockerels across the yawning fields seemed half-hearted. A dog barked once but then gave it up. They found that the door opened easily and they went in.

The floor of the barn was covered with barrels of small, bright red cider apples. They gave off potent fumes that filled the building to its ancient roof. 'Can't stay here,' said Ormerod. 'You know how drunk I get on cider. The fumes in here would have me singing and dancing in no time.'

Marie-Thérèse sniffed and acquiesced silently. They walked carefully around the old stonework at the rear of the building and came to a cart shed. Inside were three country carts, their shafts touching the floor in an attitude of obeisance, and in one corner some baled straw. They went gratefully towards that and sat down.

'We must not sleep yet,' murmured Marie-Thérèse, looking about her. It was almost the longest sentence she had spoken all night. 'We must find out if we are safe here.'

'They're French people, aren't they?' he replied a little mockingly. 'They're bound to help us.'

She said sulkily: 'Things did not go well at Granville. But we struck the blow. Le Fèvre will organize the resistance cell there.'

'If he's not already in some other cell,' pointed out Ormerod.

'I hate to tell you this, lady, but in my opinion it was a mess, a real balls-up.'

To his slight surprise she did not take offence. 'It was a pity about Dubois,' she admitted. 'He was valuable with his radio.'

'Poor old Dubious,' said Ormerod, shaking his head. 'He's heard his last Workers' Playtime, unless it broadcasts a lot further than I think it does.'

'Every time you make a joke of it,' she snapped. 'To you it is all so funny.'

Ormerod looked at her bleakly. 'All right. I'm sorry, love,' he said. 'We're in this together. Who knows, perhaps what we did last night will shorten the war. If it is only by a day. Did Dubois have a wife and family?'

'Not close family,' she said. 'It was good it was not Le Fèvre I suppose. But it is still a pity about the radio.'

He regarded her sadly. 'What's that idiotic kid's mother going to do when the Germans come knocking at her door and asking her why her lad was out all night shooting their mates?' he said.

'They will be all right,' she said. She looked far from certain. 'It was a beginning. Things go wrong in the beginning. Next time we will have some better fortune.'

They sat in silence. Ormerod felt a grim weariness overtaking him. Marie-Thérèse eventually said: 'We killed three of the Boche and we damaged the railway ending. So that is some success.' She looked at him with some sort of triumph. 'And you shot your first German.'

'From five yards,' he muttered grimly. 'The poor bastard.'

'Do you think he would have been so concerned if he had shot you?' she argued. 'Please do not moralize. Soldiers kill and soldiers die. That is their profession.'

'Where do we go from here?' he asked tiredly, surrendering the argument to her. 'Do we know?'

'There is a village,' she replied. 'Ten kilometres from here. I have been told to contact a man there. A man who will help. We must try and reach him.'

six

The first countryside through which Dodo and the Dove travelled that warm autumn was the Normandy Bocage, a landscape of small woodlands, enclosed fields and red farms. It was a region then untouched by war because the battles of May and June 1940 had ceased some miles to the east when the French surrendered following the British escape from Dunkirk.

They left their initial hiding place, the cart shed beside the apple barn, and travelled with the bins and barrels of cider apples towards Villedieu-les-Poëles and Vire. The pickers in the orchards were mostly migrant people who came every year to work in the region, some gypsies and some rough rural folk who gathered the small apples from early morning until September mist moved across the ground late in the day. It was not difficult for Marie-Thérèse and Ormerod to mingle with the apple-gatherers. Little attention was paid to them. In the early afternoon on the first day, they helped to load the barrels on to a horse-drawn dray and then, climbing aboard themselves, they went towards Villedieu, to the east.

As they sat amid the barrels with their red cargo, and as the large brown horse nodded and plodded, several German army vehicles passed them going towards Granville and the coast. Marie-Thérèse had put a coloured scarf round her dark hair and her face looked brown, like a country-girl's face, beneath it. They watched the military vehicles as they sidled by on the narrow road and Ormerod waved like some rural simpleton. Marie-Thérèse scowled at him.

There were two other apple workers on the cart, a pair of wizened gypsies, who sat on the tailboard and grunted at the German cars. They did not speak at all to Ormerod and the girl. The afternoon held its warmth, the small fields were burned brown after the dry fine summer, there were giant pumpkins in cottage gardens and the villages were lined with window-boxes full of geraniums, like bright orange flags.

But in that countryside, and Ormerod became strongly aware of it as his days there went on, something was amiss. Everywhere, in the fields and orchards, people worked as they had always worked, the slow timing of their lives unaltered, but they did not smile very often, they drank seriously and ate in silence. Sometimes in the streets there were wounded men from the lost war trying to work or trying to walk. The Germans were not in great evidence but they appeared in villages and in the towns of Villedieu and Vire, spots of grey at the ends of the streets, a military vehicle moving unhurriedly among the carts. The country-folk watched with a common expression on their browned faces that Ormerod came to recognize as defeat.

Marie-Thérèse regarded the peasants with bitterness. 'To these people,' she said while they travelled on the apple cart between the fields and orchards, 'the coming of the Germans is no different than a change in the weather. They care for nothing but their miserable fruit and vegetables.'

'You can eat fruit and vegetables,' sniffed Ormerod.

'They are fools,' she answered sullenly. 'They cannot tell the difference between a change in their destiny and a change in the seasons.'

Ormerod and Marie-Thérèse left the apple cart at a village five kilometres west of Villedieu. The driver, who had been hunched, immobile as a sack, behind the horse, stopped and without even looking at the passengers among the cargo he went into the *auberge* for a drink. The gypsies on the tailboard continued to contemplate the road as if the cart was still travelling. Ormerod glanced at the Frenchwoman and she nodded. Unhurriedly they dropped from the cart and walked by geraniums banked against the old walls of the inn.

They had seen the mouth of a lane descending from the road and they made for this unhurriedly, walking as though they were lovers. Marie-Thérèse reached over and held his hand. He glanced at her quickly but saw what he already knew, that the action was merely meant as a disguise. Once they had entered the lane, tunnelled beneath windless trees, with the air already growing damp with the progress of the afternoon, she released his fingers as an actress would release a stage lover at the end of the scene.

After a few hundred yards they saw the ghostly iron gateway to a park of some kind. The ironwork was arched and still

118

elegant but was now rusted and encoiled with creepers. The gates were fixed open, almost rooted into the ground.

An unkempt drive led from the gates and running parallel with it was a clear, narrow stream, clean among the neglect. Ormerod's feet had been aching. 'Mind if I have a paddle?' he said to Marie-Thérèse. 'Another mile and I'll be invalided out of service.'

He thought there was a smile in her nod. He returned it. The tension that had been with her in Granville had lessened as they moved further from the coastal region. The Germans seemed a long way from this peace. The stream curved away after a short run beside the drive, bending around some reedy banks cluttered with fiery old bushes. Gratefully Ormerod removed his boots and rolled up the ends of his trousers. He eased himself down the slippery grass at the bank of the stream and submerged his feet in the cold, sweet water.

'That's marvellous,' he breathed, closing his eyes to savour the moment. 'That's bloody marvellous.'

To his surprise she moved herself down beside him and taking off her shoes, put her small feet into the water beside his. 'You are right, Dodo,' she murmured. 'It is bloody marvellous.'

He laughed. 'Your English is improving,' he said. She did not answer but sat back and looked about them. Orange and yellow leafed trees filtered the last of the sunlight, the stream grunted over its lining of stones, pigeons sounded throatily, the loudest noise among the hundred small noises of that enclave. 'France,' she breathed. 'Normandy. This is what matters to me, you understand.'

He was not going to argue with her again, not then, so he said: 'It's funny isn't it, that you can come here and find peace. Right here in the middle of all the Germans. You can't find any peace in England just now, that's for sure. Everybody rushing around trying to be a hero, girding themselves for battle.' He let out a short snort.

'Patriotism is not high on your list, is it?' she said without accusation, just conversationally.

'It's there,' he said patting his heart. 'Somewhere. That's why I'm here with you instead of combating criminals in Putney. They call it "doing your bit". This is my bit. In the end the

Germans are my enemies as much as they're yours.'

She laughed quietly. 'How do you think the English will behave when the Germans occupy them?' she said.

He looked at her in some surprise. 'You really think they'll do it?' he asked. 'Invade?'

'Why not? They have got so far. Why not further?'

'You're right,' he admitted. 'Why not?'

'What will the English do?' she repeated. 'Go underground and fight?'

He sniffed thoughtfully, loud enough to set the burping pigeon flying noisily out of the tree. They both turned in alarm. 'Pigeons always seem to *fall* out of trees,' grumbled Ormerod, taking his hand from his gun. He thought again. 'I don't know whether the English will fight once they're occupied. I expect some of them will. The brave or the foolish ones. Then, in the end, the Americans will come and rescue us.'

'The Americans won't do anything,' she said with confident disgust. 'They are too fat. Too soft and too rich. So far all they have done is talk. They are best at that.'

'I don't know,' he shrugged and looked about him. 'One day they may be dying in these fields.' He took his big white feet out of the stream, shook them and plunged them back again. 'As for England,' he said. 'Well, it's the only country I've got.' He looked at his watch. 'Hadn't we better make reservations for the night?' he said. 'What about the contact you wanted to meet.'

Marie-Thérèse looked through the trees. 'He is here,' she said.

'Here? Where?'

'There is a house. A big house in this park. The people have gone, run away. But the man we have to see is still there. He was the estate manager. I received a message about him in Granville. He will help us.' She stood up, took a large padded leaf from a clump at the side of the stream and wiped her feet. Ormerod grinned at her and did likewise. The air had become even more hushed and the light was moving away. 'It is this way,' she said, pointing through the amber trees. 'Perhaps we will hear what news there is from Granville.'

His feet felt more amiable for their soaking in the brook. He had dried them with the leaf and now he pulled on his socks and shoes and followed her along the waterbank.

There was still enough light left, when they eventually turned through the trees, to see the details of a shapely house at the end of the avenue of Normandy poplars. It was really a small château, with a cone-like turret at one end, a symmetrical line of windows like framed pictures in a gallery and a stylish entrance door on a plinth of steps. In one of the upper windows a yellow light appeared.

'It is a signal,' said Marie-Thérèse pointing at the light. 'He is expecting us.'

'Where's Jerry?' asked Ormerod. 'It's a wonder he hasn't moved into a place like this.'

'The man here says it has a reputation of being haunted,' she smiled. 'Even the conquerors are frightened of ghosts.'

Ormerod's eyebrows lifted. 'I'm not all that keen myself,' he said. 'It looks a bit spooky doesn't it?' The wet evening mist was easing up from the long park in the front of the house. The grass felt spongy under their feet. From the house a dog's bark erupted into a howl.

'It was a beautiful place once,' said Marie-Thérèse untypically. She usually spoke about present things. She was not given to remembering. 'I came here one day to a wedding. All the tables were here on the grass and there was a man playing an accordion sitting beneath the tree over there. That was the day I saw my husband for the first time. He was a guest also.'

'Ah, I see,' nodded Ormerod, for some reason embarrassed by her nostalgia. 'It has memories.' They still had a hundred and fifty yards to walk to the house. The grass gave way to a paved garden, now well on its way to neglect. The dog barked from the house again.

'Where did you meet your wife, Sarah?' asked Marie-Thérèse suddenly and curiously.

Ormerod was astonished not only by the interest of the question but by the fact that she knew his wife's name. 'In a pawnshop,' he answered, after his hesitation. 'In Wandsworth. I tell her sometimes she's an unredeemed pledge.'

'I don't understand what that means,' said Marie-Thérèse. She did not sound as if she wanted to know.

'I was doing an investigation there,' said Ormerod. 'Breaking and entering. Never did clear that one up. Anyway the next week I took her to the pictures and we started going out a bit. Then we got married.'

'It is a beautiful story,' she sighed flatly. She looked across the garden in the gloomy dusk. 'Yes, the man was playing the accordion under that tree.'

'Funnily enough,' pursued Ormerod, 'the film was called *Ask A Policeman*. Quite strange that, wasn't it?'

'Fascinating,' said the Frenchwoman without a shred of enthusiasm. 'We danced here. On this courtyard. It seems so long ago. When everything seemed to be all right.'

'It did once,' he agreed moodily. 'We thought it was anyway. One minute you're in the one-and-sixes, laughing all the way. The next you're shooting and drowning Germans. It hardly seems possible.'

'It is possible,' she answered quietly. They were almost at the door now. It opened quite suddenly and quietly. A man stood there, holding back one of the largest and most fearsome dogs Ormerod had ever seen. Its eyes blazed in the dimness and its flailing red tongue seemed to glow.

'Come in,' said the man who held the monster's collar. 'He will not hurt you.'

He spoke in English for Ormerod's benefit. He smiled at the girl. '*Bonsoir*, Marie-Thérèse,' he said. 'You have come back to Mesnil-Bocage.'

She took his proffered hand and they kissed cheeks. Ormerod was introduced and he shook hands without taking his eyes off the dog. A growl was rattling in its throat. Ormerod sidled by, getting as close to the door jamb as possible. They walked into a dank, echoing hall, like a vault, the walls rising high to an indistinct ceiling. A wide staircase went up around the walls in a series of galleries. 'They call him Jacques-the-Odd,' whispered Marie-Thérèse. The man had gone ahead to put the howling dog into some confinement. 'He is a little strange.'

'I don't wonder, living here,' muttered Ormerod, looking around. 'No wonder the Germans haven't bothered with the place.'

'It used to be beautiful,' she said sadly, looking around her. They walked into a large room with a carved ceiling. A good fire was gnawing through some logs at the distant end. Jacques appeared silently behind them and turned on a single light. Ormerod felt Marie-Thérèse's nervous jump. His eyes took in the room. It was like a storehouse, crates and cases and piles of books, stacks of pictures, upturned furniture, crockery, garden tools, even a motorcycle leaning against the panelled wall. A collection of stuffed deer-heads was crowded into one corner, staring glassily into the room, curiously like animals in a pen.

'Everything is here, monsieur,' said Jacques, waving his hand at the amazing jumble. 'I guard it for the family with Honoré, the dog, and the ghosts.' He laughed. 'I think the German army is afraid of us. You would like some wine?'

He led them towards the great-mouthed fireplace and motioned them into two chairs. It was enjoyable to sit in a chair again. Ormerod felt the comfortable warmth on his face. The cheeks of Marie-Thérèse were shining in the firelight like those of a child. Jacques was a broad-shouldered man, about fifty, hair like a dish rag, and wearing the commonplace *bleu de travail* and large-toed shoes. He shuffled away to get the drink, returning with the glasses and an already opened bottle. 'It is just the *vin du pays*,' he said. 'The ordinary wine of this region, monsieur. There is some fine wine in the cellars here but I am not permitted to touch it. When the war is over some of it will be quite acceptable and some will be ruined.'

'Where is the family?' asked Ormerod.

Jacques shrugged, his shadow heaving on the wall. 'Who knows? They were going to Bordeaux, because they thought like many others that the French Government would go there from Paris and fight the Germans from the west. A lot of hope there was of that.'

'What news from Granville?' asked Marie-Thérèse more urgently.

'It is good,' replied Jacques. He sat down on an upturned flower tub. 'There was a curfew and house searches and notices posted on walls around the town, but no arrests, and so far no hostages or reprisals. It looks as though you got away with it.'

'Good,' nodded the Frenchwoman. 'If Paul Le Fèvre is still free, and the others, that means they are not looking for us. They do not realize we are here. Nobody has noticed Dubois is missing?'

'The Germans have not,' replied Jacques. 'The story is that he has gone to Rennes and has temporarily shut his business. Where did you put him?'

'In the cemetery. In a vault,' put in Ormerod, understanding the sense.

'A nice touch,' nodded the man. 'The proper place for a dead man.' He rose. 'You are hungry I expect. We shall eat excellently. I have not touched the wines, but the larder is another thing. Also I have some good Normandy tripe.'

'Tripe!' The eyes of Marie-Thérèse lit. 'That's wonderful, Jacques.'

'From Caen only today,' said the man, putting his finger in the side of his nose. 'I have a friend.'

'It is indeed a friend who brings you tripe from Caen,' she enthused. She laughed at Ormerod. 'The tripe in this region is the best anywhere,' she told him.

'We have tripe in England, you know,' he replied defensively. 'Big thing in the north. With onions.'

She made a face. 'I have seen it. It is inferior to Normandy tripe.'

'I'm not starting a war over it,' he shrugged. 'I'll surrender. Your tripe is superior to our tripe. Now are you happy?'

'Not happy. Satisfied,' she said. Jacques laughed in the deep shadows as he went from the room. The dog howled plaintively in its confinement.

'How long will we stay here?' asked Ormerod, putting his feet out towards the fire. 'I could get a liking for this.'

Marie-Thérèse did not reply. She was sitting in a wing-back chair, the shadows of the fire moving across her face. She looked weary and her eyes were closed. He thought, not for the first time, how strange it was they should be doing this thing. She appeared so small and vulnerable. It was difficult to realize that her ambition was to kill. Jacques returned through the thick gloom of the outer room bearing two more glasses of wine. It was a moment or two before Marie-Thérèse opened her eyes to take hers. She seemed to have been drifting to sleep. She smiled apologetically and took the glass. Ormerod took his and they raised them in silence. The ghostly dog appeared startlingly at Ormerod's elbow. The Englishman and the animal rolled eyes at each other. 'Ah, the Hound of the Baskervilles is back,' said Ormerod, not taking his eyes off the powerful face. The dog's jaw dropped open and its mouth glowed like a furnace.

'This estate had thirty like this once,' said Jacques, giving the hound a friendly push with his foot. 'The finest of the deer-hounds in Northern France. Now they are nothing. All gone except for Honoré here.'

The animal, as if knowing what was being said, emitted a a mixture of whine and a yawn and eased itself onto the floor like a leggy pony. Its red eyes ascended to Ormerod but they were now as soft as if it had suddenly fallen in love. The expression was one of abrupt adoration. Ormerod grinned at it. He looked up at Marie-Thérèse. She had gone to sleep. The Englishman closed his eyes also, the domestic well-being of the fire touching him. For almost the first time since he had arrived in France he wondered what his wife was doing.

Jacques prepared a meal of pâté, a casserole of tripe, with fruit and local Camembert. They ate almost in silence, enjoying the food and the rough Calvados. Eventually Ormerod asked about Bagnoles de l'Orne.

'The most peaceful place in the world,' said Jacques, wiping the tripe gravy from his mouth. 'And the safest place. If you want to hide from the war go to Bagnoles. It is a Red Cross town you understand, all the hotels and the thermal spa are in the hands of the hospitals. They have wounded from all the armies there, French, British and German, with German and French doctors to care for them. After the battles nobody is an enemy.'

'It is all very sporting, you see,' said Marie-Thérèse, opening her eyes and regarding Ormerod with her rough cynicism. 'All helping each other.'

'I suppose they've got to stop shooting at some time,' said Ormerod. 'And when you're getting short of arms and legs that's a good time to stop.'

'I have a pacifist as a partner,' Marie-Thérèse shrugged at Jacques.

'In the end he will win,' nodded Jacques. 'Any fool can fire a gun.'

The woman said nothing more, seeming tired of the argument. There was no tension at the table, though, just weariness. Jacques opened a second bottle of wine but was left to drink most of it himself. Before that he showed them where they could sleep, rooms at the extreme ends of the low, ghostly corridor, close as a tunnel. Ormerod called goodnight from his door and his voice travelled strangely under the beams. She called back, *Bonne nuit,*' and went to her room. Jacques returned to the fire, the hound and the Calvados.

Ormerod's room was large and dusty. The furniture, the enormous wooden bed apart, was draped with white sheets, giving it the appearance of a mortuary. He was too fatigued to care. He climbed into the bed in his shirt and slept quickly.

He was awakened by a movement at the foot of the bed and his hand went, instinctively by now, to the gun beneath the pillow. His eyes moved outwards and he saw a figure in white standing in the dusty gloom. It was Marie-Thérèse wearing a long nightgown. 'I cannot sleep,' she said quietly. 'The house is strange. It frightens me.'

'You've just put the wind up *me*,' he said, sitting up. 'I didn't think *anything* would frighten you.'

'I am sorry. I would like to come into that bed with you.'

A wonderful silence filled him. His hand moved from the gun to the sheets and blankets. He opened them. 'Come on in,' he muttered. 'There's room. This bed's like a football pitch.'

He was amazed at her. Gone was the toughness, the cynicism. She hurried gladly in the white nightgown to the side of the bed and jumped in like a frightened child.

Remembering how they had occupied the bed in Granville and believing that it could only be like that again, Ormerod turned clumsily away from her and said gruffly: 'Goodnight.'

'Goodnight, Dodo,' she whispered. But within a minute she had touched him with her fingers. He felt her touch his hipbone and the breath seemed to rush from his body. For a moment he did not move, still thinking it might be a mistake, that she had brushed him with her fingers in her drowsiness, but then she moved her hand forward until the small, firm palm cradled his hip. Even then he only spoke.

'Are you all right, Marie-Thérèse?' he asked.

'Yes, I am all right.'

'Good. I just wondered.'

'Please turn to me.'

He turned ponderously. He had never been a sensual man, his passions were slow after a lifetime of witnessing the passions of others. Now he did not know what to do, how to act. She seemed so small, her face like a little cheese, her body fragile in the linen nightdress. Only inches separated them but it was like a chasm. Now they had no contact. Timidly he reached out for her with his clumsy hands and touched her ribs. She murmured something he did not understand and moved to him. The touch of that slender, small body was like a shock through his system. His arms completed the circle and he pulled her with extreme gentleness to his chest. Her hands went to his waist, around his shirt, and she held on to him as he held her.

'It is just that ... I need,' she said, as though she owed him an explanation.

'I thought I didn't,' he said.

His penis came sleepily from beneath his shirt as if wondering what was going on. Its warmth touched her stomach and she gave a dark little gasp. Her hands moved deliberately from his waist and she captured it and held on to it. Her delicate fingers ran along its skin. Ormerod eased his hands, with equal gentleness, down from her ribs to the backs of her knees, then rubbed them softly up the flanks of her thighs and then on to her buttocks.

'I'm a bit out of practice,' he said.

He felt her chuckle. Her face came up from the bedclothes and she worked her way up his chest until it was against his. He kissed her dumbly. He could manage gentleness but not finesse.

He attempted it again and this time it was better. The smell of her short hair got in his nostrils and made him want to sneeze. He took his hands from the tight mounds of her buttocks and made to push them between the arch of her legs. She resisted with sleepy playfulness. 'I have other places, Dodo,' she whispered.

There were three pearly buttons at the neck of the old-fashioned nightdress. He felt her undo them and his hands went to the opening. The white linen slipped softly across the skin of her shoulders. It eased across her left breast and the nipple slid out. He felt sure it was glowing in the dark. He thought he would break his neck trying to reach it. He had to shift down in the bed and she wriggled up until his mouth was next to it. He kissed it almost politely and then drew it to his mouth. She groaned and returned her hands to caress him. He put his mouth from her breast to her neck and felt her smile. 'Is there another one?' he said.

'Somewhere,' she murmured. 'You must search.'

He put his rough lips against the outside of the linen nightdress and touched the little covered breast with his tongue. Then he sucked at it through the material. She gave a mouse-like sound and rolled on to her back, opening the arch of her slim dark legs and pulling the part of him which she held towards her. She gasped at the contact. 'I won't hurt you, love,' he said. 'I'll try not to hurt.'

'Hurt me if it is right,' she mumbled. He looked down at her tight face in the dimness. Then to the one exquisite breast shining like a small dome. The veins in her neck were like wire. Ormerod, conscious of his own natural clumsiness, staggered forward on his knees. The flats of his hands went under her backside again and he encouraged her on to him, a fraction at a time, before easing her down on to the sheet again. Then he lay against her and into her and they were entirely together. The face below him was so taut he thought she might scream.

Gradually, as he moved and she moved minutely with him, the cramped expression cleared and her skin settled. Her eyes opened fractionally. He was gazing at her face. He moved still with care, still with the fear of spoiling it.

Practical considerations still worried him. 'I'll take it out,' he said. 'I can, provided I give myself enough time.'

'Take it out and I'll kill you,' she promised. 'Leave it.'

'But . . . what if . . . ?'

'Leave it,' she sighed. 'And stop talking. We are making love.'

She left his bed sometime in the night but he did not know. He slept like a hedgehog, buried beneath the blankets, with the Normandy night wind battering around the chimneys and corners of the house. When he awoke there was no sign of her or that she had ever come to him, and he lay on his back thinking about the occurrence and wondering.

Jacques appeared at nine o'clock accompanied by the athletic deer-hound Honoré, which gave a small moan of pleasure when he recognized Ormerod in the bed. Ormerod patted him paternally. Jacques had brought a pot of coffee borne on nothing less than a silver tray. 'The service in this house is the best, monsieur,' he joked. He paused. 'Madame has gone out on business. She will return this afternoon.' Ormerod thanked him and drank his coffee. Later he went downstairs and saw in daylight the amazing store-house commodities that were packed into one large room. Crates and boxes were piled with such density around that it appeared like some unloading quay. There were garden implements standing alongside valuable paintings and tin saucepans stacked against silver jugs and coffee pots. 'How long do you think you'll be sitting on this lot?' asked Ormerod.

Jacques shrugged. 'Until the war is finished and my employers come back. I would like to be able to show them that everything is here and safe. I have made a complete list. Or until the Germans come around and shoot me before they loot the place. That is more likely I suppose. It will be many years before France is free again.'

'You believe that?' said Ormerod. He thought about it and nodded. 'I suppose you're right. If we don't kid ourselves, we ought to believe that.'

'I listen to the radio,' sniffed the Frenchman. 'It is like a game. The French radio and Laval and Pétain and all those comics. Pétain. Our old hero. *Travail, famille, patrie* – what a fairy tale. So many politicians – all with stories to tell. Fine words.'

'So you think we're cooked?' said Ormerod.

'What else is it possible to think? The only people who can defeat the Germans, my friend, are the Germans themselves. They have already made a bad mistake. They should have chased the English when they ran away at Dunkirk. The Germans should not have waited. The terrier does not give the rat time to dig a hole.'

He walked through an old arched door into the garden. It was dismal with neglect. 'I suppose the estate bailiff should be doing better things,' he said reflectively. 'But I can't find the heart. I am in an ideal position of laziness. The only trouble is I shall have to wait until after the war before I get paid.' He returned to his theme. 'The only way the Germans can lose is by foolishness, by suicide. They still fear Russia. From Russia – from the other band of villains – may come our salvation.'

'What about the underground? The resistance?' asked Ormerod.

The question brought a snort from Jacques. 'A game. Another fairy tale,' he said caustically. 'Madame will discover it. So will you. This is nineteen-forty – the people in this country do not want to fight. They have no fight left. They still have their wounds, monsieur, and the most that is wounded is their pride. But it will have to heal when it can. Maybe later they will resist, but only a fanatic is going to fight for France just now. Or a madman.'

'It all went wrong at Granville,' said Ormerod. 'It needs experience to be a saboteur.' He felt like a tell-tale.

But Jacques knew. 'What do you expect?' he shrugged. 'In French the word *saboteur* also means a blunderer.'

He said he had to be about his duties and left Ormerod wondering what they could possibly be. The Englishman went into the fresh, empty morning. The elegant countryside spread out from the house, which was built on a small plateau where the views were long and green. The loping deerhound, with the strange transfer of faithfulness that animals sometimes develop, followed Ormerod as he walked. It was almost as if the dog were showing him around. They stopped by some vacant stables and again by a large deserted pen. Ormerod guessed that was where they had kept the rest of the pack. His mind was occupied with Marie-Thérèse. He could still feel her slight body against his chest and his legs. He wondered what she would say when they next met.

There was a patchy orchard at the bottom of the initial slope of land from the house. Ormerod selected a ready-looking apple and sat on the fence to eat it. The late season sun was pleasant enough on his face. The dog crouched and put its chin to the ground. Behind him he heard a shout from the house and turned to see Jacques calling with his arms.

It had to be about Marie-Thérèse. He threw the apple down and ran heavily up the slope towards the overgrown terrace. Jacques was standing calmly. He waited until Ormerod got there. 'There's trouble,' he said. 'Marie-Thérèse has been picked up.'

'Oh Jesus, where?'

'Le Mesnil. It is a village ten kilometres from here. At the moment it is only the police, the French police you understand, and not the Germans. They are asking about her papers. It is not dangerous now but it will be very soon – when they bring in the Germans.'

'The police? Will they . . .?'

'Tell the Germans? I don't know. But I think so.'

'*French* police?'

'This is Occupied France,' pointed out Jacques. 'Which means they are probably working for the Germans. One thing is certain, if you want to get her out it will have to be now – before the Germans get their hands on her. After that, monsieur, it will be difficult, very difficult.'

Ormerod pulled in a deep breath. 'Let's go then. It's got to be quick.'

Jacques looked down at the ground. 'I cannot do this,' he said. He looked around him. 'I have to look after the house.' His watery eyes returned to Ormerod. 'Also I am afraid,' he said simply.

'So am I,' said Ormerod forcefully. 'But she's got to be got out. She's . . .'

'Can you ride a motorcycle?'

'Yes. Just about.'

'You can have that.'

'You won't come with me?'

'No. I shall join the resistance on the last day of the war. It will be safer then.'

'Bugger you,' said Ormerod. 'All right. Where's the motor-bike?'

'It is the machine in the room. With all the other things.'

'That! Does it still work?'

'Of course. I keep it in order.'

Ormerod moved towards the house, hurrying his steps. Jacques followed apologetically. 'If you are caught,' he said, 'you must say that you stole the machine from here. Please. I do not want trouble with the Germans. I have duties to perform.'

Le Mesnil des Champs is one of a group of villages, Le Mesnil-Amand, Le Mesnil Bonant, Le Mesnil-Hue, Le Mesnil Garnier and Le Mesnil Villeman, situated within the triangle formed by the road connecting Villedieu-les-Poëles, Gavreay and the cross-roads near Beauchamps. It is an area of small agriculture crossed by a web of minor roads. Le Mesnil des Champs lies almost at the centre of the triangle.

Between the two of them Ormerod and the bailiff pushed the decrepit motorcycle from the main room of the house.

'I think I can manage it,' said Ormerod, once they had wheeled it into the sunshine.

'You must,' said Jacques. 'There is no other way.' He pointed out over the landscape, giving Ormerod directions. 'There is a small square at the centre of the village,' he said. 'The police station is there. Go now.'

Ormerod started the machine. It coughed blindly and choked, then coughed again. But it started at the third attempt. He felt it wanting to go. 'Right, I'm off,' he said. 'Thanks for this anyway.'

'It is nothing,' replied Jacques. '*Au revoir*. After this moment, I do not know you.'

He gave a half salute and the deerhound howled as Ormerod departed.

He set off uncomfortably down the overgrown and rutted drive. The machine was awkward but by the time he reached the lane outside the walls of the estate he had come at least partly to terms with it.

The lanes were sunny and empty. He rattled along, afraid that at every bend he might be confronted with a farm cart or, much worse, a German armoured car. But nothing interrupted his progress and within fifteen minutes he was astride the stationary machine looking down from a steep hill onto the village of Le Mesnil des Champs. The valley was brimming with sunshine but the roofs of the village were indistinct and smoky. He eased the motorcycle forward and free-wheeled down the steep, sunny road. It was easy on the incline and within two minutes he was among the lanes and gardens on the fringe of the settlement. He dismounted and left the machine against a wall. Children played in the flowers and on the banks of the stream which descended invitingly from the hill he had just left.

He walked cautiously, but not too cautiously, through the tight cottages until they gave out onto an open space in the middle of the village. The stone houses with their vivid window-boxes and flower troughs were arranged placidly around and in the middle of the square were some young men playing football. As he went closer he realized they were German soldiers.

They were a work party taking time off from a hole in the side of the square. He passed close to the excavation and saw they had been working on some electricity cables. Their small truck and their equipment were parked nearby. They were all young soldiers, half a dozen of them, and they had taken their tunics off to play their game. One man was in goal and behind the goal Ormerod could see the entrance to the police station with the French flag and the German swastika hanging together above the main archway. That was where she was.

Attempting to look like an idler he walked around the fringe of the square, watching the impromptu footballers and carefully observing the entrance to the police station. Outside was parked a police patrol car and near this, his back to the wall, was an armed French policeman. He was watching the football too. There had obviously as yet been no particular alarm connected with the detention of Marie-Thérèse. Ormerod looked at the gateway. It was wide and completely open, a good-sized stone arch. First he had to get past the policeman.

Ormerod loitered on the edge of the football game. The guarding policeman called to him once to get out of the way because he couldn't see the play. Ormerod, hands in pockets, shuffled yards and waited. The ball was kicked about. The young men were good at it and enjoying it. Ormerod waited his chance and then trotted into the middle of the random pitch. The ball was just flying from one wing to the other. He had been a good footballer. Had he not played against the German police? As he brought the ball down he shouted one of the German words he had learnt for fun. '*Fusstritt!*' The soldiers, surprised at first at his intervention, laughed loudly at the friendly Frenchman who could play football and shouted a familiar word. Ormerod brought the ball down expertly, balanced it with his toe for a moment, flicked it forward and kicked it from fifteen yards past the goalkeeper. '*Tor!*' he shouted.

The young Germans were astonished and delighted at his obvious skill. The goalkeeper retrieved the ball and gladly threw it out once more to Ormerod. He trapped it easily and pushed it into the path of one of the players who had begun to run. The soldier struck it hard but the goalkeeper got his hands to the effort and pushed it out. It ran to Ormerod, he flicked the ball in an arc to the man on the extreme left and then waited for it to be sent back. The running winger shouted and obligingly curved the ball over. Ormerod had been watching the arched entrance of the police station. He turned to the ball now and caught it well with his head, sending it curling away and bouncing into the stone archway. '*Nein, nein,*' he shouted jovially. They all laughed, including the French policeman. Ormerod loped briskly after the ball. The guarding policeman nodded good-naturedly at the Englishman as he trotted into the courtyard. He obviously approved of fraternization. Ormerod flicked the ball with his foot as if to play it against the interior stone walls, but he allowed it to bounce through the doorway at a right angle and into a flagged corridor, so that to retrieve it he was for a moment out of their sight.

As soon as they could not see him he ran into the building, closing and locking a heavy door behind him. Quickly he went across a corridor and at once into a small office.

A junior German officer was sitting at a desk. A German sergeant and a French policeman were standing near the back wall and Marie-Thérèse was sitting in a chair opposite the German. Her face looked stiff. The officer's hand was on the telephone.

All four turned when he came into the room, gun in hand. Marie-Thérèse jumped from the chair. 'Shoot them!' she screamed.

To his own amazement Ormerod did. Twice he fired his pistol and the explosions filled the small room. The officer pitched forward onto the desk, his fingers gripping the telephone receiver; the sergeant was pinned against the wall by the bullet and slid stupidly down to the floor. Ormerod was not going to shoot the policeman. The Frenchman, horror nailed to his face, tried to raise his pasty hands in surrender. Marie-Thérèse did not hesitate. Rushing forward she pulled the officer's gun from its holster and shot her trembling fellow countryman. He slipped sideways on top of the German sergeant.

Ormerod was horrified. But there was no time for it. Marie-Thérèse picked up a bunch of keys from the desk and ran to the door. She turned the opposite way along the corridor to the way Ormerod had entered. The French policeman who had been outside was banging on the stout inner door Ormerod had locked behind him.

'There's half a dozen krauts out there,' panted Ormerod. 'At the front.'

'They have a car at the back,' she said with stiff calm. She smartly opened another door and they ran down a wooden corridor towards daylight coming over the top of a fanlight window. The girl wrenched the door open and they were in the street. It was unnaturally quiet considering the shooting. A cat scratched itself in the middle of the cobbles and a child regarded them with only minor interest from a garden opposite. A German military car was standing against the building. With some strange feminine acknowledgement she tossed the keys she had taken from the desk at him. He caught them as he ran and then they both jumped into the vehicle.

It started first time. Ormerod sent the cat scurrying away as he drove the car along the first stretch of street. He knew where the hill was. A right-hand bend and then another left the rising road before them. Marie-Thérèse turned and looked back and down at the sunlit village. The footballers were gathered foolishly at the door of the police station. There was no one to give them orders. Otherwise the streets and the square were as quiet as the smoke that eased itself from the stone chimneys of the houses.

'Good, Dodo, it was beautiful,' said Marie-Thérèse squeezing his arm.

'Lucky,' he said. 'Bloody lucky. Another ten minutes and nobody could have got you.'

'You came like an English knight in armour,' she laughed.

'I still don't understand why you had to shoot the Frenchman,' said Ormerod after a week. He had waited for her to offer an excuse, with prompting, but she had said nothing. The matter seemed to have gone from her mind. Now she shrugged.

'He was a traitor. He was working with the Germans.'

'Didn't it occur to you that he had no choice? He's a policeman and a policeman has to obey orders and do what he's told. I know that only too well.'

She sniffed. 'So he was in the way. He would have given a description.'

He did not believe that it was just that. She had wanted to shoot him. Ormerod lay on the grass beneath a horse-chestnut tree laden with autumn spikes and rich red leaves, standing out like an explosion against a cool blue sky. Marie-Thérèse sat on the grass beside him. For seven days they had been hiding and on the run. They had escaped from the small area of Le Mesnil des Champs as the Germans searched the surrounding fields, hills and hamlets.

They had carefully moved east from the immediate region and they were hiding in the modest forest of St Sever, a place of sharp little hills and dense trees. There was a winter hut for the woodman in an almost concealed valley and they had waited there for three days. Ormerod looked up at the trees and the sky. 'When are we going to move?' he said. 'I'd like to get towards Bagnoles. Albert Smales may be dead by now. I'll have come all this way for nothing.'

She smiled wryly. 'You would really like to catch him, your Smales, would you not? You have one ambition. I have so many.'

'What *are* you proposing to do next, then?' he asked. 'You're in charge.'

'My orders have come from Paris. I received them at Mesnil just before the police took me in,' she said a trifle stiffly. 'It would not be good for both of us to know everything, but I will tell you that a man will come here. They call him by a code-name, Jean Le Blanc. He will be a great resistance leader. Perhaps it will take a year yet, but he is the one. I have great faith in him. He will put some iron into these people. He will make them resist.'

A bird flew high against the stainless sky and Ormerod followed it with his eye until it had cleared the horizon of the trees.

'Jean Le Blanc was the famous horse of the Perche region,' she said quietly. 'He was the stallion who was the father of the Percheron horses. This man comes from that region. That is why he has taken this name.'

'Have you ever played conkers?' asked Ormerod, gazing up into the trees.

'No. What is conkers?'

'Every English kid knows how to play conkers,' he said.

'I was a French kid, remember?'

'All right. Sorry. I'll show you.'

He stood up in his heavy way and walked down the slope from the tree. Many of the green, spiky horse-chestnut cases had fallen among the dying leaves down there. The interior of the husk was like white velvet. The horse-chestnuts shone as round and smooth as the finest wood. He bent and picked up two, rejected them and carefully selected another pair. 'They have to be exactly right,' he said.

When he turned up the incline again he saw she was smiling indulgently towards him. He returned the smile and went back to where she was sitting. 'We need some string,' he said. 'Or better still ... here ...' He sat down and began to remove the

137

laces from his boots. At that moment two German armoured cars and two companies of troops in lorries were moving along the forest road, a mile away and several hundred feet above them.

Ormerod went into the hut, his now laceless boots flapping comically on his feet. He returned with a slim nail and made a central hole in each of the hard chestnuts. Marie-Thérèse watched him with tolerant amusement. The sun striking through the high trees touched her face and neck. The forest stirred. Above them the German soldiers left their trucks and began to move along the rutted hunting rides, the split sunlight making chevrons on their bodies as they advanced. Ormerod threaded the bootlaces through the pierced conkers and secured them with a tight knot at the end. He held them in his hands. 'Choose,' he invited. 'Take one.'

Marie-Thérèse picked one up and admired its warm gloss. 'It is a pity they cannot be eaten,' she said. 'They look very good to the appetite.'

'Eaten? Oh God, where's your soul?' he sighed. 'Conkers are for playing conkers. Hold it by the lace and I'll show you.' She did as he said, standing small and smiling while he took a pace away and considered the target. He drew back his conker on its string and aimed. He looked up and grinned at her. 'This takes me back, I can tell you,' he said. 'Way back. I had a conker once at school – a hundred-and-oner. That means it had beaten a hundred and one conkers.'

'Conquered them,' she said, pleased with the joke.

'Very good. Right, ready . . .'

He drew the brown nut back and struck at her suspended conker. He missed, the lace becoming entangled with hers. 'Now your turn,' he said. 'Take it steady, aim carefully.'

Mare-Thérèse put her tongue between her teeth, her eyes narrowing. With great precision she drew back her conker and swung it quickly. It caught the target beautifully, with a clear crack, splitting it into four or five pieces which scattered to the earth. Ormerod stared at her, disconsolate.

'Beginner's luck,' he muttered.

'My killer instinct, as you say,' she smiled. Her eyes wandered for an instant and she saw the German soldiers moving against the treed skyline. 'Boche!' she hissed. 'Quick!'

Ormerod turned and saw them too. He swore. 'In the pipe,' he said. 'Get everything from the hut.'

She was already on her way. Running at a crouch through the trees, up the slope to the woodman's hut. He was right behind her. Fortunately there was little to collect, a haversack with some food, two tin mugs, and two small boxes of ammunition. They gathered them quickly. They had slept in their clothes on the two bare mattresses, part of the equipment of the hut, so there were no blankets to give them away.

Ormerod got to the door again first. The skyline seemed clear, then the flat cap of one of the armoured cars appeared, moving gracelessly against the woods. Ormerod crouched. The vehicle rumbled on. Now he could hear its ungainly engine. But the horizon was blank. 'Right – now,' he whispered to Marie-Thérèse behind him. 'Run.'

At a crouch they scampered across the open ground around the hut, half running, half tumbling down the grass slope and into some firs beyond the horse-chestnut trees. The lack of laces in his boots made Ormerod's descent both difficult and comic. There was a wide-mouthed drainage pipe half buried in the ferns and brambles down there. He reached it, turned and helped the girl to wriggle into its aperture. She went in feet first. He could hear her panting breath echoing from within the tube. 'Voilà,' she whispered. Ormerod flattened himself and wriggled in backwards.

It was dank and full of smells in there. He pulled some of the dying ferns across the opening at his end and lay face down against the curved bottom of the pipe. They waited. There was nothing else they could do. He could hear the girl breathing near his heels.

It took the Germans another half an hour to reach the hut. Throughout that time the forest sighed and stirred above the culvert and the tube and the air within the enclosed space became fetid. Insects of various sorts promenaded in front of the fugitives' noses. Then they heard a bird call out in alarm and the sounds of the soldiers' steps and voices coming through the woods. Someone called an order when they spotted the hut and the troops clumsily surrounded it, taking cover while a sergeant and two men approached and first looked cautiously through the window before kicking in the door and entering with a great deal of dramatic noise.

Ormerod heard the sergeant shout that the hut was clear. He felt the soldiers moving again. A pair of German boots appeared almost at the opening of the pipe, so near that he could have tied the laces together. First the heels were pointing in his direction. Then the man began to urinate. Ormerod grimaced horribly and tried to turn his head. He could not. The urine ran in a river into the pipe, flowing right past the nose of the hiding man.

The sergeant gave an order for the men to take a five minute break and they sat around the hut in the striped autumn sunlight, smoking and talking. Another man relieved himself against the pipe. It was amazing that they had to find somewhere vaguely lavatorial when they had the entire forest at their disposal. Ormerod, lying in the pipe almost below their feet, was all but overcome by the stench of urine. Because his body almost blocked the pipe it had soaked into his jersey. He closed his eyes and tried to think of happier times.

Eventually there came the sound of further orders and the German soldiers, grumbling, prepared to move away. Ormerod and Marie Thérèse lay stiffly while they heard the boots moving through the ferns and trees. The forest fell to silence. They remained imprisoned in the pipe, shifting only an inch one way or another, for a further two hours. They were aware of the daylight seeping away. The birds began their final chorus before darkness came down. Then, when they thought it was safe, the man and the woman emerged like animals from their burrow.

'I wonder if they were looking especially for us,' said Ormerod when they were in the hut again, the blank black night closed in all around them. 'Or was it just routine?'

'Does it matter?' she shrugged in the shadows. 'We are caught here and in some way we must move. But before we move we must wait for Jean Le Blanc. Let us hope he gets here soon, Dodo. We need him.'

It was thirty hours later that a forest worker on a bicycle came bumping down the forest path. They heard him a good distance away and as a precaution concealed themselves again in the pipe. He stood in the clearing and imitated the call of the turtle dove. The fugitives emerged from their concealment.

'Jean Le Blanc,' said the man dully, as if he did not want to show enthusiasm for the message, 'has arrived in Villedieu. The Germans are quieter now. Tonight you will make your way to the road at the top of the forest, by the crucifix, and you will be met by a man who will take you to Villedieu. His signal will be the call of the dove.'

seven

Villedieu-les-Poëles was, in 1940, a town of just under four thousand inhabitants, noted for its copper utensils (Poëles means pots and pans) and its milk churns, used throughout the dairy country of Normandy. It also had, and indeed still has, a bell-foundry, in the Rue du Pont Chignon, which was first established in the twelfth century. When the Germans occupied the town in the summer of 1940 three large bells were being cast for a church in the Pyrénées-Orientales *département* of France.

The German commandant of the area which included Villedieu, General Wolfgang Groemann, was, by chance, a campanologist, and took much interest in the casting of the three bells in the long barn-like building. When the church in the eastern Pyrénées, in the Unoccupied Zone of France, decided that, because of the national situation and the lack of funds, they could not after all take delivery of the bells, General Groemann contacted the ecclesiastical authorities in his home town, the cathedral city of Minden, and arrived, very pleased, at the bell-foundry one morning in his staff car to personally purchase the bells (at a bargain price it should be said) for a church in the German city. The work on the casting and finishing was completed in September and a date in early October was fixed for their transportation by rail to Germany.

For hundreds of years it had been customary for bells cast in the foundry to be blessed in the centre of the little town and to be carried off in procession on the first part of their journey to the church where they were to hang. Because of the circumstances in October 1940, it was doubted in Villedieu that this ceremony would take place, in fact a great number of the townspeople were against it; but General Groemann was insistent that it should be as always, with a religious ceremony and a colourful procession through the narrow streets. And this time he and his soldiers would take part. (A photograph of the bells being taken away, incidentally, appeared in a Free French newspaper and a number of British newspapers under the heading 'Nazis Loot Bells from French Town'.)

When the killing of the German officer, the sergeant, and the French policeman took place in the police station at Le Mesnil des Champs, it was thought in Villedieu, the nearest town of any size, that the bells ceremony would be postponed. Large numbers of troops were deployed over a wide area of the Normandy countryside but had failed to pick up the assassins. Roads were still being watched and there were systematic searches in the surrounding towns, but it was felt by the French authorities and the Germans themselves that the man and the woman they were hunting had gone in the direction of Paris. In any case, General Groemann had promised the bells to his bishop. He wanted them delivered.

The first Sunday in October was designated as a suitable day for the ceremony. The great bells would be carried by cart from the foundry, blessed in the square, and then borne in procession to the Villedieu railway station where they would be loaded on special wagons for their journey to Germany.

On the Friday before the event, Ormerod and Marie-Thérèse were brought into Villedieu concealed in a cavity made under a pile of logs in the back of a cart drawn by two dray horses. The man who had met them on the high forest road with the call of the dove took them straight to a small house. It was here for the first time that they met the fanatic, Jean Le Blanc.

During Ormerod's years as a policeman, he had cultivated, as policemen do, a nose for a villain. It was not the size, not the shape of a man; not what he said, nor, often, what he did. A man could be a criminal without being a villain. Ormerod always considered that the eyes had something to do with it. And there was a sort of aura, an atmosphere, a smell about a villain. In all his life, he had never seen a more natural-born villain than the man who called himself Jean Le Blanc.

He was thick and tall, very powerful, with a big, domed, bald head. His hands were fleshy. The skin on his arms and face and head was as white as if he had never been out in the fresh air in the whole of his life.

Ormerod and Marie-Thérèse had been taken to a house near the bell-foundry in the town. At his briefing and instruction at Ash Vale, although Villedieu had been one of the towns detailed, no one had mentioned the bell-foundry. From a guide book, Ormerod had learned that the town gave its name to vaudeville, because of a comic actor who once lived there. Ormerod remembered thinking at the time that this information, while not generally useful in war, might turn out to be appropriate in the circumstances. And so it was.

The 'safe' house, where they were to hide, had a loft fitted like a room. They had climbed directly from the log cart up through a trapdoor and into the concealed place.

There were three men and a woman waiting for them. One of the men was Jean Le Blanc. He was wearing a pair of blue overalls. On a box in front of him was a German tommy-gun, which he was dismantling, and several detonators and sticks of explosive. Also on the box was a wad of something that Ormerod took to be putty. The other men were also in their working blue; the woman was silent and lined with worry. She went off to get some food and drink. Le Blanc picked up the putty-like material and began to work it around in his fingers.

'You have met with the plastic explosive, monsieur?' he inquired, his sleepy eyes making the effort to look up at Ormerod.

'Oh, that's it,' said Ormerod. 'I thought you were making a model of Hitler. To stick a few pins in.'

The joke was not appreciated. 'Well, it just looked like that,'

143

he mumbled. 'Should you be rolling it around in your hands?' he asked. 'Explosive?'

Le Blanc smiled dryly. 'It is safe to do this.' He threw the handful of plastic straight at Ormerod's chest. Ormerod jumped apprehensively and he caught it. Carefully he returned it to Le Blanc who dropped it on the table. 'It is like a magic toy,' he said. 'It can be easy and without harm, it can be fixed into any space and in any form. But when it explodes it is very, very big.' He looked around at the four faces in the lamplight. 'This, my friends, is what the Nazis will come to fear in France. It is our greatest weapon.'

Ormerod half turned to Marie-Thérèse and was not surprised to see her eyes shining in the half-light. 'If we had this at Granville,' she said, 'there would have been no accident.' Her expression was not merely for the explosive, however, Ormerod could see that. Her admiration was also for the man.

Afterwards, when the others had gone and he and Marie-Thérèse were left alone in the dark loft, she said, as if she felt compelled to explain: 'This man is from my region in Normandy. He is from the Perche. Jean Le Blanc, the famous Percheron stallion, was also powerful.'

'What does he do for a living?' asked Ormerod grumpily in the dark. 'Bend iron bars with his teeth?'

'Like me, he also was a schoolteacher,' sniffed Marie-Thérèse. 'But he was the head of a big school.'

'I bet the kids loved him,' muttered Ormerod. 'Fancy him swinging a cane.'

'He is what we need now,' she said solemnly. 'He is what France needs. Strength, what you in English call guts. Someone who is not afraid. In this country we have had enough of our cowards.' He could hear her sneer in the dark. 'They were going to defend Paris to the last corner, to the last lamp-post. Instead they gave up at the gates.' She shifted alongside him. 'Did you see the poster they have put on this wall?'

He remembered seeing the poster fixed at the other end of the loft but away from the light. 'What was it?' he said.

She switched on her torch and swung it around. 'There,' she said as its beam settled on the poster. It was a picture of an optimistic French soldier. 'The words beneath say: "France will win because she is strong",' recited Marie-Thérèse. She kept the torch steady. 'It is a bad joke,' she said. 'These were put upon the walls in France. How the Germans must have laughed. The people here have brought it inside this place because they believe that one day it will be true again.' Suddenly she turned the torch on his face, making him blink and raise his hand. 'Perhaps it is difficult for you to understand, Dodo,' she said. '*You* have not been disgraced. Not yet.'

Blackness enveloped them as she switched off the beam. They were lying in two sleeping bags on a rough rug laid across the floor. He heard her lie down, disgruntled, beside him. He knew if he put his hand out he would quickly touch her. All through their days in the forest together they had never made love. After that first time in the château she had reverted to her former self and Ormerod thought it would be better to wait until she invited him again. But now, in the dark, before the beginning of another adventure, he reached out and touched her. Her hand must have been lying waiting for him because his fingers found hers immediately.

Clumsily he turned towards her. He felt her turn inwards also. Their faces stared at each other in the dark.

'I wish to talk to you, Dodo,' she said solemnly.

'Oh blimey. I thought we might make love.'

'Yes. That also, I need too. I shall come in with you because it will be easier.'

Ormerod, his heart banging in the darkness of his body, made room for her in the sleeping bag. He could hear her taking her shirt over her head and then she slid in beside him, slim as a young animal.

They held each other as if they were the last pair on earth, her mouth against his neck, open and wet, his hands around her buttocks, pulling her thighs against his. When they coupled she eased herself above him, lying like a swimmer on his wide chest. She shuddered as they climaxed and then lay there as if she had gone to sleep. Ormerod had cramp in his leg. He moved it to ease it.

'In Hemingway,' she said, 'in *For Whom the Bell Tolls*, they made love like this in a sleeping sack.'

'It's not exactly a double bed,' he said.

He felt her smile. 'And was it good enough now, for us?'

'It was all right, as a matter of fact. Was it all right for you, Dove?'

'It was good,' she replied, still smiling. '*For Whom the Bell Tolls* is very right, also, Dodo. For us.'

'Why's that?'

'Tomorrow we are going to hide under the bells. We are going to escape from this region beneath two bells from the foundry.'

'Jesus. Is that so?'

'It is so. We have to move from here. But all around are the Germans. You want to get to Bagnoles and there is something Jean Le Blanc wants to do there also.'

'Don't tell me he's after Albert Smales?'

'No. Something much bigger. But the roads are still being checked around this area. We need to get further east, to Vire, so that we can move more freely. Tomorrow three bells from the foundry are to be taken from here by horse-pulled cart and then by rail. They are going to Germany. The Boche have stolen them. The plan is for you and I, Dodo, to hide under the bells and be taken to the railway and then to Vire, where we will be released by local men. The bells are set upon bases, pallets, and there are round holes in the pallets, so we shall be able to breathe.'

He listened, astounded. 'It sounds clever,' he admitted. 'But I can't say it appeals to me much. Appeals – bells. That's a joke.'

'It is a joke I do not understand,' she said disconcertingly. 'And now is no time for it. There is to be a procession for the bells. Church people and the Germans – hah! That will be the joke. And another joke is that we will be hiding below the bells.'

'We're sure that someone is going to turn up at Vire and get us out from underneath?' said Ormerod. 'I'd hate to be stuck under there for long.'

'In that matter,' she said slowly in the darkness, 'I think you will have to trust Jean Le Blanc.'

146

Even then the thought came to Ormerod that trusting Jean Le Blanc would be a difficult thing.

In post-war years the Blessing of the Bells has become a charming attraction in the town of Villedieu-les-Poëles. When the long and precise process of casting and moulding a new bell or a clarion is complete the beautiful bronze workmanship is brought from the foundry and shown by the proud craftsmen to the townspeople. There is a religious service, children's choirs sing in the modest square, and there is a procession through the deep grey streets of the town.

On that first Sunday of October 1940, many of the townspeople were reluctant to take part in the ceremony because of the participation of the Germans and the fact that the bells were bound for Minden. Others felt that it was necessary to behave as though things were as near normal as possible, not to antagonize the occupying forces, and to keep the foundry working. The children, who in the main could not understand politics, were eager for the ceremony because it was always a special day in their little town.

Before dawn Marie-Thérèse and Ormerod were roused, given a cup of thick, bitter coffee, and taken from the loft of the house near the foundry. The two local men who had been in the loft the previous night conducted them across the courtyard and took them by a small door into the foundry building.

They entered. Ormerod stood immediately within the door, surprised and awed. It was as he imagined Hell might look. A wide, high, hot cavern, brimming with brimstone and shadows, grit and ghostly glowing from the furnaces. A scaffold of thick and ancient wooden beams spanned the building and standing below them, silhouetted in the inferno like a trio of misdirected bishops in their robes, were the three great bells.

They were already placed on a long flat cart which two dray horses would pull along the cobbled streets to the railway station. They stood, as Marie-Thérèse had said they would, each on a thick wooden pallet with cup-sized holes drilled through the wood. These pallets were raised on blocks so there was air beneath them. The two local men moved ahead of Ormerod and the girl. They lifted the first bell clear of its base by means of a suspended chain tackle. Then they motioned Marie-Thérèse forward and she went, uncertainly at first Ormerod imagined, then more quickly, towards the first bell clear of its pallet. One of the men nodded '*Voilà*' at the woman. She smiled a thin smile at Ormerod and said : 'See you in Vire, Dodo.'

'With bells on,' he answered grimly.

She crawled below the mouth of the cloche and squatted, like a pixie, while the casting was lowered over her. One of the men crouched and looked below the pallet supported on the blocks. A slim finger appeared through one of the holes, the sign that she was all right.

One of the men now glanced at Ormerod as if sizing him up, before he moved forward to the second, larger bell. There in the dim half-light he had a strange memory of once, in the course of his duties, being present at an exhumation. Waiting for them to lift the bell was something like waiting for the tomb to open. Except that this was *his* tomb. If Jean Le Blanc chose, they need not lift the bell at Vire and the bells might take weeks to go to Minden and be unloaded. What comment the curled up body of a London policeman would cause in that town in Germany!

The men moved the chain tackle along its gallery high overhead and attached the hook to the top of the bell. The chain rattled and the casting eased its way an inch at a time clear of its pallet. When there was a three foot space the men both nodded at Ormerod and he gave them a little salute. Doubtfully looking at the great bronze mouth hung above him he climbed onto the pallet and crossed his legs, endeavouring to form himself into a pyramid. He heard the chain creak and bit by bit even the dim light disappeared. The bell descended carefully and at last sat properly upon its pallet. Ormerod pushed his finger through one of the holes to show he had no serious complaints. But he did not like it in there and the thought of spending several hours like that did not appeal at all. He looked around the close-walled darkness. 'Fucking ding-dong,' he muttered.

At eleven o'clock on that October Sunday morning a booted

148

and helmeted German band with glockenspiel and sun-reflecting souzaphone stomped melodiously into the modest town. Some of the people had come out in their best clothes to see the ceremony of the bells, not as many as usual but sufficient to crowd the main square. Germans or no Germans, the bells had been made there in Villedieu and must be properly blessed and sent on their way. A platoon of infantry marched after the band and drilled noisily on the cobbles, forming a rectangle around the three *cloches* standing on their cart. The crowd waited for the priest and the German General Wolfgang Groemann.

At a window overlooking the square, like a disgruntled protrait in a frame, sat Jean Le Blanc, his domed head hidden beneath a trilby. He watched cynically as the despised Germans paraded. From the edge of his mouth, but without ceasing his watching, he spoke to a Frenchman stationed within the room. 'One day,' he said casually, 'I think I would like to blow up a German band.' The souzaphone was yawning almost below the window. He took a last draw at his cigarette and dropped the stub into the mouth of the instrument. A thin finger of smoke curled from it.

Beneath the shell of his bell Ormerod listened to the muffled music and tapped out time with his finger. It was very hot inside the bell and he was sweating heavily. He rested his forehead against the metal. He heard the boots of the soldiers striding on the cobbles and then the orders as they halted and stamped around into their ceremonial formation. He was, he reflected unhappily, surrounded.

General Wolfgang Groemann, the burgher of Minden, delighted with his bargain purchase of the bells, arrived smiling in an open staff car. Jean Le Blanc, observing from his window, could easily have shot him through his medals. But there was time for that and very soon. The general acknowledged the salutes of his soldiers, did the statutory *Heil Hitler*, although he did not much care for the slogan, particularly in the middle of a conquered town, and stepped down to be greeted by the mayor.

The religious procession followed, the priest and the ecclesiastical officials with the decorated cross, and a bobbing line of surpliced choirboys. The German beamed when he saw them. He began to think that the occupation might, after all, be peaceful and a success. Jean Le Blanc watched him, seething within like a cat unable to touch a fat canary. He consoled himself with the promise of what was to follow.

The priest had a troubled conscience about the ceremony, but he argued inwardly that the Germans had so far behaved themselves in the district. And the town needed to sell bells. He had given permission for the church to take part as normal, after consultation with his bishop, but he had personally baulked at the ringing of his own church bells. They remained silent. He told the general that the belfry was discovered to be unsafe.

While Ormerod and Marie-Thérèse sweated under their respective bronze covers, the ceremony proceeded. They were grateful that it was not protracted. The prayers and responses came to an end while the sweat ran into Ormerod's eyes. Then the band played 'La Marseillaise,' followed more loudly by 'Deutschland, Deutschland, Über Alles', and the hidden couple felt the cart shudder beneath them as the decorated dray horses were hitched. Then the muffled band began a rousing tune and the bells began to move. As the wheels began to grind on the cobbles, the general, feeling pleased with the day, the bells and the ceremony, stepped forward and gave each one a small tap with his knuckle. 'Good,' he nodded. 'Off you go – home to Minden.'

Ormerod rested his head against the casing, fatigue and relief consuming him. He wondered how Marie-Thérèse was feeling. The people were wordless as the three domes moved from town. Usually this was a signal for rejoicing, but today it was not the same. The crowd dispersed with bleak expressions and bowed heads. Only the children made any sounds as the Germans marched away.

The priest and his procession returned to the church, bright colours and silent faces, and with the band in front and the platoon of infantrymen behind, the bells were borne to the railway station.

General Wolfgang Groemann went home to lunch, well satisfied with the sunny morning. He had rarely felt so much at peace in a conquered land. On his desk was the memorandum confirming that the following Thursday morning he would be visiting the wounded in the hospitals in the Red Cross town of Bagnoles de l'Orne. From that visit he would not return.

At Villedieu the three bronze bells on their pallets were hoisted aboard a special truck on a goods train that left the same afternoon for the east. It made its unscheduled stop at Vire, twenty-eight kilometres towards Paris, in the early evening. It was becoming dark when six men arrived at the goods yard adjoining the station and climbed onto the wagon carrying the bells. Jean Le Blanc watched from a bicycle propped against the quiet wall of the station.

The men manoeuvred a small rattling crane alongside the wagon and hitched its hook to the first bell. The crane creaked and the cable tautened. The bell was raised a few inches at a time. Marie-Thérèse, like a curled-up baby, tumbled out into the arms of one of the men.

The crane was then moved along to Ormerod's bell. Gratefully he felt it being raised a few inches at a time and he knew his ordeal was over. He could scarcely move his limbs and the men had to help him to the ground. The bells were quietly replaced and the men took the Englishman and the Frenchwoman with them into Vire.

They went through the shadows of the small town to another 'safe' house where a young girl gave them some food, a stew and bread and a bottle of wine. Several furtive people arrived and departed during the evening. None of them spoke to Ormerod, nor could he understand anything that was said. It was like watching a shadowgraph.

His body was still stiff from the hours beneath the bell and eventually he nodded to sleep in a rough wooden chair in the main downstairs room of the house. He had been sleeping for almost an hour when Marie-Thérèse woke him firmly.

'We leave soon,' she said.

'Oh God. Tonight?'

'Yes. You should be glad. We go to Bagnoles.'

'Ah,' he said, sitting up stiffly. 'That's more like it.'

There was an oil lamp in the room. She allowed herself a

151

smile in its light. 'There is time for you to wash and shave your-self before you go,' she said.

Ormerod blinked. 'My disguise not pretty enough for you, eh lady?'

'You look as you are, a fugitive,' she said. Ormerod rose clumsily.

'If it's to Bagnoles we're going, I ought to get myself cleaned up. I want to look tidy for Mr Smales.'

'Ah, Smales, there is another thing,' she said.

'What other thing?'

She regarded him steadily. 'We have an important operation in Bagnoles,' she said. 'Nothing must get in its way ...'

'Oh, now, look here ...' he began to protest.

'Everything will be okay,' she assured. 'But let *us* find Smales for you – our local people will know where he is, or they can find out. You are not the most silent of men, Dodo, and we must tread carefully.'

Ormerod studied the girlish face in the lamplight. 'Le Blanc's put his spoke in, hasn't he?' he guessed. 'He's the one. Well I've come for Smales, and I intend to get him. So the Percheron bloody horse can stuff that ...'

'We are under Jean's orders,' she told him bluntly. 'Nothing can go against that. But we will discover about Smales. I prom-ise, Dodo.'

He rose grumpily. 'I get the feeling I'm being buggered about,' he said. 'What if I don't agree?'

'Jean Le Blanc will shoot you,' she said simply. 'Then you'll never get to Smales.'

Ormerod knew where the toilet was. He had heard the flush going. He sighed. 'All right. I don't like it, but I'll go along with it.' He regarded her small face seriously. He could not resist touching the cheek with his finger. 'You promise, then,' he said. 'About Smales?'

'I promise,' she said. She put up her hand and held his finger against her cheek. 'At Bagnoles,' she said. 'It will be something amazing.'

They travelled to the fringe of Bagnoles de l'Orne in a but-cher's van taking meat to the hospitals. In the hour's journey

Ormerod was knocked first one way and then the other by sides of pork swinging from hooks. It was not a refrigerated van but it was very cold. He and Marie-Thérèse crouched together in the darkness.

Once they were stopped at a German check-point but the driver of the van was either convincing or the soldiers were lazy because they did not open the rear doors. Ormerod and the woman breathed with relief among the pork.

At the conclusion of the journey they left the van stiffly and were conducted by a young priest to the organ loft of a church on the outskirts of Bagnoles. Ormerod sat on the floor next to Marie-Thérèse who was bowed with exhaustion. He looked about him. The pipes of the organ came like silver fingers through the floor, the roof went up into medieval dimness inhabited by shadows, spiders and báts.

A man came from the town with bread and cheese and coffee. Two mattresses and some blankets were hauled up from below and the fugitives were left there in the dark, the autumn wind snorting through the cracks and crevices in the ancient roof. Marie-Thérèse had hardly spoken a word. Her white face could be seen in the dark. Ormerod arranged the mattresses side by side and helped her to lie down. Then he stretched out gratefully beside her, held his large arms about her slim form, and they slept.

In the morning the furtive man who had previously brought the food returned with more bread, cheese and coffee. Ormerod sat up achingly. Birds were fluttering high up in the ceiling and splinters of daylight showed through the roof. 'The diet is a bit unvaried,' said Ormerod as he and Marie-Thérèse faced each other across the mattresses. 'No one can say you eat well as a spy.'

'We are *here*,' she pointed out. 'That is a victory for us. It was ingenious, don't you think, to get us away beneath the bells?'

'Ingenious but uncomfortable. Now I know how the clapper feels. Anyway, this is Bagnoles. Just think, chummy Smales may be just around the corner.'

She smiled, but seriously. The dusty light in the loft suited her face. 'You will get your chance,' she assured him. 'Smales will be found. But first, as I told you last night, Jean Le Blanc has some plans for Bagnoles.'

'Can't say I like the look of friend Jean,' admitted Ormerod. 'He puts the wind up me a bit.'

'The winds up you?'

'Not winds, wind. One wind. It means I'm worried about him.'

'Worried? You mean he frightens you?'

'Well not quite, but it will do. He looks the sort who is capable of anything.'

'That is why we need him. There are too many old women in France. He hates the Boche as I do. It made me sick when I heard French people singing songs with the Germans yesterday. This country is grovelling on its stomach. Now we even give our church bells to the Nazis.'

A noise came from below and Ormerod's fingers went to the gun. It was Jean Le Blanc. His bold dome came through the trapdoor. 'Ah, it's Humpty Dumpty,' said Ormerod.

'*Ca va?*' the man said, climbing like an agile giant through the trapdoor. 'It goes well?'

'We are recovered,' answered Marie-Thérèse. 'Are there no alarms?'

'It is quiet,' Le Blanc nodded. 'We have spent all night booby-trapping the bells. When they get to Minden they will explode.'

'Christ, you think of everything don't you?' said Ormerod grudgingly. 'Let's hope nobody moves them in Paris.'

'They are the general's special plaything,' said Le Blanc. 'And the bombs will only blow up when the bells are moved from their bases.' He smiled like somebody remembering a kindness. 'They will make only one sound, those bells, and it will not be ringing.'

He turned his back on Ormerod as though he had nothing more to say to him. He faced the girl, sat down and they conversed rapidly in French for ten minutes. Eventually he seemed satisfied and rose from the mattress. '*Au revoir, Monsieur l'Anglais,*' he said to Ormerod as he opened the trapdoor and descended the ladder. 'Soon there will be important work for you to do.'

154

'I can't wait,' nodded Ormerod dryly. The dome began to descend. 'Mind your head,' he called after it. 'They'll never put it back together again.'

For three days Ormerod remained in the church loft. He was simply left there while Marie-Thérèse spent hours away, returning late to sleep exhausted on her mattress on the floor. They seemed to have no use for him; or they had concluded that he was too high a risk. He was bored but not sorry.

The man who had brought them food came back twice a day and replenished Ormerod in the manner of a zoo keeper feeding a captive bear. He put the food over the top of the trapdoor, muttered a scattering of indistinguishable phrases and went away again. Ormerod grumbled to Marie-Thérèse when she returned unexpectedly in the middle of the afternoon. She appeared white and drained.

'I'm beginning to feel like the housewife who only ever sees the milkman,' he complained. 'Off you go to work and I'm stuck here all day waiting for you to come back.'

She understood the wry joke and she smiled faintly at him. 'I am sorry Dodo,' she said wearily. 'We are getting men together here. It is very good. We are organizing something ... something very big. We will need you then.'

Ormerod looked at her through the dimness. He wondered, not for the first time, how someone so slight could be so concerned with violence. 'I wouldn't mind something to read,' he said. 'My eyes are getting used to this place now. I can even spot the bats on the ceiling.'

She nodded tiredly. 'I will see if there is anything in English,' she promised. 'I will get them to bring it here.'

From the shopping bag she carried she took out the pieces of a sub-machine gun and began slipping it together. She went out an hour later and the man brought the food in the evening and pushed an additional carton through the aperture, shoving it towards the seated Ormerod with ill-grace, like a worn-out Father Christmas delivering a present to the final child in the world.

In the box were assorted books and magazines and a thoughtfully provided candle and matches. Eagerly Ormerod took his prize to the enclosed part of the organ loft and there he lit the candle. The organ pipes were close together and all around him. It was as though he were sitting in a barred cage with no space between the bars. He delved into the box. He held the candle eagerly to the first book he took out. His heart dropped. '*Bunty Bunnikins and the Naughty Gnomes,*' he read miserably. 'Oh, sod it! I've read that.' The next offering was just as unpromising: *Super Tales for Girls*, then *A Manual of Organic Chemistry*. Groaning he put his hand in again and came out with half a dozen English boy's comics. Relief flooded through him. '*Hotspur, Champion, The Wizard!*' he whispered to himself. 'That's a bit better.'

The candle spun shadows around the organ pipes. He had forgotten the food. He settled back and began to read 'Rockfist Rogan', eating every word slowly so that the adventure would not come to a conclusion too quickly. He exhaled deeply at the end of the story. Now for 'Wilson the Amazing Athlete'. Then the 'Wolf of Kabul' with the lethal cricket bat wielded as a club. Ormerod read hungrily. He began to chew a lump of bread and cheese as he read. The frustrating moments came at the end of episodes of serials. He finished the last sentence then stared out into the great darkness of the Normandy church. What happened next? He was so entranced that he only heard Marie-Thérèse arriving when she was almost through the trapdoor.

She laughed outright when she saw him, knees up to his chest, bread in hand and mouth, eyes glowing at the story. 'Ah,' she said. 'They found you some English reading.'

'I'll say,' he grinned. He glanced at the date on the comic paper he was holding. 'I'm catching up on years of neglect.'

Indulgently she moved towards him, and absently taking some bread and cheese from the box, she leaned over and read across his shoulder. Her tension had gone.

'Red Fury,' she recited. 'It is about Communists?'

'It's about a Red Indian,' sighed Ormerod. 'A boxing Red Indian. Kids don't go a lot on Communism.' He was aware of her chin on his shoulder. There was a faint dry smell about her, like old lavender. 'The trouble is,' he said, 'some of the stories are serials, see. You have to break off just when it's really getting exciting.' He glanced at the date on the comic in his hand. 'I mean, you don't suppose the people who gave you these might have the *Hotspur* for May 14, 1938, do you?'

She laughed pleasurably and suddenly leaned over and kissed him on the forehead. Then, after a pause, on the lips. He sat retaining his hold on the edge of his comic.

She withdrew her face a few inches. 'In the whole world,' she said with slight mockery, 'there is war and hate, and here you are, Dodo, reading schoolboy adventures.'

He shrugged. 'There was nothing else except *Bunty Bunnikins and the Naughty Bloody Gnomes*,' he told her seriously. 'Or *Organic Chemistry*.'

She sighed deeply and sat down, resting her flank against his body and her head against his shoulder. 'I am so *fatiguée*,' she said. 'We have been doing so much. Everything is organized. Now all that is left is for it to go right or wrong.' She turned and looked into his steady face. 'I need you to lean on, Dodo,' she said. 'Sometimes it is all too difficult and too much for me.' She closed her eyes. Her face was very pale in the candlelight. In an almost fatherly fashion he awkwardly put his arms about her. They easily encompassed her. She drew close to him and kissed him again. 'I am not too tired for you,' she said, opening her eyes to him.

Pushing aside *Hotspur*, *Bunty Bunnikins* and *Organic Chemistry*, Ormerod stood up, lifted her and carried her with great care to the mattresses lying on the organ loft floor. Their shadows in the candlelight were cast hugely upon the walls ascending into the cave of darkness. When they had got there and he had laid her down, he stood, in his unskilful way, seeming not to know what to do next. She looked up and noted his expression. She smiled, understanding his clumsiness, and quietly, as if she were alone, began to take her clothes off. He found himself gazing down at her naked shoulders in the opaque light, the graceful arms, the slim neck, the calm breasts. She pulled one of the blankets around her like a habit. He took his upper clothes off also, watching her all the time except when his jersey, his shirt or his vest was covering his eyes. In his preoccupation he omitted to properly unbutton the shirt and it became fixed over his head. She laughed with hardly a sound and, standing up, put her fingers beneath the material and released it from the inside.

'Thanks,' he said. 'My mother was always having to do that.'

She considered his whole body, touched his arms and the middle of his chest and then his throat. When she leaned against him her short hair was just below his chin. 'It is so cold in here,' she said. 'Keep me from being cold.'

He stood with his arms warming her, letting her do the next thing. She did, unbuckling his belt and deftly undoing his front buttons. The slim flats of her hands went down the hair of his loins and the thick tops of his legs. He leaned to her and let his hands caress her back, rubbing her infinitesimally, gently scratching her backbone, letting his fingers run along the tight skin cleft between her buttocks. She became at once limp and drowsy and encouraged him to the floor. He bent with her and almost fell on top of her. Regaining his balance he lowered her to the rough mattress. Lying there, fragile with his large body arched on hands and knees above her, she looked up and, reaching out for his neck, pulled him carefully down on top of her. He pulled the second blanket over them.

'You are a very considerate lover, Dodo,' she said eventually, when they were quiet afterwards.

'It's my nature,' he smiled at her in the half-light. There were dark circles round the notable eyes.

'I think it is,' she said. 'You will never achieve anything.' She kissed him goodnight. 'We must sleep. Pull the blankets across us. Tomorrow there are things of importance for us to do.'

In the early summer of 1940 the Normandy spa of Bagnoles de l'Orne was declared an Open Town, a Red Cross centre for the wounded of all armies from the fighting in Northern France, and, since all sides acknowledged this, it remained untouched by either troops or bombers. French, German and British wounded were taken there from the last dying battles of France and were treated by Germans and French doctors.

The town had long been a delectable situation, in the embrace of a large forest, with a lake at its centre and the famed thermal springs along the road going towards the twin resort of Tesse la Madeleine. Before the war it was a place of invalid carriages, some of then steam-propelled, hotels of the upmost gentility, a demure racecourse, a casino, and widespread parks and lawns where those who had come to take the cure could sit or walk as well as they were able.

The thermal bathhouse was closed in 1940, one of the more unusual casualties of the war, and as the armies fought, advanced, retreated, won and lost, so the wounded and the maimed were brought into Bagnoles. For them the healing spa waters would have been to say the least, inadequate. But all the hotels were requisitioned and turned into hospitals or quarters for medical staff. The six storey Grand Hotel in the Avenue Phillipe du Rozier, facing the central lake, became a hospital for officers, all belligerents agreeing that commissioned wounded men were distinct from non-commissioned wounded.

At Tesse la Madeleine an ambitious mock-Renaissance château, towered and turreted and set amid some of the most imposing trees in Europe, became the headquarters of the German medical staff. The château, built on a shoulder of rising ground, was approached by two wide, circling roads, with lawns descending through the strong trees and flowering shrubs.

It was at this place, on the first Thursday of October 1940, that General Wolfgang Groemann, the military commander of the district and the man who had bought the bells at Villedieu, arrived at ten o'clock in the morning at the start of a visit to the medical establishment, where he was to meet French and German doctors and talk to the wounded of all nationalities in the hospitals.

Three hours before the general's car arrived at Tesse, before it was light, Ormerod was woken in the organ loft of the church by a touch on his cheek. He sat up to see Marie-Thérèse crouching a yard away clicking pieces of the sub-machine gun together. 'It is time, Dodo,' she whispered through the chill, leaden light. 'We must be on our way.'

'You haven't been doing that jigsaw puzzle all night have you?' he yawned, pulling a face at the gun. She permitted herself a smile but she did not look at him. Eventually the trapdoor opened and the Frenchman who always delivered the food came in. He had coffee and rolls. 'Room service,' said Ormerod.

They drank the coffee silently and Ormerod put one of the rough rolls in his pocket, thinking he might need it later. They descended the wooden stairs into the vestry of the church. Even as they went down Ormerod saw the white, bare head of Jean Le Blanc almost illuminated in the half dawn. The ponderous eyes came up to meet him. In them he saw disdain and trouble. 'Morning,' said Ormerod politely.

'It is important,' said the big, pallid man, ignoring the greeting, 'that you today get into the Grand Hotel, which is now, of course, a hospital. There are some wounded British in there so it is possible that you will find the man you are looking for.' He glanced up, looking for the interest in Ormerod's eyes. He saw it. 'But most important is that you get into the room – the ward you call it – on the top floor of the building, the sixth floor, and that you remain there until members of our group arrive.'

Ormerod looked at him suspiciously 'What's going to happen? Am I allowed to know?'

'Later you will know,' said Marie-Thérèse at his elbow. 'It is important that the way to the ward is kept open. That there is no one who would stop us getting in there.'

'How do I get in?'

'We have a French doctor who has agreed to help. It was difficult,' said Le Blanc, 'but we were able to get him to assist us in the end. He will meet you and he will see you get to the ward. It may be that you are disguised as a casualty.' He smiled thinly. 'You will be able to spend the day in bed. Leave your gun here with us.'

Ormerod felt the doubts filling him. He glanced at Marie-Thérèse. 'There need be no worry on your conscience,' she said, knowing the meaning of the look. 'The Boche have no conscience when they take people to their concentration camps. They have already started doing that to people in Paris. The Jews in Paris now wear a yellow star.'

Ormerod nodded. 'I'm here to do what you say anyway,' he shrugged. 'Is it possible to know what the plan is? What you are going to do?'

Jean Le Blanc shook his large head. 'You will see in time, *Monsieur l'Anglais*,' he remarked in his mocking way. 'Until

160

then you will have to imagine. *We* know what we are doing and that is the important matter, you understand.'

'All right, I understand,' said Ormerod, who did not. He stood waiting for them. There was still no light over the streets although the thin echo of a cock crow could be heard from what seemed like miles away. They were waiting for something, apparently listening.

'I heard a cock crow,' he said helpfully. 'That wasn't a signal was it?'

Marie-Thérèse looked at him impatiently. 'A cock crow is not a good signal at this time of the day,' she said. 'Many cocks crow. It would be confusing.'

Whatever the signal was, Ormerod never heard it. Perhaps they were waiting for a set time. They stood like people deep in thought or prayer. Then Jean Le Blanc raised his eyes and nodded. 'It is time now,' he said. 'There is a man outside with a bicycle for you. He will take you to the Grand Hotel where our comrade the doctor is waiting. He will know what to do.'

Not much surprised Ormerod now. He touched the side of Marie-Thérèse's hand with his thumb and said: 'Good luck.'

'Good luck, Dodo,' she answered soberly. 'For all of us.'

He went out into the stiff morning air. Just outside the door was a man who looked like a farm labourer or a road digger, his rough coat tied round his middle with string, his head covered by a beret like a black mushroom. Ormerod felt he ought to give the man a nod, which he did although it was wasted because there was no response. Instead the man pushed a bicycle towards him, a skeletal machine, the like of the one he had himself.

'Forgot my clips,' apologized Ormerod, tucking his trousers into his socks. 'Hang on, will you.'

He took the bicycle from the man and mounted it uneasily. He could feel the rust coming off on his hands. Fortunately it took his weight and he wobbled off down the grey and vacant street, the wheels bumping irritably on the cobbles. The man rode a yard ahead, his machine emitting a low rheumy squeak as he pedalled. The journey was less than a mile. They saw no movement except a dog scratching itself by the chilly lake. There were some weary, early lights showing from intermittent windows in the hospital buildings all around. Eventually the Frenchman's bicycle trembled as he slowed down and turned into a tight alley behind a building that Ormerod could see was the Grand Hotel. The neglected lettering above the curved doorway showed in the illumination of a central lamp over the yellow brickwork. The rest of the building was oblong and institutional, facing the main road and with its back looking out across the lake upon which the initial glimmer of the October day was feeling its way with exaggerated caution.

The Frenchman muttered '*Là*', the only word he ever spoke to Ormerod, as an indication that they had arrived. Ormerod found the brake on his machine reluctant to work and he had to stop it with his feet. They had arrived at a doorway, squares of anaemic yellow light showing through the panes. A man in a white coat was waiting inside and as soon as the bicycles had arrived he came hurriedly but furtively out of the door. He looked at the two men, decided which one was Ormerod and said: 'Please.' He turned and walked back into the building. Ormerod lifted a half wave in the direction of his previous escort but the man was already pedalling away.

Inside the door it was much warmer. The white-coated man gave him a smile like death itself and nodded towards a side door. Ormerod went in. It was a bare room except for three wooden chairs, a cupboard and a pyramid of grim plasma bottles. Deciding it was too early in the day to study them Ormerod turned towards the nervous doctor and said: 'Well?'

The Frenchman had a filed down face, with two little rabbit teeth jutting over the lower lip. His head was a route of ashen skin from forehead to crown. Ormerod had never seen anyone's eyes appear to tremble before but this man's did.

'I speak English a little,' he muttered. 'I am frightened very much. What I have to do I wish to do *toute suite*, you see?'

'Right,' said Ormerod, feeling sympathy for the frightened man. 'Let's get on with it. What do I have to do?'

The doctor rummaged in the cupboard in the corner and brought out a drab dressing gown and a pair of creased flannel pyjamas. 'They are unclean,' he said apologetically. 'A little blood. But it is not possible to get clean things. They count each one. And it is better that you should be a patient who has been here for some time.'

Ormerod looked disgustedly at the garments. 'What happened to the last bloke?' he said.

'Gone away,' muttered the doctor, holding out the pyjamas impatiently.

Ormerod caught the look in those shaking eyes. 'Dead, eh?' he said.

'He was bad,' shrugged the doctor. 'Please hurry.'

'Looks like he could have died of septic poisoning wearing these,' muttered Ormerod, looking at the dirty garments. The pyjamas made him angry. He took them from the thin anxious fingers, and began to take off his clothes. 'Turn your back please,' he said ill-humouredly to the doctor. The doctor almost spat at him in his hurry. Ormerod rolled his clothes up under his arm. He wanted to have them near when he needed them. The pyjamas stank of disinfectant. He could hardly bear the touch of them on his skin. He took the robe, only marginally less repellent, and put it on. By the time he had done this the Frenchman was already urging him from the door.

'All right, I'm coming,' grumbled the Englishman under his breath. He followed the man down a yellow-brick corridor, then into a noisy lift. To his horror there was a dead man lying on a stretcher in the lift, his face taut with the nastiness of his going. The doctor took no more notice than he would have taken of a bag of laundry. Ormerod grimaced and wondered which army the man had died for. He had a sudden, outlandish feeling that the cadaver might be Smales. That would be poetic. But not even death could diminish the muscles of Smales that much. He decided it was not. They went to the top of the building and the Frenchman opened the gates with increasing nervousness. 'Please,' he kept whispering. 'Please, s'il vous plaît.'

They reached what was obviously the door to a ward and the doctor put a cautious hand out to slow him down. He had to look like a casualty. The man's hand shook so violently on the muscle of his arm that Ormerod had to put his other hand on it to steady it. He thought a brief moment of gratefulness appeared in the Frenchman's eyes.

163

Now they were at the paned door of the ward. Looking through Ormerod saw the double line of beds, the wan daylight coming through the big windows and lighting the room as it might light a graveyard. The Frenchman pushed at the doors and attempted to guide Ormerod in. There was a male nurse at one end of the ward in a yolk of yellow light. He saw them coming and obviously expected them although whether he was part of the conspiracy or not Ormerod never discovered. He came down between the beds and nodded towards a vacant iron bedstead where the sheets were already drawn back. Ormerod was relieved to see that they were apparently clean for they were straight and sharp on the mattress.

The doctor pushed him towards the bed and he obligingly climbed in. He pushed his clothes in the locker at the side. The two Frenchmen exchanged glances, which may have been official or not, and the doctor, with the briefest last look at Ormerod, went back through the double doors. The orderly pulled the bedclothes up around Ormerod's neck. 'Now you sleep,' he said, indicating it was an order. 'For some time.'

The warmth of the bed pressed itself around his weary body. He looked out, over the horizon of the sheets and along the ranks of the still, snoring figures of the wounded soldiers. His body was filled with a swamp of apprehension.

eight

When Ormerod awoke four hours later it was to a sense of some excitement and expectancy in the ward. Orderlies were hurrying about sweeping and polishing and one was arranging a large bowl of rich autumn flowers on the central table. He watched all this activity over the snowline of his sheets, carefully turning his gaze to take in all the rows of heads in the line of beds opposite. Over there they looked like an opposing army deep in the trenches. He turned his look to the left and saw a grey-faced young man returning his glance.

'There's a Jerry general coming,' said his neighbour. The voice was middle-class English. The young man had only one eye. 'They didn't think he'd come up here to see the enemy, but he wants to. So they're having to rush about to tidy up the place. Quite a joke really, I suppose.'

He paused and surveyed the room with his eye. 'You must have turned up very early this morning,' he said, returning to Ormerod. 'Didn't see them bring you in.'

'Very early,' said Ormerod cautiously. 'Still dark.'

'My name's Bailey,' said the young man. 'Charles. Lost my eye. See.'

'Yes,' nodded Ormerod. 'Nasty.' He thought he had better give a fictitious name, although Ormerod would still be meaningless. 'Steel,' he said. 'George Steel. Feet. Shot feet.'

'Where did you get that lot?'

'Abbéville,' said Ormerod, trying to think where the last battles had been. 'Around there,' he added cautiously.

'I was in the St Valéry fuck-up,' said Bailey bitterly. 'Tanks – except if you remember, we didn't have any.'

'I remember,' lied Ormerod. 'Royal Artillery, me. We didn't have any guns.'

'They always seem to leave you short of essentials. What's your rank by the way?'

'Lieutenant,' said Ormerod, trying to sound like one. He had not expected to be questioned by a fellow countryman. 'Can't see me getting promotion now.'

'Same as me.' Bailey turned his head to take in the whole ward. 'Damned difficult getting used to seeing with one eye,' he said. 'The bloody nose keeps getting in the way. I never realized before now how big my nose is. Where have you been up to now? Which hospital?'

'Caen,' answered Ormerod. He realized his feet should have been bandaged, but it was too late now. He turned around carefully to look at the bed on the other side. The occupant was asleep, a head swathed in dressings, like a pudding, lying on the pillow. Turning back to Bailey he said: 'Brought me down here because they thought the air would be better for my feet.'

He grinned and the young man laughed. 'It's not bad

really,' he said. 'In fact the Jerry doctors and what-have-you are better than the French. I think the French have got it in for us a bit. They've got the idea that we ran away.'

'I know,' said Ormerod. 'They keep telling me.'

Bailey turned his one eye around. 'Do you think we did? Run away?'

Ormerod was surprised at the need for reassurance. He sniffed. 'Well ... no. We evacuated. That's different altogether.'

This appeared to give Bailey further cause for thought. Eventually he returned to Ormerod. 'I haven't told my mother I've only got one eye yet,' he said pathetically. 'Or my girl, my fiancée. I'm only twenty you know. I look older don't I? When you halve your eyes I think you double your age.'

He looked almost comically miserable. Ormerod felt quickly sad for him. 'Your mother won't mind. Mothers don't. And if your girl's anything of a girl, she won't either. She ought to be proud of you.'

The younger man grinned uncertainly. 'You think so? You think she'll still marry me? I'm like bloody Cyclops.'

'Of course. I shouldn't worry about it, son.'

Bailey hesitated. 'You're very decent,' he said. 'Very good. Can I ask you a favour?'

'You can ask.'

'I'm finding it difficult to see properly to write. It's getting used to it. You don't realize how awkward it is at first. I keep trying to push this damn great nose thing out of the way.'

'You should have your nose off as well,' joked Ormerod, trying to cheer him.

'Oh God,' smiled Bailey. 'That *would* have done it. No nose as well. That would have been goodbye to my girl. You couldn't expect her to put up with that, even if she puts up with being one eye short. No ... what I wanted to ask was – could you write a letter for me to her? Just telling her. I haven't had the guts to ask anybody up to now. It would only mean a short note, an explanation really. I think I ought to come clean about it. If I don't tell her and spend God-knows-how-long in a Jerry prison camp and then go home and she's

166

been waiting and she sees I'm missing an eye, well ... it could be a big disappointment.'

Ormerod, engulfed with pity, stared at him. He reached across the space between them and patted the young man's hand. 'I'll do that for you,' he said. 'I'll do it right now. Have you got a pen and some paper?'

Bailey looked at him eagerly. 'That's very decent of you,' he said.

At that moment an orderly appeared in the ward and threw a clean pair of pyjamas on Omerod's bed. 'Oh good,' he said. 'I could do with these.'

'You can thank the Jerry general for that,' said Bailey.

Only then did it hit Ormerod. *That's what was happening!* That's why Jean Le Blanc was in Bagnoles, that's why Marie-Thérèse was there. That's why he had been planted in the hospital. His face grew cold. Jesus Christ, they were going to kill the German general right here.

Almost mesmerized by the realization, he put his hands slowly to his pyjamas. He took off the dirty jacket, the smell of it hitting him as he pulled it over his head. Bailey noticed the blood on the front.

'Thought it was your feet,' he said. 'You've got blood down the front of that.'

'Cut myself shaving,' said Ormerod in what he hoped sounded like a jovial voice. His inside was ringing. God Almighty, what were they going to do? They couldn't assassinate a man, not even a German general, in a *hospital*. With a loaded heart he decided they could.

Dumbly he put the pyjamas on, keeping his supposedly wounded feet out of sight. Bailey said: 'There's all British and French officers in here. I hope this Jerry hasn't come to gloat.' He handed a pen and a writing pad across to Ormerod. 'Here it is then,' he said. 'Are you sure you don't mind?'

General Wolfgang Groemann left the front entrance of the mock château at Tesse la Madeleine at eleven o'clock that morning, after having coffee with the senior medical staff billetted there. It was a bright day, with the autumn sharpness gone from the air by that hour, and the lawns and trees around the building bathed with mild but comforting sunshine. There were red squirrels on the lawns and a group of German nurses were sitting by the trees, in the sun, waiting to see him as he went by. He spotted them and walked over to exchange some words with them before returning to his staff car. His aide, Major Hans Einder, was now impatient with the delay. He was happy when the timetable was strict and was just as strictly observed.

The general got into the car. Einder tapped the window and the driver turned the large grey vehicle down the easy curving paths towards the Rue de Jolie, which joins the twin resorts of Bagnoles and Tesse. 'It has been arranged that you visit soldiers of all nationalities, as you wished,' said Einder primly. He himself did not approve, although he admitted there was a certain one-upmanship in a German general inspecting vanquished enemies. 'The French and the British are in one unit that was a hotel, by the racecourse, and there are some officers of those nationalities in a ward at the Grand Hotel. You wish to visit both of these places?'

Groemann nodded as if nothing else had ever occurred to him. 'We are all in the war together, Einder,' he said, philosophically. 'We are all to some extent casualties. Yes, I will do that.'

'There is another matter,' said Einder. 'A suggestion from the News and Propaganda Department . . .'

'I am not standing on my head for Dr Goebbels,' said the general firmly.

Einder looked serious. He was occasionally worried about the general's future. 'It is not standing on your head, sir,' he said pedantically. 'The suggestion is that you should go out in a small rowing boat with two German wounded. If you just sit there for a few minutes, just a short distance from the shore, then the news photographers can get some pictures. A field officer in a boat with two wounded men would be a nice touch, don't you think?'

Groemann brightened. 'A good idea, Einder,' he nodded. 'I haven't been in a little boat for years. But I want to *go* for a row on the lake, not just pose for photographers.'

'It will not be necessary for you to row, sir,' said Einder hurriedly.

'Why not? It won't be very good publicity if the wounded men do the rowing, will it?' insisted Groemann. 'Not with the general sitting in the boat.'

Einder sighed. 'Yes sir,' he replied.

The car turned along the curve in the road beneath an outcrop of boulders called the Rock of the Dog, because a dog was said to have jumped from it years before and been saved by a miracle. On the top of the rock a Frenchman, working in the gardens of one of the former hotels, now a medical hostel, watched the car turn towards the centre of Bagnoles de l'Orne. He raised his arm in a clear signal. The car went over a little bridge and the central lake of the spa smiled invitingly in the fine morning sun.

At ten minutes before noon General Groemann entered the ward for British and French officers at the former Grand Hotel. So far his tour had been as successful as it had been informal. In Bagnoles the Occupation Forces expected no trouble from any direction. He had, of course, a military escort, but even that was not to the taste of the mild man of Minden. Frequently he made unexpected detours or instructed Einder to keep his escort at a distance.

Ormerod, propped nervously up in the bed half way down the ward, turned his head with all the other patients as the German general entered the room with his entourage. 'Good morning everyone,' said Groemann at the door. His English was firm. Various 'Good mornings' were said, or in most cases tentatively muttered, from different parts of the ward. Groemann smiled at the hesitations. Ormerod thought he looked like a reasonable man. He wondered what exactly Jean Le Blanc had planned for him.

Groemann was on the short side and slightly rounded with it. He came down the lines of beds and talked to the wounded men, not standing over them but sitting on the edges of the beds as he did so. Ormerod heard laughter coming from the far end of the ward. He waited unhappily.

The visiting party came up the other side of the room and

Ormerod and Bailey watched them approach. 'Doesn't seem a bad old stick, does he?' commented Bailey. 'Not like you would think.' He had his letter, his confession of having lost an eye, now sealed on his bedside locker.

Ormerod decided he did not like the aspect of the young, leaner officer at Groemann's side. The man's cane moved irritatingly against his uniformed leg and he watched the patients with something like quiet mocking. A French and a German doctor followed the party but only came forward if some technical explanation was needed. In the background Ormerod suddenly saw the furtive doctor who had brought him into the ward in the dark morning. The man looked whiter than his coat. His eyes seemer to stand out from his skin.

The visiting general moved unhurriedly along the iron bed-rails. The man with the bandaged head next to Ormerod had not awakened all the morning and now slept deeply. Groemann laughed quietly and put his finger to his lips as he crept by the bed on mock tip-toe. He arrived at the bottom of Ormerod's bed. The Englishman's heart seemed to slow and he could feel his hands sweating.

'Good morning to you,' said the German.

'Good morning sir,' said Ormerod. His mouth seemed to be on a hinge like that of a ventriloquist's doll.

'Too good to be in bed in a hospital,' said Groemann genially. 'I expect you would rather be in England playing cricket.'

'Well, sir,' hesitated Ormerod. 'I'm not one for cricket, and it's the wrong season. But I wouldn't mind being home.'

'Nor would I,' sighed the German reflectively. 'Perhaps one day we can all go home. Where do you live in England?'

'London. Putney.'

'I know, I know,' smiled Groemann. 'It is on the River Thames. Putney Bridge is it not?'

'That's right, sir,' nodded Ormerod. Groemann sat on his bed.

'I was in London,' said the German officer. 'At the embassy in 1936 and 1937. I had a very good time there. And my wife also. My God, I like London better than Berlin!' He laughed at his joke. Ormerod thought Einder grimaced. 'What is your wound?' asked Groemann.

'Feet,' said Ormerod, suddenly terrified he would be asked to display them. He saw the frightened French doctor move tentatively forward in case a quick explanation was necessary. Groemann merely nodded. 'Not a good place for wounds,' he said. 'Not the feet. You cannot escape. In the First World War men on both sides used to shoot themselves through the feet so that they could miss the fighting and be taken home.'

'I wish I'd thought of that,' said Ormerod.

The German grinned. 'I hope you are better soon,' he said. He stood up and moved on. He shook his head sadly when he saw Bailey's youth and his wound. Ormerod watched him sorrowfully. He had a very strong suspicion that this would be General Wolfgang Groemann's last day on earth.

Lunch was served in the ward and Ormerod began to wonder when anything was going to happen. Without any hope he asked Bailey if he had ever heard of a man called Smales who had been at Bagnoles. Bailey shook his head. Ormerod wondered how far he could trust Marie-Thérèse's word that Smales would be located for him. Not far, he had to fancy. Not when she had her own business occupying her mind. And today, after whatever happened, he knew they would have to be on the run and in hiding again. At two o'clock precisely the frightened French doctor came through the ward and gave Ormerod a small, petrified glance. Something was going to occur. Almost at once the sleeping man in the next bed sat up. Turning to Ormerod as if he had known him for years he said in French-English: 'Get your clothes on you.'

Ormerod stared at him. The man looked amazingly like a baby in the swathes of dressing. He had a young, puffy face and blue eyes. Ormerod glanced towards Bailey, already feeling somehow ashamed at his cheating. Fortunately, Bailey was dozing. Like a man who knows he is descending into the chaos of a nightmare but can do nothing to stop himself, Ormerod rose from the bed and removed his clothes from the bedside locker. Hardly taking his gaze from the bandaged man in the next bed he began to dress. An afternoon somnolence had settled on the ward. Sunshine through the big windows lay unrolled on the floor and across the beds. The bandaged man said: 'I am Henri. Do as I tell you.' He was putting his own clothes on now, a hospital blue jacket and trousers and a grubby white shirt. For some obscure reason Ormerod wondered if he would take his bandages off. He did, quickly releasing them and unwinding them like some resurrected Egyptian mummy.

'Lock the door at the end of the ward,' ordered Henri. 'We have arranged as far as possible that nobody will interrupt, but we don't know. You have no gun?'

'No, I thought it would look silly in here.'

Henri did not appreciate the cynicism. 'They will bring guns for us,' he said. He turned and looked out of the window to where the green lawns of Bagnoles stretched down to the shore of a calm water that reflected the cruising October clouds. 'This,' he said with satisfaction, 'is the perfect sniper's window.'

'Oh, Christ,' said Ormerod quickly, realizing fully what they were going to do. God, he would have given half his expected life to be out of that place then. But he was trapped with it. He stared at Henri with a mild misery. 'I said lock the door,' repeated the Frenchman.

'We're not going to get away with this business,' Ormerod whispered desperately, as if he had to make some sort of protest.

'Do not be afraid, my friend,' smiled Henri. 'There is nothing to stop us.'

The Frenchman began pulling his shirt over his head. He looked through the aperture of the neck at Ormerod and stared at him as if surprised he was still there. 'Monsieur,' he said, hard and quiet, 'go to the door.'

Ormerod looked stupidly about him. Their rising and their conversation had all but gone unnoticed. He walked unsteadily to the ward door, the terrible feeling of the thing beginning to grasp him. He closed it with casual carefulness and slotted the bolt. He turned and saw Henri regarding him with suspicion. He nodded as if to say, 'I've done it,' then shuffled back between the beds. Henri was standing watching the door as if expecting someone. 'My friend,' he said, when Ormerod was near enough, 'today you are with us or you are against us. We do not need a referee. Be careful. Because either we will shoot you or the Germans will shoot you. Or perhaps both.'

A light jumped into his eyes and Ormerod saw that Jean Le Blanc had come through the door at the other end of the ward, his head wobbling like that of a carnival giant. Marie-Thérèse entered after him and then a third figure, a man unknown to Ormerod. This man carried a case in which Ormerod guessed immediately was a rifle with a telescopic sight. He was right.

The intruders had still caused little stir in the ward. Most of the patients still dozed. Now Marie-Thérèse closed the door behind her and called out: 'Will everyone please pay attention.' She said it first in English and then in French. The wounded men awoke, grumbling at the interruption. Some sat up to see what was happening, some had to remain flat. Ormerod watched Bailey wake and painfully turn his good eye onto the group. He saw the unique expression of single surprise in the eye as the young man saw he had dressed and was with the intruders.

'What's happening?' he asked Ormerod. 'What's going on?'

'We are friends,' Marie-Thérèse said loudly so all the ward could hear. 'Comrades. We have come in the name of France and England and their allies. All we ask is that you stay where you are in your beds and do not move or try to interfere. Everything will be done quickly and nobody here will suffer. It is all part of the war for which you have been wounded.'

While she spoke Jean Le Blanc had gone to the window. He looked down onto the lakeside and a satisfaction came into his face. Marie-Thérèse walked to Ormerod and handed him a pistol. He felt almost ashamed as she gave it to him and he let it drag down by his side. He could see Bailey staring at him disbelievingly with awful lonely eye. Marie-Thérèse knew he needed to be told. 'It is all right,' she whispered. 'It is the correct thing, Dodo.'

It was too late to argue anyway. Henri had also been given

a gun and had stationed himself by the door through which the group had arrived. He sat at the bottom of a bed nursing a pistol and watching the stairs outside. The man who had carried the case now undid it and brought out the rifle in two parts, plus a tripod and, lastly, after he had assembled the the other components, a telescopic sight. He briefly laid the sight on the bed that had been Ormerod's and the Englishman looked at it with slightly more apprehension than he looked at the rifle.

Bailey suddenly started to get out of bed, only slowly, but it was enough to make Jean Le Blanc turn on him and point his pistol. The young man sat down. He was ashen, his eye strangely seeming to be in the centre of his head. 'But you can't,' he whispered. 'You can't shoot anyone here. Not *here*.'

'You will see,' said Le Blanc. 'Return to your sheets.'

'Who?' Bailey said, not appearing to have heard. 'Who is it?'

'Bailey, son, get back into bed, please,' pleaded Ormerod.

A man sat up abruptly across the ward. 'I know,' he said in a strangled way. He had a dressing around his throat. 'They're after the general! The man who came in here.'

'He is a German,' snapped Marie-Thérèse. 'Stay in your bed.'

Ormerod was looking wildly about. The patients were moving and muttering.

'The general?' Bailey was aghast. 'You can't. For Christ's sake, this is a military hospital. You can't do that *here*, I tell you.'

'This hospital is covered by The Hague Convention,' said a British officer across the room. His words were slow, and said with difficulty. 'They have kept to it. So must you. I am ordering you to leave. Get out!'

Jean Le Blanc raised his pistol but Ormerod pushed him quickly and fiercely aside and hurried across to the man in the bed. 'Listen, sir,' he said, 'for fuck's sake shut up. He'll kill you. He's a right bastard, believe me.'

The man appeared not to hear or even see him. He was staring at the gun they were assembling at the window. He moved forward. Ormerod felt Le Blanc raise the pistol almost at his ear. He rushed forward, stumbled against the British officer, clumsily embracing him. The man also had a wounded leg and it gave way under him. With Ormerod still clutching him he staggered back almost comically and sat down heavily between the beds, bringing Ormerod with him. They lay on the polished floor, Ormerod on top. 'Sorry,' he gasped. 'Sorry about the leg.'

He got to his knees and looked around. Jean Le Blanc still had his pistol levelled at the British officer. Ormerod turned and raised his own gun at Le Blanc. 'Shoot him and I shoot you,' he said simply.

The domed Frenchman looked at him with incredible disgust. 'Today who I shoot is no concern for me,' he said. 'As long as I kill the Nazi. Nobody else matters.'

The interlude had enabled the British officer to get to his knees. Ormerod using one arm helped him to get back into his bed. 'Stay there,' he pleaded. 'For God's sake, stay there.'

The Englishman looked at him with a sort of dull hatred, but he did as he was instructed. From across the ward Bailey said to Ormerod: 'How did you manage to get mixed up with these bastards?'

'Our Government sent me,' said Ormerod succinctly. 'The same Government that sent you.'

'*Voilà*,' said the man who had been assembling the gun. He had taken no notice of what had happened behind him. Jean Le Blanc turned eagerly. Marie-Thérèse was still facing into the room, looking at the hostile men in pyjamas grouped around the walls. She had not looked at Ormerod at all. Henri was still watching the door. Now everything was still. An autumnal fly buzzed insidiously against the window but that was all.

With two or three flicks of his eyes Le Blanc saw that the gun was right; securely on its tripod and with the telescopic sight correctly aligned. He crouched and looked along its bare barrel. Even as he did so two German staff cars pulled up alongside the lake below. A fissure of a smile opened on his face. 'He is come,' he muttered. 'The man is here.'

Below them, six storeys below, General Wolfgang Groemann, having lunched at the officers' mess, stepped from his car onto the sunny grass. Einder was fussing again. Where was the boat? Where were the wounded soldiers? Where were the photographers?

He need not have worried. The News and Propaganda Department knew how to assemble its props and parts. As the general descended from the car a smart white rowing boat appeared, nudging its way around to the small bay where the cars had stopped. Two German soldiers, one with each of his arms in a sling, the other with a theatrical-looking bandage across his head and eye, were sitting on one of the crossboards. Another soldier pulled back the oars.

'We shall not need the crew,' asserted Groemann as the boat came to the bank. 'I shall really do the rowing. I will not have it said that I only row for photographs.'

Annoyance flushed Einder's face. Any lowering of what he felt ought to be the general's prestige he looked upon as a lowering of his own. 'Are you sure, sir?' he said anxiously.

'Oh, for God's sake Einder, don't be such a washerwoman. Of course I'm sure. I've rowed a boat before, you know.' He looked out to the level, shiny waters of the lake.

Einder shrugged and grunted something to the sergeant holding the painter of the boat. The sergeant gave an order to the man at the oars and he left the boat smartly. The photographers took some pictures of the group on the shore, and then the general by himself. He was smiling after the photographs and began to take off his tunic. Einder's eyes were raised in shock. 'Sir!' he protested. 'Surely ...'

'Yes, surely,' Groemann affirmed stiffly. 'I cannot row a boat done up like a turkey.'

'But it will not look *correct*,' protested Einder. 'Your *medals*. Your medals will not show.' He leaned closer to his superior. 'And, forgive me, my general, perhaps your lunch will.'

He knew he had scored his point. Groemann was more than conscious of his increasing stomach. No, Einder was right, it would not have been proper. He nodded his acknowledgement. 'All right, so I *am* a turkey.' He climbed into the boat, ignoring the helping hand offered by the sergeant, sat down and smiled at the wounded soldiers.

The two men facing him sat as white as their bandages. He grinned at them. 'After this you get a medal,' he joked. 'You must be very brave to volunteer for such hazards. Maybe you have to swim.'

They smiled uncertainly. Not being able to salute or click their heels or come to attention they had no notion of how to confront the general. He eased their apprehension by shouting to Einder: 'Where are those photographers then? Come on, we want to be sailing.'

Obediently a larger boat propelled by an outboard motor came throatily around the grassy head of the park. Aboard were half a dozen men with cameras and a newsreel cameraman. 'We are to be film stars,' said Groemann encouragingly to his stiffly sitting passengers. 'Always I have wanted to be a film star.'

Awkwardly he began to row away from the bank. He could not remember at first which oar guided the boat which way and Einder watched apprehensively and with a certain measure of disdain. He did not think that a man of Groemann's rank should be so obviously enjoying himself with such pursuits and in such company. If it were necessary for propaganda, then do it; but to enjoy it was undignified.

Forty feet from the bank and the general finally remembered how to steer the little craft. The oars made pleasing patterns on the polished water. The general smiled and the wounded soldiers smiled diffidently back. At that moment the boat cleared a hanging willow which had been obscuring it to the window of the hospital ward. 'Très bien,' whispered Jean Lo Blanc who was crouched behind the sniper's rifle. The words were to himself. 'Très bien, très bien.'

If he had intended to squeeze the trigger then, he had to change his mind, because the little craft on the lake swung erratically as the general rowed and Le Blanc was abruptly afforded only a view of the soldiers' backs as they sat in the passenger seat. Then the target cleared again, only to be once again obscured by the cutting across of the photographers' boat. He cursed through his teeth.

The photographers, with their traditional scant regard for authority, were shouting across the water to the general to manoeuvre the rowing boat to one side so that they could get their first shots. He did so good-humouredly. This brought the larger boat directly in front of Le Blanc's target. From the elevation he might have fired over the first boat and the photographers' heads with a good percentage chance of hitting his man. But he wanted it to be without error. He breathed shallowly and waited. By now Ormerod was watching the scene with horror and fascination. The window sash had been lifted over the barrel of the rifle and the afternoon breeze came in sweetly. Marie-Thérèse still faced the patients with her gun in her small hand, but now the British and French men just sat dumbfounded around the ward waiting for the shooting to happen. The fly buzzed impatiently against the imprisoning window. Ormerod moved to squash it against the glass. Marie-Thérèse snapped: 'Be still.'

It was like a slow, locked dream. From the door of the ward Henri emitted a click of the tongue. Someone was coming up the stairs. He raised the nub of his pistol. In through the doors came a white-coated doctor, a Frenchman. His eyes glazed as they came down on the hole of Henri's pistol. Speaking quietly Henri told him to sit down on the nearest bed. He sat down, his trembling hands trying to find the iron bedfoot to steady himself.

At that moment it became right. On the lake the photographers swung their boat for a picture at a different angle. It brought Groemann facing the rifle, with his two passengers slightly to one side and clear of the field of fire. Jean Le Blanc recognized a right moment when he saw it. His sight was on the centre of the general's chest, just to the side of his double bank of medals. He checked his breath. He pressed the first pressure of the trigger and then, almost at once, the second. The single sharp explosion burst around the lake and its buildings, sending birds screaming from the trees. General Wolfgang Groemann, a sudden blood-red flower spraying outwards on his tunic, remained upright for several seconds, then his body seemed to leap on some spring and fall backwards into the bottom of the little boat he had been rowing. 'Take a photograph of that,' muttered Le Blanc. The boat trembled and crazily turned. It was five seconds before the shouts went up. The wounded soldiers, like two comedians, tried to stand up and tipped the boat first one way then the other. The one with the bandaged arms fell over the side and was drowned, although nobody noticed at the time.

'Depart,' said Jean Le Blanc in the ward. They knew what to do. There was no time to dismantle the rifle. It remained where it was like a piece of modern sculpture, cold and impersonal. The resistance group began to back away towards the door. Ormerod looked for the last time at young Bailey. The young officer was sitting speechless on the side of the bed, tears running surrealistically from his one eye. Ormerod felt an overwhelming need to apologize to him.

'Bastards!' called the other officer across the ward. 'Bastards!'

The French doctor who had intruded suddenly stood up and ran screaming towards Le Blanc, who shot him without compunction. His pistol exploded and the man's white coat was ripped apart by the shot. He fell down, bloody and grotesquely spread out in the middle of the ward. They went out. Standing in the open door of a lift on the landing was the French doctor who had first taken Ormerod into the ward. He seemed mesmerized with fear. Le Blanc pushed him aside as they got into the lift. Before the doors closed Henri fired two shots towards the ward door to discourage pursuit.

The grating closed and they descended six floors. Only the heavy sound of their breathing filled the cage. To Ormerod it seemed as though they went down in slow motion.

Le Blanc and Henri ran out into the sunshine, ready to shoot. But the road at the side of the building was vacant. An ambulance stood against the kerb, its engine vibrating. The French doctor ran like a rabbit to climb into the cab and the rest of the group hurried into the back and closed the doors.

The vehicle started with a jolt that all but toppled them from their feet. Ormerod felt sick. Marie-Thérèse put her hand on his wrist and he felt her vibrating. He did not look at her.

The ambulance took the upward sweep of the road which sent it over the modest hill below which were parked the staff cars which had brought the general and the others to the lakeside. Everyone was at the water's edge, the photographers' boat frantically towing the rowing boat towards the shore. In the general's boat the wounded soldier was bending over the dead Groemann, weeping from fright and shock. His comrade's body had gone below the smooth surface. Men were running from buildings all around. As the ambulance turned up the incline and away from the scene. Einder was running up the slope shouting: 'Ambulance! Ambulance!'

Four miles out of Bagnoles de l'Orne, going east on a minor road below trees, towards Sées and the Forest of Ecouves, the ambulance was stopped by the first of the road blocks which the Germans were frantically throwing across all roads leading from the spa town. As the route bordered the small lake, the Etang de Vie, a three-man Wehrmacht motorcycle team appeared by the side of the road. They had only just arrived and Jean Le Blanc, looking through the small window into the driver's cabin of the ambulance, cursed as he saw them ahead. Another two minutes and they would have been there first. Now it all depended whether the Germans knew they had escaped in an ambulance. He watched two of the three Germans come forward towards the vehicle and he knew by their attitude that they were not aware that an ambulance had been used in the escape. Had they known, he had no doubt they would have fired on it first. Now they walked forward unsuspectingly and spoke to the driver. The third man remained by the motorcycle and sidecar in the centre of the quiet road. They had not had time to erect any barrier. The lemon sun was filtering through the bordering branches and birds sang undisturbed in the cool air.

'I am going to Sées to pick up a patient,' said the driver to the first soldier. 'What is the trouble?'

'Nobody tells us anything,' grumbled the soldier. 'We have to check all vehicles, that's all. But it's something big by the sound of it. Who's in the back?'

'Just the orderly.'

The soldier was about to turn away and wave the ambulance through when the man who had remained with the motorcycle shouted: 'Go and check the back.' He must have been in charge because the two soldiers shrugged and turned back towards the vehicle. The face of the driver tightened.

'They are coming to look,' Jean Le Blanc whispered to the others. He nodded to Henri and the other man who had taken the rifle to Bagnoles. They moved quietly so that they were standing inside the rear doors, their guns pointing directly towards the back. Jean Le Blanc moved in just behind them, a sub-machine gun carried like a baby across his stomach. Ormerod and Marie-Thérèse crouched in the furthest interior of the vehicle. The Germans began to undo the door.

It rattled and creaked and then both doors swung open wide. Ormerod had never seen such expressions appear on the faces of any men. One was in the middle of a sentence when he looked up and saw the guns. Henri and the other Frenchman fired at once and both soldiers fell down heavily out of sight. Immediately Jean Le Blanc, with the agility of a gorilla, jumped to the ground and, swinging around the flank of the ambulance, fired one burst from the sub-machine gun at the third German by the motorcycle sidecar. The man had not had time to react to the killing of his comrades before he was flung over by the bullets. The petrol tank of the motor cycle caught fire and blew up with a hot, small explosion. Nodding to the ambulance driver Le Blanc ran around to the back of the vehicle and treading on one of the dead Germans as if the body were a step, he climbed back in and closed the door. The vehicle was already moving forward.

'After today,' muttered Ormerod almost to himself, 'the Red Cross is not going to seem quite the same.'

The Forest of Ecouves covers sixty square miles of hills in the triangle between Bagnoles de l'Orne, Alençon and the cathedral town of Sées, in Lower Normandy. It is the highest land in north-western France and its pinewoods, its deep cleft valleys of oak and beech, are thick and remote, the home of roebuck and deer. The main road from Sées to Alençon cuts along the eastern flank of the forest and there is a secondary route that goes through the area, but the rest is traversed by primitive tracks, many only known to woodmen and hunters. It is a good place to hide.

181

The fugitives entered the forest after leaving the ambulance in a barn near the village of Rouperroux on the western boundary of the trees. It would take a thorough search to discover it. The furtive French doctor who had driven the vehicle now went on some pre-arranged way which eventually led him into the hands of the Gestapo and a merciful death. The remainder of the party went into the trees in the late afternoon as the first rain since the middle days of September came across the hills with the evening clouds. It thickened as they went deeper down into the rifts and the coniferous slopes of the hills, until even the trees afforded only a little shelter from its force.

Henri, who came from that region, led the group, with Le Blanc immediately behind him, a woollen hat protecting his skinned head from the cold downpour. Marie-Thérèse came next, her face wet and calm, and then the third Frenchman, who they called Poëles, because he had been a tinsmith at Villedieu. Instant streams filled the paths and the slopes became thick with mud. Twice Marie-Thérèse slipped and Ormerod had to hold her. She did not acknowledge his help, and when he himself missed his footing and slithered down a slimy bank into a mass of dead, wet leaves, they left him to recover himself and catch up with them along the dark, narrow track. Nobody spoke while they walked for two hours.

Eventully a light showed in the rainy blackness ahead, a signal light blinking deliberately. The party paused and Le Blanc signalled back with a pocket torch. 'Home sweet home?' muttered Ormerod hopefully.

They had reached a considerable chasm right at the heart of the forest. It was so dark that it was not possible to estimate how far it descended. Ormerod could only hear the pounding of a newly replenished river down there among the rocks and boulders. The path narrowed even more and seemed to Ormerod to be skirting the drop perilously. With great caution he followed the slight shadow of Marie-Thérèse just in front of him. There were more flashes of a torch and eventually they climbed a last difficult incline to a hard, dark ledge and Ormerod saw that there were some caves ahead. A man with a torch was standing at the mouth of the largest cave. He greeted them quietly and said to Le Blanc. 'I hear you have done well. Come inside.'

Within the cave it was warm and damp. Ormerod slumped down with the others on the uneven floor, his cold, wet clothes sticking to him all over his body. Then a second figure came from further within and Ormerod, with no great interest, saw it was a woman. She called to them softly and they followed her. It became warmer and wider as they went deeper. A glow appeared and Ormerod was grateful to see a small fire burning, its smoke being drawn up through a hole in the ceiling. There was a large container of coffee and roughly cut sections of deer were grilling on an iron spit. Ormerod's nose opened to the smell. There was a pile of old blankets in one corner and they each took one. They crouched, still barely speaking, around the fire.

Ormerod looked across at Marie-Thérèse. The strain of the murderous day had drained her face and she looked small and surprisingly wizened. Her glance came up to him. 'Well?' she said.

'I was thinking it was a pity I never had the chance to see if my friend Smales was around,' grumbled Ormerod. 'You're getting greedy.'

She looked at him sullenly. 'We did what was needed,' she said. Then she added: 'We made the inquiries about Smales, as I promised. I have known for several days about him, but I did not want the matter to get in the way of the operation at Bagnoles.'

Ormerod looked at her steadily. 'And where is he then?'

'I was informed that Monsieur Smales escaped from the hospital two months ago. He is now in Paris. He is a member of the resistance, Dodo.'

'Fuck my luck,' muttered Ormerod.

They remained in the cave for six days. German patrols were seen in the forest moving along the old hunting rides and occasionally opening fire on animals they thought might be the men they sought. But they never came to the vicinity of the cave.

'We are very fortunate here,' said Marie-Thérèse to Ormerod on the third day. They sat looking up at the bat-hung ceiling of their concealment. 'The first Frenchmen, the cave dwellers, made this place for us. They even put a little hole in the roof for the smoke to get out.'

He sniffed. He had a heavy cold from the long trek through the rain. 'It's hardly the Savoy, I suppose,' he said. 'But it's better than nothing. What are we going to do next, blow up the Eiffel Tower?'

'I do not know,' she said seriously. 'It is Jean Le Blanc who is in command now. In this part of Normandy the resistance will be very good. It is better organized.'

'It would take a lot of Germans to track them down here,' said Ormerod, looking out of the mouth of the cave to the tree tops of the forest.

'There are many places such as this,' she said. 'And as we get nearer to Paris, so we will find the resistance movement is stronger. The news is travelling through our network. Already the workers at Dreux have had meetings to decide their actions. And at the Citroën plant there has been sabotage. At Chartres two Germans were shot and thrown into the river. At Argentan, only to the north of here, the house of a collaborator had been burned to the ground. France is waking.' She went into the inner cave and returned quickly with a photograph. She handed it to Ormerod. 'This was brought by one of our people,' she said. 'The late General Groemann – taken by one of his own Nazi photographers by the lake just a few minutes before he died. See how he smiles. Our network is getting very good you see. We can obtain such things. You can keep that copy as a souvenir.'

'Thanks. I'll try not to wave it in front of the Gestapo.' He regarded the image of the convivial, plump man in the photograph. 'Poor old Wolfgang,' he said.

'He was a Nazi,' Marie-Thérèse pointed out.

'All right. He kept bad company. He paid for it.'

'As many others will,' she said. She threw a stone down into the chasm.

'How long before we will be in Paris, then?' he said. 'I'd like to just set eyes on Mr Smales. Just once.'

She smiled wryly. 'If Mr Smales is valuable to our movement then it might be difficult for us to permit you to take him away.'

'That had occurred to me,' he said. He looked at her steadily. 'In which case I might have to smuggle him away.'

'As the situation is at the moment,' she continued, ignoring the comment, 'we will, I think, need him more than you. But there may come a time when we will be glad to hand him to you.'

'There's nothing going to stop me getting to him now,' said Ormerod doggedly. 'So you can get that straight.'

'If anything is to be straight, Dodo,' she replied quietly, 'it might be *you*. If you are less valuable than Smales then maybe you will be the one to be eliminated. For myself, you understand, I would not do it.'

He saw she was looking at him seriously. 'Thanks very much,' he said.

She leaned closer. 'But listen, please listen. In a few days I will leave you for some time, only a short time, but you must be careful. Be careful of Jean Le Blanc. I have been protecting you, Dodo, telling him that you have an essential role to play in Paris, where he has no command, that you cannot be expended. But when I am away you must watch him carefully. He can be very violent and very selfish.'

'Oh, he's *selfish* as well is he?' said Ormerod, wondering at the understatement. 'And what do you mean about me being "expended". I don't altogether like the sound of that.'

She watched his face. Then she moved her face forward so that their cheeks touched briefly. 'Ever since Bagnoles,' she said quietly, 'he has wanted to kill you.'

Eastward from the Ecouves Forest the countryside becomes less wooded, but still with many sharp hills and deep-lined valleys. This is the beginning of the Perche region, given over to small enclosed farms and the breeding of horses.

It is a landscape not easily travelled at night, but after five days the group split up and left the forest caves; Ormerod, Marie-Thérèse and Jean Le Blanc moving towards Montagne-au-Perche. It took two nights travelling and they hid during the day in a barn on the fringe of the village at Longpont. It rained all through the day and the strange trio lay in the stored hay, hardly speaking, eating little food. Ormerod watched Le Blanc carefully. When Le Blanc went to sleep, then Ormerod went to sleep. When he awoke Le Blanc had gone.

'Well,' he yawned. He felt himself all down his chest. 'He didn't kill me this time.'

Marie-Thérèse smiled grimly. 'He is from this region. He is gone to visit his family.'

Ormerod raised his eyes at the revelation. 'Family?' he said. 'Never thought of our Jean as a family man.'

She ignored the sarcasm. 'You know I am from this region also, the Perche, my children are near. I am going to see them tonight. You must wait here for my return.'

He looked at her strangely. This would be the first time they had been parted for more than a few hours since they had landed in France. She smiled at his expression. 'The man here, the farmer,' she said. 'He is a friend. He will bring some food. But if the Germans should come he will not know you are here, you understand?'

'Just let the Germans come over the horizon and I *won't* bloody well be here,' he assured her. He touched her face. 'Be careful won't you, love. Since Bagnoles they've turned nasty. They'll be on the lookout. Don't get caught again. Please.'

She regarded him intently. 'I thank you for your concern and your tenderness,' she said. 'You are a very kind man. I will be safe.'

'Make sure you are,' he replied. He stood up and they came together and kissed as lovers. 'Give my love to the kids,' he grinned.

'If anything should happen to me, if I do not return by tomorrow night, then you must make your way to Paris. Go to the vegetable market at Les Halles and find the man they call the Monkey – *Le Singe*. He will look after you.' As if realizing the seriousness of what she was saying she tried to smile and make a joke. 'It will be boring for you here, Dodo. Without me and without your dear friend Jean Le Blanc.'

He grimaced. 'It's never boring when he's around. There's

always the diversion of having your throat cut. You're right, though, I'll not have a lot to do. I wish I'd brought my comics.'

She kissed him again, briefly this time, a signal that she was going. 'You're a good man,' she said again.

'There's not many of us left,' he said softly. 'Goodbye, take care.'

'*Au revoir*, Dodo.'

'And you, Dove. Don't be long.'

When she had gone he lay back unhappily and slept fitfully in the straw. Then his general weariness, built up over those fugitive days, overcame him and he descended into a deeper sleep. Marie-Thérèse, returning at three in the morning, woke him as she entered the barn. He had his pistol pointing at the door when her shadow whispered tiredly. She lay down at his side, her body against his as if she needed comfort and protection.

'How was it?' he said.

'It was wonderful,' she whispered. It sounded oddly unconvincing. 'The children are so beautiful. My mother is with them.'

'I bet she was surprised to see you,' he said conventionally.

'Yes, she was very amazed. She thought I was dead. I am supposed to have been killed in a flying accident in England, you see. It is part of the cover. She could not believe it was truly me.'

'God. I bet. I didn't know about the flying accident story.'

'There is much you don't know,' she sighed. She pushed her face into his neck. 'But my children are beautiful and safe. That is good. My mother cares for them well.'

'Any news of your husband?' he said with caution.

'He is still with the Germans.'

'They're still holding him?'

'Yes,' she said carefully. He detected her reluctance to talk about it. 'Tomorrow,' she said, 'I have told my mother that we will visit her. You will like her. She was an actress once, years ago. Then you can see my children also. We will eat there. In my house.'

He could not understand what was wrong. It was her voice. 'That would be nice,' he said, as though it were an invitation to tea in Surrey. Then doubtfully: 'How about food? Do they have enough to feed us all?'

Her head nodded against him. 'Yes, there is plenty of food. They are not short of anything. My husband sees to that.'

Ormerod remained silent. He could not understand. Then he said: 'I thought you said the Germans had got him.'

'They have,' she replied hollowly. 'They *have* got him.' Suddenly she began to sob against his neck. He could feel her tears running down inside the collar of his jersey. 'Oh, Dodo,' she said. 'I thought my husband was a patriot. Instead he is a collaborator.'

The village of St Luc au Perche was only two miles down the wooded valley. It was a haphazard place with the dwellings spread out over three or four meadows and a single cobbled street, part of the road from Longport to La Menière. There were no Germans stationed there, only occasional security patrols, although these had increased since the assassination at Bagnoles.

The house of Marie-Thérèse was not difficult to reach, a matter of leaving the valley track and going across two wet fields to the small back garden and the rear door. They went in the dark at eight o'clock and half an hour later were sitting in the comfortable room at the table. Marie-Thérèse sat between the two children, Clovis and Suzanne, looking as though she had never been absent. She talked to them sweetly and she kept touching their hair, her eyes hardly ever leaving their animated faces. Watching her Ormerod wondered how this could be the same woman who had drowned two men in a fishing net, who had shot a policeman, her own countryman, and had been at the assassination at Bagnoles de l'Orne.

Marie-Thérèse's mother, Madame Le Couteur, the former actress, looked across the table at her resurrected daughter with quiet but unending wonderment. 'A miracle,' she kept whispering to Ormerod. She was thin and lined and grey, only her eyes indicating her youth.

She had provided a good meal; soup, veal and vegetables, fruit and local cheese, with a large bottle of wine. Ormerod did not care that it was by courtesy of the Germans and he ate gratefully. Marie-Thérèse was asking Clovis about school. The boy was seven. He answered eagerly. He had almost forgotten his mother. Suzanne, who was six, was anxious to join in the conversation. She spilled her food in her excitement.

'Mama, we are learning a new nursery rhyme,' she announced. 'It is like Boule Boule.' Marie-Thérèse smiled across at Ormerod. 'That is French for Humpty Dumpty,' she explained.

'Back to our friend Le Blanc,' he observed. She grimaced at him. The little girl was anxious to tell more. 'It is like Boule Boule,' she repeated. 'It is called "Humpelken-Pumpelken".'

Ormerod saw the little girl's mother go pale across the table. 'That is German,' she whispered. She stared at the girl. 'They tell you that?'

Suzanne did not realize the tone. 'It is funny,' she said enthusiastically. She began to recite. 'Humpelken-Pumpelken...'

'No!' Marie-Thérèse almost shouted at her. The two children turned quickly to face her, frightened. The grandmother looked astonished. Ormerod regarded her stonily. 'No,' she said more softly. She touched the little girl's hand. 'It is not good, a rhyme like that.'

The grandmother's mouth trembled. 'It is good for *her*,' she said, her voice low, but with a touch of threat. 'She is the one who has to go to school.'

The boy Clovis stood up and went moodily to the window. He lifted the curtain and stared out a few moments. There was still silence at the table. The boy said casually, without turning around: 'There are soldiers in the street.'

Madame Le Couteur moved more quickly than either her daughter or Ormerod. The door was already bolted. She pulled the boy away from the window. 'Quick, go to your bed.' Then to Marie-Thérèse, 'Go up and get under the children's beds,' she said sharply. 'Perhaps they will not trouble the children.'

She began frantically to clear the extra plates and dishes from the table, taking them into the small kitchen and almost throwing them into a cupboard. Ormerod followed Marie-Thérèse up the narrow stairway. His heart seemed to echo against its close walls. The children had two neat nursery beds against opposite sides of the room. They were already quickly undressing and getting between the sheets. Marie-Thérèse crawled beneath her daughter's bed and Ormerod squeezed narrowly beneath the boy's. He drew his large feet up so that his knees were against his chest. His bulk was pressing into the bedsprings above him and swelling the mattress under the child's body. He lay still, sweating, afraid for all of them.

After two or three minutes there came a knocking at the door. Ormerod's breath seemed to die in his lungs. He heard the grandmother hurrying up the stairs. 'Clovis,' she whispered to the boy. 'Go down and open it. Don't speak to the man. Just let him in.'

Ormerod felt the boy leave his bed. He thought the grandmother had gone to the adjoining room. He wondered why she had not answered the door herself. He waited, his pistol against his chest. Beneath her daughter's bed, Marie-Thérèse had also drawn her gun. She held it against her cheek as she lay on her stomach facing the door.

Clovis went down the stairs, a slight figure in a white nightshirt and bare feet. He made some play with the bolt of the door and then eventually opened it. Two German soldiers were standing in the street. They seemed nonplussed at being confronted by a small boy. *'Papa?'* asked one. *'Mama?'*

'Grandmère,' corrected the boy. The soldiers moved nearer.

'We must come in,' said one. They were both ordinary private soldiers, carrying rifles. They scanned the room. Clovis turned away from them and hurried back up the stairs.

'Grandmère,' called one of the soldiers politely. They went into the room and he called loudly, *'Grandmère!'*

The second soldier looked at the table. 'Grandmother drinks a lot of wine,' he said, picking up the near-empty bottle that remained on the cloth.

'You are a wonderful detective,' said the other unimpressed. 'She has probably drunk it for two days.' He called again, *'Grandmère!'*

Her reply came from above them, up the stairs, but they did not hear what she was saying. The soldier gave the other a nod.

They went, still civil caution at each step, mounting the stairs, one behind the other. The stairway went directly into the children's room. The two men in their helmets went in and stood looking with embarrassment at the wide-eyed Suzanne. '*Grandmère?*' said the first soldier again.

The answer came immediately. Around the door jamb leading to the other room came the elderly Madame Le Couteur. She was naked and she had unravelled her long ghostly hair and taken her teeth out. In her hand she had a cracked glass of wine. She was skinny and leathery, her bones projecting all over her body, her belly distended, her legs like sticks, her breasts like lolling dog's ears. '*Bonsoir, mes petits soldats,*' she murmured seductively. She took a swig of wine and rolled it horribly around her toothless gums.

'My God, Herman,' muttered the first staring soldier.

'I cannot believe it,' said the other. 'It is terrible.'

The crone began to advance on them. She left the support of the door jamb and staggered across the floor. The little girl began to screech. Clovis, who was clever, shouted: 'Leave the soldiers, grandma. Don't hurt them!'

Madame Le Couteur grinned wolfishly. She swayed her boned hips and made her eyes glisten. The horrified Germans backed towards the stairs. The first man got his sidepack and his waterbottle caught in the narrow entrance. Herman gave him a push. They both clattered metallically, half falling down the stairs. Madame le Couteur reached the top and stood there like a sexual nightmare. '*Mes petits soldats allemands!*'

The two Germans were still gazing up the stairs, stupefied. The old lady began scratching herself violently. That was the end. They opened the door and fled into the dark street. One got his rifle jammed in the door as he went.

When Marie-Thérèse and Ormerod emerged from their hiding places they went down the stairs where the children were already with their grandmother. She was sitting with the table cloth like a cloak around her, bent over the table, her old head in her bony hands. She was weeping.

Her daughter fetched a blanket and wrapped it over her shoulders. She kissed the children and sadly sent them upstairs again. Eventually the old woman was able to speak. 'It is as well I was always a good actress, a *comédienne*,' she sniffed through her tears.

'It is indeed,' said Marie-Thérèse softly. 'There has never been a performance like that.'

Ormerod was without words. He put his hand on the blanket on the grandmother's shoulder. She looked up at her daughter. 'You must go now,' she said stiffly. 'You will only bring disaster to this house. Go away and do not return until the war is finished. Then and only then can you decide what rhymes your children must sing at school.'

That night, in the enclosed darkness of the hay barn, they lay together on the bales. She needed his comfort and he needed her warmth. Sadness lay heavily upon her after seeing her children and knowing her husband was a traitor.

'He is in Rennes,' she said to Ormerod in the dark. 'He returns to see the children once a month. The rest of the time he is working for the Germans.'

'Maybe he is working undercover against them,' suggested Ormerod without much hope. 'There must be some who have infiltrated. They're the bravest of the lot.'

He felt her shrug in the dark. 'It is not so. I would be lying if I tried to tell myself that. I should have known. He was not interested in politics or the serious life. I was always. He was only interested in comfort. Now he gets that by treason.'

As though it were something to do with what she had said, as if it were some symbol against her husband and her marriage, she slowly undid the buttons of her trousers. Then she lifted the front of her thick jersey to expose her sleepy white breasts. 'These are yours,' she whispered to Ormerod. 'Suck them.'

He put his mouth to the dim, small nipples and touched them with his tongue. His large hands went inside the parted trousers and he slowly and firmly pulled them away from her thighs and down her slim legs. His hands enclosed her buttocks.

'You are good to me, Dodo,' she said wearily.

'And you are good for me,' he said, adding, 'Dove.'

'You have kindness,' she said. 'I can never have kindness.'

'I have never enjoyed a woman before,' he said. 'Not before.'
'We give something to each other then.'

They loved and then lay against each other in the dark, warm-smelling barn. Ormerod slept fitfully and then, in the first light, he heard a movement outside. He lay still, hoping it might be a fox or a stray cow. But it had the sound of a man. He touched Marie-Thérèse's face to warn her. She sat up in the shadows holding her pistol, while Ormerod, his gun in his hand, eased himself down to the floor. Outside it was chill and scarcely light. He moved cautiously around the side of the barn and then around the back. As he turned the corner Jean Le Blanc rose from behind a derelict farm cart and struck him on the back of the neck.

The blow missed the vital point by a fraction because Ormerod had just begun to turn and because Le Blanc had been drinking cognac. It knocked Ormerod sideways against the barn door. He looked up to see a boot travelling towards his hand and his gun. The gun took most of the boot's force and went spinning across the muddy yard. Le Blanc's bald head had a dull shine like lead in the dawn light.

Ormerod rolled away from the wall and got behind a rusty wagon to gain some respite. The heavy Frenchman came after him, but Ormerod dropped down and crawled beneath the wheels. The boots tried to kick him again. He doubted if Le Blanc would risk shooting him. Almost absently he wondered what Marie-Thérèse was doing. She was, in fact, standing in the shadow of the barn, watching, her fear of Le Blanc holding her. 'Jean,' she said in only a whisper. 'Leave him. Why do that?'

Her countryman turned and spat in her direction. She backed away as if the gob was a bullet. 'No,' she pleaded again. She walked out into the slimy yard and Le Blanc, moving at her, gave her a fierce push which sent her backwards against the barn wall. It knocked all the breath from her, but her interruption had given Ormerod time to breathe. Now he came out from beneath the farm cart and staggered forward as Le Blanc turned away from the girl.

The big bald man seemed surprised to see him. He may have been confident that he had damaged Ormerod enough to knock any fight from him. Now he stood with the early light settled on his unpleasant face. He was one of the few men that Ormerod had ever seen who looked worse when he was smiling. He had a smile now. Ormerod swung his fist in the direction of the smile but Le Blanc hardly needed to move to duck it. The two big men collided and Ormerod had some luck because the Frenchman slipped on some dung in the yard and fell backwards. Ormerod fell on top of him and rising away from the other man's body quickly punched him full on the jaw before he had time to move his head away.

For a moment, even in that poor light, Ormerod saw his opponent's eyes glaze. He tried to think of an unarmed combat ploy he could use. He abandoned the idea and settled for crudely hitting Le Blanc on the jaw once more.

The Frenchman's head went back and Ormerod thought that was the end. But as he climbed away from the prostrate man, Le Blanc's foot came and caught him a sickening kick between the legs. The force of the blow sent him stumbling back, holding his groin. It took Le Blanc some moments to get up, but even that was ample time. He went for Ormerod with cold rage, throwing another kick at him which the Englishman managed to avoid by staggering out of range. He needed to get his breath back. The old farm machine standing there was a reaper with circular pointed tines sticking out like a wheel of rusty needles. Ormerod retreated behind this and rubbed his crotch. He bent almost double with the sickness and looked up to see the Frenchman coming after him again with that look that only a truly evil man can summon.

It was like a slow comedy scene, Ormerod dodging around the farm machinery while the Frenchman stalked him. Both were coated with dung and mud. The stench was in Ormerod's nose, making him want to retch more than ever. But he had gained some time. Suddenly, as Le Blanc followed him around the flank of the barn, he leapt out as if he had been waiting in ambush. The sheer ferocity of the attack surprised Le Blanc who fell back under the battering of Ormerod's large fists. For a moment he swayed and Ormerod grasped him like a bear and forced him back onto the pointed tines of the old machine.

They stuck through Le Blanc's clothes and punctured the skin on his back. He was hanging there and Ormerod gave him a final punch to settle it.

Ormerod staggered back, swaying like something caught in the wind, then moved towards Le Blanc, and, watching for the leg trick this time, pulled him across his shoulder in a fireman's carry. There was a dung heap portioned off with a stile-like fence. Breathing in sobs he pushed the Frenchman against the wooden railings.

'Dodo,' Marie-Thérèse spoke behind his back. He half turned and saw she was twenty feet away levelling her pistol at him. 'Whose side are you on?' he gasped.

'Leave him now,' she ordered. 'It is enough. We are all in this together.'

'I only want to kill him before he kills me,' answered Ormerod, glancing back at the sagging Le Blanc. 'Is that unreasonable?'

'He has orders *not* to kill you,' she said. 'Orders from Paris. He would not dare to do it now. But we need him also. You have done enough.'

Le Blanc was a dead weight against the fence. Ormerod let him drop to the muddy ground. 'All right then,' he said. 'But just let him try it once again and I'll shoot his ugly bloody head off.'

He bent and put his hands under the Frenchman's armpits. With a grunting heave he lifted him onto the top cross-member of the fence. Then, steadying him with one hand, punched him backwards into the soft dung.

'Humpelken-Pumpelken,' he said drunkenly. 'Had a great fall.'

Then he collapsed on the cobbles.

The small town of Moulin-en-Ceil lies south-west of Paris, twenty kilometres from Chartres. The countryside is flat as an ocean there, running for miles to the sky, with Chartres Cathedral rising like a great and distant ship.

The harvest had been taken and the fields were rough with stubble, some of it now being burned, the annual ritual, so that the placid vista looked as if some recent battle had taken place. Coils of oily smoke, with red eyes of fire at the base of each, climbed into the flat October air.

Ormerod and Marie-Thérèse moved carefully across country over two nights to reach Moulin-en-Ceil. Jean Le Blanc had left before them, sullen and bruised as Ormerod was bruised, instructing Marie-Thérèse that he would be bringing orders to the town.

The little town, like the cathedral on the other horizon, is to be seen from a good distance. It sits on a plateau of slightly rising land, so modest that it might have been made by man not nature, but clearly seen because of the flatness of the country. The windmill from which it takes its name stands up against the sky.

They arrived there in the early morning and went at once to the house of a man called Louis Brechet, who lived above his grocer's shop almost at the tail of the main street. They slept deeply in his storeroom, among bags of beans, and in the evening Brechet's wife came into the storeroom and said there was a message for Marie-Thérèse. The wife was suspicious of them, in the way that wives have for scenting trouble in other women.

Ormerod was left with Brechet, who was a dark-jowled, sociable man, solidly eating Normandy tripe and nosily drinking Muscadet. He found it difficult to start a conversation, even though the Frenchman spoke some English. In the end, his mouth filled with tripe, he asked, 'And how's business?'

Brechet looked unsurprised at the unorthodox yet mundane question, in fact he seemed to welcome it. 'Not bad,' he said. 'Not bad at all. At the moment we have enough goods to put in the shop. Later it will be difficult.'

'Are the Germans good customers?' inquired Ormerod cautiously.

Brechet looked at him in astonishment. 'I am a Jew,' he said. 'The Germans are not permitted to buy from me, thank God. That is their own law. They look in the window sometimes because I have some things they like to put in their bellies, but I have a large notice saying "This is a Jewish Business" and I wave it about in front of their noses and they go away. It works both ways.'

He drank his wine appreciatively as if it were a new and unusual vintage. 'Some of the shops must have made good money from the Boche,' he said. 'Very good. The Occupation is the best thing that has happened to their poor businesses. They are nothing more than Kollabos.'

'Kollabos? What's Kollabos?'

'Collaborators, licking the boots of the Nazis,' sniffed Brechet. 'You should have seen them when they realized the Germans *paid* for goods. They thought that the troops would just take everything, loot it, so they locked up their miserable shops and hid in their rooms. Then the Germans began looking through the windows and waving money. Ah, that was different. Soon the doors were unlocked. Even patriotism does not shout louder than money, my friend.'

Ormerod nodded sagely. 'I bet you're glad you're Jewish,' he said. 'Not having to serve them.'

'I am,' said Brechet sincerely. 'But when food gets short I shall be the one who is looted. You just see.'

Marie-Thérèse reappeared in the storeroom, climbing over the bags of beans like an elephant boy over the backs of his charges. 'I have a message from Le Blanc,' she said. She glanced at Ormerod as she said the name.

'I'm surprised he's still talking to us,' commented Ormerod. 'Well, to me, anyway.'

'Forget that,' she said, sharply enough to make Brechet glance at them questioningly. 'That is past. I told you, it must be forgotten. There are more important things. Jean Le Blanc is our leader and he must be obeyed because of that fact. Nothing more matters.'

'The fifth-form bully wins again,' muttered Ormerod. 'What's the news?'

'We are growing very strong in this region,' she said with a serious smile. 'The information from Dreux is that many of the workers in the factories are forming resistance groups. There has already been sabotage. In Paris things are being organized very quickly. Before long the Nazis will know it is *we* who have *them* the prisoners. They will not be able to move a single metre without fear.'

She glanced at Ormerod and then at Brechet, her face full of enthusiasm. 'Tonight,' she said, 'we have a rendezvous with Le Blanc, with some of the leaders from Dreux and two men from Paris. Our plans are looking well.'

'Perhaps your Paris boys will know the whereabouts of Smales,' said Ormerod without much hope. He looked at her. 'You remember Smales?' he said.

'Something I have to tell you, Dodo,' she said stiffly. 'Monsieur Smales has been told that you are looking for him.'

Ormerod felt his indignation rising. 'Oh thanks. Thanks very bloody much. Well, I'll still get him, you wait and see.'

'You may not be permitted to get him,' she said quietly. 'I told you that before. Or *he* may get *you*. Also, there is another thing. Motte, the doctor who smuggled you into the ward at Bagnoles; he was arrested and is now dead. They tortured him and he fortunately was able to commit suicide. But they got one thing from him first. They have your full description.' She looked abruptly dejected as she said it. 'They now know the face they are looking for. So from now on you must be more careful than ever.'

Ormerod looked crushed. 'That's bloody lovely that is,' he said. 'Bloody lovely. I think I'll just pack up and go home.'

The rendezvous was at an almost derelict mill house built over the stream at Moulin-en-Ceil, a stream which springs almost at the heart of the modestly elevated town and, because of the immediate slope to the flat country all around, runs at a fast rate down to the agricultural plain.

It was a cold place for the meeting, noisy with the rushing mill brook, but the large old building was ideal for posting look-outs and an escape way was planned along the stream if the Germans found them there that night.

These precautions were explained immediately by Jean Le Blanc to those sitting in what had been the machinery room of the mill. There were four men from the factory committee at Dreux and the pair from Paris, all quiet, threatening-looking men, squatting and listening to Le Blanc. As Marie-Thérèse, Ormerod and Brechet came in Le Blanc's eyes drifted up for a moment to those of the Englishman. Ormerod performed a mock affable wave. 'Feeling better?' he asked. The Frenchman did not answer. Nor did his expression alter. Ormerod squatted down with the rest. He could feel the cold air coming up from the dashing water below.

'I am here to tell you that the first operation of the resistance group in this area has been planned,' said Le Blanc, his bald head strangely like some extraterrestrial orb in the gloom. 'It will be a very special operation and it will show the Nazis that there are still those who will not tremble before them. We plan, gentlemen, to blow up a German military band.'

Marie-Thérèse translated in a whisper and she watched as Ormerod's jaw dropped. Christ, he thought, wasn't that just like Le Blanc. An assassination at a hospital, an ambush from an ambulance, and now the destruction of a military band. He nearly said: 'Why?' but Marie-Thérèse restrained him with her hand on his arm. She watched Le Blanc seriously.

'It will be poetic, I think,' said the Frenchman. 'It will also be practical. On Sunday the Boche are holding a parade of troops in this region. They will march through several villages, to show off their strength, and then through the streets of this town, Moulin-en-Ceil, and across the bridge which can be seen from this very place where we are now sitting. The water that you hear under our feet has run down from the bridge which is only two hundred and seventy metres upstream. The bridge can be well observed from this mill in daylight. The plan is to explode the bridge and to escape by means of the stream itself. We have some small canvas boats being brought from Chartres for the purpose. It will be a very swift escape. Our Paris friends here have arranged the boats and are experienced in using them. We leave immediately after the action, dropping through the trapdoor there and below to the side of the water. The boats will carry us downstream and we will leave them just before the main Chartres road.

'There is a railway station at Nogent le Roi. There is a train to Chartres at noon on Sunday. The group will be on the train. There is a connecting train to Paris at one o'clock. We will be on that. It is as well that the French railways are still good. There is no other way of travelling quickly. We will, obviously, split up. I will travel alone, our friends from Paris will go together and our friend Dove and her friend Dodo ...' his eyes went to Ormerod like a slow dart, '... they will go as lovers to Paris to see Notre Dame.' His smile was icy.

Ormerod thought: 'You're jealous too, you bastard. Jealous because of her.'

'Brechet will not be required to take part in this operation. He is too valuable in this region to take the risk. There are plenty of us anyway. Nor will our friends from Dreux. You have things to do there. Your turn will come. The small details of the operation will be given to those taking part just before we commence.'

Marie-Thérèse had been whispering a translation to Ormerod. Now he leaned forward in the gloom. 'Question?' he suggested diffidently. 'May I ask a question?'

The white-skinned Frenchman glowered at him. 'What is this question?'

'Well ... why blow up the band? I mean if there's a column of infantry why not wait until *they're* on the bridge?'

For almost a minute Le Blanc looked at him like dull steel. Then he said: 'Because I *say* we blow up the band. I *want* it to be the band.' His nasty smile severed his lower face. 'I have no ear for music.'

Sunday saw all the stubble fires in the fields at last extinguished. The flat pan of the countryside was black with ash. The harvest was finished. It was traditionally a day for thanksgiving. On the Saturday night, in the days of peace, there had always been harvest suppers in the villages of the plain and a church service on the Sunday in the onion-domed church at Moulin-en-Ceil. The people from the villages would walk in procession up the gentle gradient roads to the town carrying with them the rewards of their work; bread and barley and vegetables, and singing songs that had been sung beneath those pale autumn skies for as long as anyone could remember. In this October of 1940 the people's thanksgiving was muted. There were no harvest suppers, the men instead just gathering in the village inns and bars to drink one or two glasses of wine or cognac before quietly going home. Nor were there the traditional trailing processions across the used-up plain making the ascent to Moulin-en-Ceil. Instead the village churches each held their own quiet thanksgiving, each sending a prayer that there would be some kind of harvest to gather the following year.

The parade of the German soldiers through the villages of the plain was watched by a few people in the streets and many more from their windows. Few of the inhabitants wished to be seen standing to watch the Germans march by to the jolly music of their band, although children, to whom soldiers and music and marching are a fascination without prejudice, watched the conquering platoons excitedly.

The October sun was warm enough for the marching troops to sweat as they left the roads of the flat country and began the gradual ascent of the streets of Moulin. They were glad of the band with its cornet and drums, its oomphing souzaphone and its charming, chiming glockenspiel. As the musicians entered the enclosed streets of the town its sound altered as the music filled the narrow spaces between houses. All the shopkeepers – excluding Brechet – and most local businessmen had come out to watch the parade with their families, one or two of them waving tentatively. Some of the girls eyed the striding Germans speculatively. The occupation, they argued within themselves, was likely to last a long time.

The rumbustious music and the sound of the boots on the cobbles alerted the local German commander at his saluting base outside the town hall. The mayor of Moulin and his councillors were present because they had been ordered by the occupation authorities to be there. But they refused to wear their robes. Now they stood behind the German colonel and his senior officers as the music and the boots came near. The band swung jauntily into the main square and the German commander raised his arm in salute. His fellow officers stood to attention with clicked heels. The mayor and the town council stared ahead with sombre interest. For them it was not a good day.

Because it was Sunday and the place was peaceful, the German troops were not wearing steel helmets, neither did they carry arms. It had been decided to parade in this fashion as a reassurance to the French population. There had been no trouble with the people of Moulin-en-Ceil and the occupation commander wanted it to remain like that.

The column of troops was not long, the band and three platoons stretching four abreast over perhaps three hundred yards of cobbled streets. They went smartly through the square. The band played well in the brisk air. Crouching in the old mill building, Le Blanc and the others heard it approaching. The charges had been placed beneath the bridge over the mill-stream since early morning. Waiting with Le Blanc were Marie-Thérèse, Ormerod and the two men from Paris. Ormerod realized he was the only one who was trembling. Below them, visible through a hatch in the floor, two canvas boats waited, pulled up clear of the swift millstream onto the stone foundations of the mill building.

The bridge upstream was not the solid stone arch to be seen in so many French towns in that region of small rivers. It had been built only just before the war to replace a stone bridge which had been damaged by flooding through many winters. It had metal spans and rails but the bridge itself was of wood. The charges were quite sufficient to blow it to small pieces.

The music increased, the tinkling glockenspiel somehow sounding above the other more strident instruments like a happy bird in the field. Then they saw the grey but jaunty band rounding the last corner of the town and making for the bridge, the platoons of infantry following it. Because of the screening hedgerows they could only see the heads and shoulders of the bandsmen and the marching troops. They could not see at all the children of the town who, as children will, had followed the band. There were a dozen or more, most of them small and in their Sunday best, running along by the legs of the band, smiling and skipping and jogging to the music. At the edge of the town most of them hesitated and then went back to their parents at the centre. But three, a boy and two little girls, continued to follow the band. From the mill they could not be seen.

The parade had only three hundred metres to go before it reached the bridge. Ormerod felt miserable and sick. He sensed the bodies of those around him grow tense. The trigger button was at the hand of one of the Parisian men. He looked the coolest of the lot. The top of Le Blanc's head was shining with pale sweat.

They watched. The music tinkled and oomphed. The bridge drew nearer. The Parisian with the trigger waited calmly. The others had frozen. Then, unbelievably, the band halted, the music ceased, the rest of the troops stopped. Their heads were ranged along the top of the hedgerow. Ormerod learned a new French swearword. Then he realized what was happening. He remembered from his army time.

'They're not going to march over the bridge,' he told them. 'They have to break step. Otherwise the whole lot collapses. It's normal military procedure.'

For once Le Blanc looked as though he valued something that Ormerod had said. 'They will still go?' he asked. 'They will not turn and go back?'

'Maybe they will,' replied Ormerod. 'They just won't *march* over. Look, they're doing something now.'

The German band had, in fact, broken into two lines that were now forming up one each side of the footway, along the length of the bridge. The rest of the troops were at a halt. The three French children stood smiling and wondering at the Germans. Once they were formed, the band, stationary in two ranks facing inwards, began playing a lilting waltz-like tune. The infantrymen were then ordered into single file and began crossing the bridge in broken step.

In the mill house the man from Paris carefully returned his hand to the button. Almost at the same time Ormerod saw a flash of a pink dress as one of the little girls moved forward towards the bridge with the soldiers. He reached out and took the binoculars from the hands of the second Parisian. Putting them up to his eyes he saw the three children among the soldiers. Frantically he reached across to the Parisian. 'No, mate, no,' he shuddered. 'There's kids ... *enfants* ...'

At the same instant a combined act of God and the German sergeant-major saved the children's lives. The sergeant-major had not objected to the children marching with the band, for the band was a childish thing, but now he did not want them marching over the bridge with the soldiers. He called and roughly ordered them back. They looked at him doubtfully, then returned from the wooden cross-boards. He pointed back towards the town and told them to go home. They looked at him with shy sulks but he repeated the instruction sternly and began walking away. When they were seventy metres back towards the town, the Parisian, who had not seen them anyway, decided that the correct moment had come. He pressed the button.

The charge below the bridge coughed apologetically for a split second. Then, with a huge roar and a flash of red light, the bridge was lifted up into the air in thousands of pieces, carrying the entire German band and all the infantrymen stepping across it at that moment. The children and the soldiers who were waiting their turn to cross were blown over by the force. The sergeant-major had both legs blown off and died before they could move him. The little river was suddenly full of bodies and blood. From the town the French people and the German officers began to emerge to see what had happened. A coil of smoke hung over the carnage.

'Time to depart,' murmured Le Blanc.

'You bastard,' said Ormerod. 'The kids.'

'The children were safe,' put in Marie-Thérèse swiftly. 'The Germans sent them back. Come. We go.'

The others were already dropping through the trapdoor into the cellar with its running water. As he followed them Ormerod saw the water was stained red and when he reached the side of the canvas boat two bodies floated past. He heard the man who had pushed the button laugh. The Parisians knew what they were doing with the boats. They launched them quickly and easily, holding them still while Ormerod, Marie-Thérèse and Le Blanc got aboard. Ormerod put his head between his legs. Nausea rolled over him. They pushed off quickly. From upstream they could hear the commotion that had followed the explosion. Whistles were being blown and the noise screeched across the fields.

Their escape was swift, for the river ran quickly through meadows and well below the level of the grass. They crouched in the bucking boats and without hindrance reached a small landing stage a mile downstream. They climbed ashore and coolly lifted the canvas craft from the water after them. The others moved decisively but Ormerod felt slow and dazed. He looked across the square landscape to where the hairline of smoke was still hanging in the distant air.

Within two hundred metres of where they landed was a sheltered path between a clutch of cottages. It led, with a slight elevation, to the platform of the railway station. They had timed it perfectly. The afternoon train for Chartres was steaming easily in. The Parisians quickened their pace so that the group split up, Le Blanc walked briskly some distance behind them and Ormerod and Marie-Thérèse followed. She held his hand, for effect, and found it was still trembling. 'Come on, *chéri*,' she whispered. 'We are going to Paris.'

nine

Paris in the autumn of that year was gradually emerging from its stunned summer. The cafés were open and so were the shops, cinemas and theatres. Performances began mid-afternoon and were finished by early evening. The Opéra was beginning a new season. A different sort of music was provided by a German military band playing Prussian marches which strode every morning at the head of a picked company of troops around the Arc de Triomphe and down the broad and vacant run of the Champs-Elysées. Parisians tended to find they had business elsewhere during the hour of this bombastic display by the conquerors.

Red and black swastika banners were displayed throughout the city, even hanging from the girders of the Eiffel Tower and there were military pillboxes and sentry posts at the main junctions. Random identity checks were made at all hours, on a population which had hardly had time to believe its senses, let alone resist. There was a curfew at midnight. Anyone caught abroad after that time was arrested and questioned and usually released the following morning after spending a night performing menial cleaning tasks for the German sergeants. In the later years of the occupation some curfew-breakers were shot by firing squad as a reprisal for acts of force by the resistance movement. But this was all in the future. The Germans in those first months of their triumph had inherited a cowed city.

To the eye the most obvious change in the life of the capital was that, overnight, motor vehicles, apart from German military transport, had vanished from the streets that had once been among the most congested and clamorous in the world. An occasional car or taxi, propelled by gas generated from a towed wood-burning boiler, could be witnessed coughing along the boulevards, but the people, in general, had taken to the bicycle and the Métro. Former taxi-drivers emerged with little carts towed by one or two bicycles and known as *vélo*-taxis. Food was not yet in short supply and there was almost as much drink available in the cafés and bars as usual. Newspapers, naturally censored by the occupying power, were available at the inimitable street kiosks, together with new journals sponsored by the Germans and French sympathizers.

German troops went sightseeing and strolled along the avenues, their jackboots treading in the russet leaves of another autumn. Everywhere there were posters showing a German soldier holding a French child in his arms. They were smiling at each other.

For the most part the Parisian treated the invader as if he did not exist, walking by him in the street, looking straight ahead and never speaking to him unless he asked for directions. Then he was freqently sent the wrong way. It was a small act of revenge, but it was something.

The Place Denfert-Rochereau is in the fourteenth *arrondissement* of the city, south of the Luxembourg Gardens. Beneath the street in that district run the dark tunnels and communication caves of the Paris Catacombs. Established in the eighteenth century when several million skeletons from a dozen old cemeteries were brought there, the caves date from Roman times when there were quarries below Montparnasse, Montrouge, and Montsouris, the three hills of Paris. The connecting tunnels stretch out to the Porte de Versailles and the suburb of Gentilly. In the deep darkness of this grisly place are dozens of galleries, all lined with skulls and attendant crossbones. During the German occupation it eventually became the safe headquarters of the resistance.

In October 1940, however, the movement had scarcely begun to stir. The Communists, who formed a powerful and fanatical part of the eventual strength, were showing no inclination to fight the invader, for Germany and Russia were still embraced in a treaty of friendship.

But there were other men, shamed patriots and national fighters, who had held clandestine meetings, formed committees of action, and explored the possibilities of the Catacombs.

It was to Denfert-Rochereau that Ormerod and Marie-Thérèse went after arriving in Paris on the evening of the blowing of the bridge at Moulin-en-Ceil.

They left the train at the Gare St Lazare, walking in the thick of the crowd. A group of German soldiers and French policemen were examining identity cards at the exit. Ormerod glanced at Marie-Thérèse. She took her card from her pocket and pushed forward, presenting it to one of the soldiers. They were having trouble checking everyone because the train had been crowded. Ormerod followed immediately behind Marie-Thérèse, hoping his papers would not be asked for. But the official arm of a gendarme moved out towards him and caught him by the elbow. Ormerod's mouth went dry. He stared at the policeman, a small and bluish face under a large cap, and the Frenchman looked at him closely. 'Carte,' he said stiffly.

Ormerod fumbled and produced his forged identity card. The policeman examined it. Ormerod was conscious of Marie-Thérèse lingering ten yards away. He wondered what she would do, shoot or run. The French officer sniffed over the card. Something was wrong. He regarded Ormerod again. 'Ce n'est pas signée,' he said, tapping the card. Ormerod saw that the line for his signature was empty. 'Oui,' he managed.

The policeman looked at him strangely now. Ormerod saw Marie-Thérèse move. She stepped two paces closer, then deliberately pushed a woman carrying a baby into the back of the policeman. The Frenchman turned, a swearword breaking on his lips. His action knocked the child from the unbalanced mother's grip and it fell half-way to the ground. The policeman

207

and the woman caught it between them in a flurry of exclamations and curses. The infant was hanging upside down when its fall was eventually arrested. The mother began shouting at the policeman above the baby's howls. The man protested that it was not his fault. Ormerod, left unattended, walked away.

Outside the station they hurried through the dusk. Marie-Thérèse's face was white. 'No signature,' she cursed under her breath. 'For God's sake!'

Ormerod realized he was still trembling. They had reached a newspaper-seller's kiosk outside the station enclosure. A man reading a magazine touched the arm of Marie-Thérèse and she put her hand out to stop Ormerod.

'I am Raymond,' said the man quietly. He was thin and studious. His face stooped towards them. 'Is there trouble?'

'Some trouble,' replied Marie-Thèrése.

'We will leave quickly,' said Raymond. Two bicycle-taxis were at the kerb. Raymond called to them and they pedalled towards the trio.

'Take that one,' said the newcomer. He was careful and calm. Ormerod and Marie-Thérèse climbed into the odd cart. Ormerod had a quick vision of getting into one of the cars of the big wheel at a fairground. The bicyclist began to pedal laboriously. Raymond was in the *vélo*-taxi in front. 'Follow him,' Marie-Thérèse said to the driver.

It was a strange, slow-motion journey. It had rained and the city was damp and cold. Ormerod wondered if the policeman at the Gare St Lazare would have searched for him, raised an alarm, or just dismissed the matter as a minor occurrence. He felt like the slowest fugitive in the world.

The bicycle rider puffed in the moist air as they travelled through the almost vacant city. Few people were on the pavements. There was a light in the door of a church and the Sunday afternoon worshippers were coming out, turning their collars up as they left. An occasional military vehicle, the stark black cross on its flank, moved through the gloom.

The journey ended in the Rue des Plantes, a street in a district afterwards renowned for its resistance activities. The adjoining Avenue Jean Moulin was named, in later times, after the most effective and dauntless underground agent of all those dangerous years, a man who died in triumph at the hands of the Gestapo. The Avenue du Général Leclerc, re-named after another hero of the Free French, is in the same vicinity.

In a third floor apartment in the Rue des Plantes, Ormerod and Marie-Thérèse once more found themselves in the company of Jean Le Blanc. The two men who had gone to Moulin-en-Ceil from Paris were also there, and three others, excluding Raymond. As Ormerod came through the door after Marie-Thérèse he smiled wryly at Le Blanc. 'Had a nice day?' he said.

'An excellent day, *Monsieur l'Anglais*,' said Le Blanc with his own cleft smile. 'Twenty-three Nazi soldiers killed, according to our information, and eighteen more wounded. They will play no more tunes in that band.'

'What about the French children?' said Ormerod, sitting down. 'They got clear?'

'Every one. They were not harmed.'

'No thanks to you, mate.'

'We did not know they were there,' shrugged Le Blanc bluntly. 'In any case, French parents should not let their children run along with the occupier's forces.' He looked around the room. 'It was a good victory,' he said in French. 'The best so far against the Boche.' He turned to the tall Raymond. 'The trains are running well, Raymond,' he said. 'The Germans make them run on time.'

'It is as well,' replied Raymond. 'Moving about in France today, and especially moving quickly, would be impossible without them. You had no trouble?'

'Nothing,' smiled Le Blanc. 'They just checked papers at the Gare St Lazare. I even sat in a compartment with three Nazi airmen. We travelled together from Chartres. I smiled at them all the way.'

Ormerod sat looking at the group. The three additional men did not look like the nucleus of a guerrilla group. One was young and staring through heavy spectacles, a second had the premature roundness of a grocer and the third kept picking his nose nervously. For his part, Ormerod, while not encouraged by the aspect of the company, felt suddenly more assured himself. In a city, once more in surroundings with which he

209

somehow felt familiar and comfortable, he began to feel like a policeman again. It was as though he had abruptly grown a new coat. He had gone through all the death in the countryside and all the running and now he was there in Paris. And in Paris was also Albert Smales.

'We have a committee of action in each *arrondissement*,' said the stooping Raymond, looking at him and speaking in English. He seemed anxious to establish their credibility. 'Each college and factory has its committee. I am a tutor at the university and I know that the students are planning a demonstration in the Place de L'Etoile and the Champs-Elysées – on Armistice Day next month. The Germans are nervous. They have some foolish hope there will be no trouble in Paris. We are planning a newspaper to be circulated secretly. Acts of sabotage are to be co-ordinated. There is a supply of weapons and ammunition which is growing each day. Yes, our conquerers are very anxious.' He laughed quietly. 'I think they have us just where we want them.'

The girl and the others were watching him closely. But Ormerod was impatient. When Raymond paused and looked around Ormerod interrupted. 'I find all this very interesting, monsieur,' he said with his finger raised like a schoolboy. 'But I would like to ask a question.'

Raymond raised his scholarly eyebrows. He was not used to being interrupted. 'Monsieur?' he said a little testily. Marie-Thérèse looked impatiently towards Ormerod. A sneer wriggled across the face of Le Blanc.

'I am looking for a man called Albert Smales,' said Ormerod in his best police manner. 'I have reason to think you know where he is.'

Raymond looked at him over the top of his spectacles. Just as formally he said: 'I am aware, monsieur, that you have an interest in Albert Smales. This has been transmitted to me. He has been here in Paris working with us for some time. At one time we considered he would be a valuable member of our group.'

Ormerod felt the hair on the back of his head twitch. 'Smales,' he said slowly, 'is wanted for questioning in connection with a murder in London.'

The men all smiled at that. Raymond's smile was of exaggerated patience. Marie-Thérèse looked embarrassed. Raymond glanced at the others, then made his own decision.

'Monsieur,' he said, 'we are aware that this man Smales is a criminal. We are also aware of something we did not know before – that he is a risk to our security. He is a man who, if the circumstances were right, if he were in a trap or if he were offered enough money, would betray us. We have needed to watch him very carefully. So we are not, as you say, very fond of him.'

Ormerod sniffed. 'He's a difficult man to like.'

'Exactly. But for the moment we need him. You see, in this district as in all districts of Paris, we are just beginning to be organized. And to be organized and to carry out the warfare that we want to carry out against the Nazis, we need money. In the future we hope that our friends in England and other places will provide it. But for the present we must find it ourselves. And the only way we can obtain enough money for our needs is by robbery.' He watched Ormerod's reaction. The English policeman regarded him sternly. Raymond smiled and continued. 'We plan to take some cash from a French bank in the next few days and for this we need your friend Smales. We need an experienced criminal, monsieur. We are from several professions, but none of us is in the profession of crime. Smales is. Already he has planned the raid in detail for us. After it is all over and we have the money – then you can have him, monsieur. He will be all yours.'

Ormerod took it all in. Eventually he said: 'Well, you couldn't have a better villain than your friend. I must say I never thought I'd be told the details of an armed robbery before it happened. That's war does that, I suppose.'

'War changes many things,' agreed Raymond. He looked hard at Ormerod and said, to the Englishman's surprise, 'I can arrange for you to have a conversation with Smales if you like.'

'Oh, can you?' beamed Ormerod. 'Now that would be very nice. I'd like that. Where is the bastard?'

'I will take you to him. It will be expected that you leave your gun behind.'

Ormerod shrugged. 'That's all right. I've never questioned a suspect with a gun yet. Will he have his?'

'No. We will make sure of that.'

'Good. All right then. I'll look forward to it.'

'And there is one more thing, monsieur. You said a few moments ago that you had never been told of a robbery before it happened. As a policeman, are you worried about your attitude to a criminal act like this?'

'Well you must admit, it's a bit odd. It's civil crime, even if it is a good cause. I'm not sure what my position ought to be.'

'When the time comes,' smiled Raymond without humour, 'we will tell you your position. You will be taking part.'

On the following afternoon, when it was getting towards the early dusk, Raymond called at the apartment in the Rue des Plantes. 'Monsieur Smales will be able to see you in half an hour,' he said.

'Very good of him,' said Ormerod. 'Was it difficult to get an appointment?' He had slept in a small room in the company of four rabbits in a cage. Raymond smiled.

'You had plenty of friends last night.'

'You're not joking,' grumbled Ormerod. 'I didn't realize rabbits made so much noise. God knows what they were up to in the dark. And they smell a bit too.'

Raymond shrugged. 'Many houses and apartments have rabbits now,' he said. 'Or even chickens. In this apartment we hope to have them breeding. Before very long they may be our meat for Christmas dinner and other special days.'

'I suppose I should be grateful it's not goats,' said Ormerod. He followed Raymond from the door and they descended the straight staircase to the street.

They walked together studiously through the misty district. 'Smales is in an unusual place,' said Raymond quietly. 'Not a very pretty situation. But very safe. You will see.'

They reached the circus of the Place Denfert-Rochereau, ghostly with all the traffic gone. A few bicycles wheeled slowly around it and there were pedestrians moving like shadows on the pavements. 'This was once called the *Place d'Enfer*,' said Raymond. 'The Place of Hell.'

Moments later Ormerod understood why. From the damp street they descended some leaf-thick steps into a dark and gloomy passage. Raymond opened an iron grille door and a strange smell assailed Ormerod's nostrils. He had smelled it before but not in that particular bouquet. It was the smell of death.

'Where's this?' he said in a seemly whisper. 'A graveyard?'

Raymond produced a torch and led the way down a long, ominous passage sloping below the ground. The Frenchman kept the torch just ahead of his feet but after a few minutes he stopped Ormerod with a touch of his hand and then turned the torch and swung it around the walls. Ormerod jumped. They were in a galleried chamber, and everywhere, grimacing down, were skulls, row on row on row, each with their attendant crossed bones. 'Bloody hell,' breathed Ormerod. 'Where's this?'

'Hell, as you say,' replied Raymond, sweeping the torch about the grisly ranks. 'The Catacombs. All the ancient dead of Paris. It is quite a population. This is going to prove a useful place for the resistance movement. Here we are to make our headquarters.'

'Smales is down here?'

'Yes. You will need to find him. But he is somewhere. We brought him here today to meet you.'

'Appropriate place,' sniffed Ormerod, still looking around. 'Are you staying to hold my hand?'

Raymond laughed dryly. 'No, I shall leave you with the torch and with Monsieur Smales. You must become acquainted. But, please remember, there must be no violence. We need him.'

'The British copper doesn't do that,' said Ormerod smugly. 'We don't believe in roughing people up. Not all that much anyway. Not generally.'

Without a further word the torch was placed in his hands. Raymond muttered a casual '*au revoir*' and walked away from him up the macabre passage. Eventually, in the distance, the iron grille door closed. Ormerod was surprised to find himself sweating. He swung the torch around the great grinning gallery of skulls. 'Evening everybody,' he recited.

He began to walk slowly, deeper into the ossuary. His

clothes felt damp inside. The skulls and the bones went on and on like some nightmare wallpaper. It was amazing how alike everyone looked after a few years of death. 'Smales!' he suddenly shouted. 'Where are you, Smales?'

The echo seemed fragmented as if it were jumping in and out of the thousands of human crevices. There was no reply. He stepped a few more paces. He attempted to console himself by grinning back at the skulls as they came into view. 'Smales, lad,' he called again with professional mock-persuasiveness. 'Come on out. It's the police.'

Abruptly there was a movement like the brush of a shoe on the ground. Then another. 'Just a few routine questions, Smales!' he called again as he paused. 'Nothing to worry about. Just routine.'

'Fuck off, copper!' The cry seemed almost a scream. Ormerod swore he could hear the bones shifting. 'Go on – fuck off!'

'Offensive words and behaviour,' called Ormerod in his best official voice. 'And in *here*. I wouldn't be surprised, blasphemy as well. Where are you? Come on son. Come on out, there's a good lad.'

A pile of skulls suddenly rolled down from a shelf like loaves of stale bread. They bounced about his feet. He turned the beam of the torch up swiftly. There was a gap in the grisly wall from which the skulls had been pushed and standing in the gap, his face loaded with hate and viciousness, was Albert Smales, the man he had come so far to see.

'Hello, Albert,' said Ormerod softly. 'What's a nasty boy like you doing in a nice place like this?'

'What you want?' demanded Smales. 'What you after? You've nowt on me. Nowt at all.'

Ormerod looked up at him. He kept the torch off his face, but flicked it to and fro. Smales covered his eyes with his hands. Ormerod intoned: 'I told you, lad, routine inquiries. Concerning the death of one Lorna Smith in London on ...'

'You must be fucking mad,' growled Smales. 'What do you think you can do here in bleeding Paris? There's Jerries everywhere. What hope have *you* got?'

'I've done all right up to now, Smalesy,' smiled Ormerod.

'You're here and I'm here. I've come a long way for this.'

Smales suddenly picked up a skull and threw it at him. Ormerod was expecting it and caught it like a rugby ball. 'No respect for the dead!' he bellowed, hurling it back. It smashed against the stone wall. Smales was suddenly gone, his shadow flying along the wall and the curved ceiling. 'Come back you bastard,' said Ormerod more to himself than to Smales. He began to trot cautiously along the grim passage. He stopped and waited. He could hear the other man breathing among the bones. 'Smales!' he called 'Come on out. I want you, Albert. I want you.'

'Well you ain't going to fucking get me!' The words came in a screech. They were followed by a fusillade of bones, old legs and arms and then two skulls. Ormerod covered his head. But the direction from which the bombardment came showed him where his quarry was. Carefully he went along the corridor shining the torch on the floor, until he reached a short flight of stone steps going up to the gallery. He crept up the steps having the passing thought as to who originally had the task of arranging all those grinning skulls and criss-crossed bones. At the end of the gallery he saw the half shadow of Smales. A policeman always knows by instinct when he has got his man. Ormerod knew he had got Smales. He went forward one small step at a time.

Smales knew he was coming. He was waiting with a skull in his hand. As Ormerod rounded the end of the gallery he brought it down on the policeman's head with all his strength. Unfortunately for Smales it was one of the older inhabitants and it splintered like dry bread on contact with his pursuer's forehead. Ormerod staggered back, his head resounding with the force of the blow, his knees buckling for a moment. But he did not fall. Instead he used his bent knees as a spring to bring him up forward again. At last the unarmed combat was going to come in useful, even if it were not against the Germans. He came up on a powerful rebound and grabbed Smales with both arms forcing him back against the wall. Smales was not as big as Ormerod, but he was years younger and he was frightened. He butted at the policeman but Ormerod managed to pull his face back away from the blow. He banged Smales against the stones causing half a dozen skulls and their attendant bones to collapse in a gaunt heap. Smales fell backwards, pulling Ormerod with him, and they lay on top of each other, panting and sweating. Smales got his hand free and grabbed another skull. He lifted it to strike Ormerod but the policeman caught the other side of the skull and they wrestled with it like two men with a ball. 'You bastard – this could be somebody's mother,' panted Ormerod. He knew he had him.

Smales collapsed back on the floor, sweat pouring from every pore in his face, his eyes swimming in it. Ormerod leaned off. 'Right, now, what were we saying?' he began.

Smales opened his pale eyes and blinked as the sweat ran into them. 'How ... ?' he gasped. 'How do you reckon you're going to get me out of Paris?' His chest heaved. 'You must be looney.'

'Do you wish to make a statement?' Ormerod gasped formally.

'Let me get up. Let me just sit up will you? You're killing me.'

Ormerod should have learned from Le Blanc. He eased himself off Smales and even sportingly helped him to his feet. As the soldier stood up he brought up his knee and caught Ormerod the second most powerful blow he had ever felt in the crotch. He gasped and staggered back. Then Smales hit him across the head with a tibia selected at random from the many piled around them. It was a good bone and it hurt. His face sagged. Smales rushed forward and pushed him.

The English policeman fell backwards down a flight of stone steps, his arms outstretched and sweeping down with him a crowd of skeletons who ended up in a gruesome embrace with him at the foot of the steps. Ormerod blacked out. Smales, laughing wildly, ran.

Raymond was a man who spoke in the same manner as he walked, a stooping, hesitant delivery, everything careful and considered. Ormerod wondered how he would ever be able to handle a sub-machine gun when the time came. 'I must tell you again, monsieur,' he said, sitting in the room of the apartment át the Rue des Plantes, 'that the man Smales is important to our plans for the next two days. We need the experience of the criminal. After that he's yours. He is not somebody we can trust.'

'Right,' nodded Ormerod. His back hurt from his fall down the stairs and the human tibia had given him a large contusion on the forehead. 'I just want him long enough to make a statement about the murder he committed.'

'And after that – what?' asked Raymond.

Ormerod shook his head painfully. 'That I don't know,' he admitted. 'My whole object has been to find him. But as to getting him out of here and back to face a court, well, that is going to be bloody difficult, I've got to admit. I'll be lucky to get myself out as far as I can see. And Smales would shop me to the Germans the first time he had a chance. He'd rather spend the next few years in Germany than go to a necktie party in Wandsworth.'

Raymond looked puzzled. 'What is this necktie party?' he inquired.

'Hanging,' said Ormerod simply. 'When he's convicted they'll hang him at Wandsworth prison in London.'

'Ah, of course we have the guillotine, you know.'

'Don't like the idea of that,' grimaced Ormerod. 'Dit messy I should think.'

To his considerable surprise Raymond said: 'I expect we could get Smales out of the country for you.'

'You could? How?'

'Well, you know, France is still operating, if you understand me. Everyday life still goes on all over the country, here and in the unoccupied zone – already we have transported a man in a coffin to Switzerland, a live man, I mean, with air holes in the coffin and food. He reported that the journey was very comfortable. Also everyday transport methods are often easy. The fruit and vegetables coming in from the country to the market at Les Halles. Several men have arrived amid a pile of cabbages. That method is called *"mon petit chou"*. Then there are the trains. The Germans make checks on trains but mostly they are not very thorough. We hid a wanted man on the footplate of the engine all the way to Perpignan, you know, disguised as the fireman. The Boche checked everybody on the train except the driver and our friend. Oh yes, there are ways.'

Ormerod looked at him with new admiration. Raymond smiled at the recognition. 'And for the moment,' he said, 'there is Unoccupied France, Vichy France. There are many comings and goings over the long border, believe me. The Germans may be sitting in our house, monsieur, but the basement is full of Frenchmen.'

Raymond left his chair and poured them cognac. 'Provided you give the appearance of going about your everyday business, you can move in Paris with some freedom. I still carry on my teaching at the Sorbonne without interference from the Nazis. At present that is. The only difference is that my Jewish students are now more recognizable. They have to wear a yellow star. Sometimes there are a dozen or more Jewish boys and girls in a lecture. There are so many stars that I say it is like teaching astronomy. We have to make a joke of it. Sometimes the other students, just to protest, wear the stars as well. The Germans don't like that, but they have done nothing about it yet. They are very busy trying to learn to be occupiers.'

Ormerod looked at him steadily. 'When will you do your bank raid?' he asked. 'That's if you can tell me.'

'Some time in the next three days,' said Raymond. He was not being cautious. He did not know. 'It will be difficult, but we need the funds. It will be interesting because I have never done anything truly criminal in my life. War gives a man strange opportunities.'

Ormerod nodded: 'It certainly does. Strangely enough, I've never done anything really criminal either. It's a bit frowned upon in the Metropolitan Police. Do you still want me in on it?'

'Yes I do.' Raymond regarded him seriously. 'We do not have enough people or enough experience to carry out this sort of thing. Jean Le Blanc has been called to the Vichy Zone, to Lyons. He will be back in two or three days. It is a pity, but it was urgent. He would have been useful.'

Ormerod sniffed: 'Yes, a useful bloke our Jean. I shall miss him.'

Raymond smiled thinly. 'He is not a friend for everybody,' he said. 'What is your expression – not everybody's cup of tea? I think he is a hard man. But, monsieur, France has had too many soft men. Soft men do not win wars.'

'He's a tough bugger all right,' said Ormerod thoughtfully. 'And without a lot of sportsmanship. He'd make a marvellous Nazi.'

'As I say, we need him,' repeated Raymond calmly. 'We need men of every sort in the resistance. All politics, all beliefs. Believe me, before Paris is free again they will be fighting each other as well as fighting the Boche. As for myself, well I am a patriot, pure and simple. All I wish is to see France free. For that I would sacrifice everything. It is, you must understand, very embarrassing to be a slave.'

Ormerod regarded him with admiration. 'I hope it all works out for you,' he said with his customary inadequacy.

'Thank you. But for now we must consider the bank robbery. It is, I repeat, a great pity that Le Blanc is not here. Also I have told your comrade Dove to stay out of this. In a direct way, that is. She has too much to do in the future. We cannot risk her on something like this.' He spread his hands. 'And so we have got what we have got,' he said. 'Novices. In the future, as we become tougher, more accustomed to this life, it will be different, but at the moment, the men attached to the group, patriots though they are, are not criminals. Smales is a criminal and you are a policeman. We need men of your background and calibre.'

Ormerod grinned. His bruised mouth hurt when he did so. 'I'm not sure whether to take that as a compliment,' he said.

'It is,' smiled Raymond. 'We have a part for you, monsieur. It requires some coolness but it will not involve you directly in the robbery.'

'That's a relief anyway. I never really fancied myself with a mask over my nose. What do I do?'

Raymond went to the bureau in the corner and took out a map of Paris which he spread on the low table between them. 'One of the great difficulties of any kind of action like this in France, and particularly in Paris, whether it is a resistance operation or a bank robbery, is getting away from the scene quickly. There is no quick transport available. And in any case, a car hurrying through Paris in these days would be picked up in a moment. As you see there are very few civilian cars on the roads and we could hardly escape on bicycles.'

Ormerod acknowledged the fact. 'I've travelled to Paris in just about every way except camel train,' he said. 'As you said the other day, thank God the railways are running.'

'Exactly. And this is what we plan to do with the bank robbery. Not the railway – the Métro.' He pointed to the map. 'See, here is the location of the bank. It is in the Rue de Babylone. Here.' He looked at Ormerod quizzically. 'I have to tell you, monsieur, that we will have a little co-operation from inside the bank itself. The assistant manager is a patriotic Frenchman and he knows the money is for a good cause. He is making sure that it is conveniently together and that there will be no resistance, so nobody will need to be shot.'

Ormerod sniffed. 'Not unless our friend Smales gets trigger happy,' he warned. 'Albert would really enjoy shooting a bank cashier. Especially if he thinks it's in a good cause. Right up his alley that is.'

'If he shoots anyone unnecessarily then he will be tried by our own court and will be executed. I'm afraid we would have to cheat you, monsieur. It has been made clear to him.'

'What do I have to do?' asked the Englishman. 'My non-combatant role?'

'You,' said Raymond, 'will be the carrier of the suitcase. After the robbery it is arranged that the money, in a leather suitcase, will be taken into the Métro station at Sèvres Baby-lone. You will be waiting on the platform – on the Direction Mairie D'Issy platform – at exactly ten-fifteen. The Métro closes at eleven o'clock each morning so the operation must be complete by that time. The money will be brought down from the platform by another of our members who will set it down next to you. You will pick up the case and get into the third carriage of the train that will come in. On the train will be your colleague Dove. You will not speak to her. Just set the case down next to her and she will take it from the train at Notre Dame des Champs which is two stations down the route. You will remain on the train and change at Montparnasse

Bienvenue for the train to Denfert-Rochereau, it can be either Direction Porte D'Orléans or Direction Nation. From Denfert-Rochereau you will return to here on foot. Later today you will be taken to the Métro so that you will know the route.'

'Sounds simple,' said Ormerod, relieved he did not have to take a direct part in the hold up.

'It sounds simple,' agreed Raymond. 'Perhaps it will be.'

The raid on the Rue de Babylone branch of the Paris Commerce Bank took place at ten o'clock the following day. It was a grey, drizzling morning with little in the streets but bicycles, bicycle-taxis and a few horses and carts. Pedestrians, weighed down it seemed by the weather and the times, walked with faces averted. Cafés were open along the Rue de Babylone, their lacklustre candlelight flickering in the dimness of the day.

At nine fifty-five four men in overcoats and trilby hats left four different cafés in the street and the adjoining Rue Sèvres and walked unhurriedly to the premises of the bank. They entered through doors at each side of the bank, pulled silk scarves up to their noses and produced guns.

Ten million francs in notes, worth then about £25,000, was conveniently stacked in the office of the assistant manager who, at the point of a gun, handed it over with an agreeable smile. The raid was completed within two minutes. Some people in the bank were not aware that it had happened.

On the platform of the Sèvres Babylone Métro station at ten-fifteen Ormerod stood more nervously than he had ever done during his lifetime's activity on the proper side of the law. He wondered what his superintendent at Wandsworth might think if he knew that he was about to take delivery of a consignment of stolen banknotes. On the platform were thirty or so waiting people, spread out along its length. Ormerod was amazed to see Smales striding along towards him with a leather suitcase. Smales obviously did not expect to see him either for his expression abruptly altered, he halted and then moved hesitantly towards Ormerod again. He put the suitcase down next to Ormerod, never taking his eyes off his face. 'Hello Albert,' said the policeman. 'Partners in crime, eh?'

Smales did not reply. He went hurriedly along the platform and out of the exit. The thought occurred to Ormerod that the messenger was supposed to go by Métro in the other direction. He shrugged and picked up the suitcase. A green train with 'Direction Mairie D'Issy' on its indicator board clattered through the tunnel. The third carriage came to a stop almost at Ormerod's feet. He glanced up and saw Marie-Thérèse sitting tight-faced inside. He took the suitcase and stepped in casually.

There were a dozen other passengers in the compartment, including a fat German soldier curled in sleep, his face perspiring gently beneath his cap. He looked like a tired village postmaster. Ormerod sat down and studied a poster showing a grinning blond German helping an old lady across the road. He smiled speculatively at Marie-Thérèse but she did not even look at him. At Notre Dame des Champs she stood up and, picking up the case, left the train.

Ormerod followed the instructions and changed at Montparnasse to get a train to Denfert-Rochereau where he left the station and walked casually to the apartment on the Rue des Plantes. They had given him the key. He went to his bedroom, patted the rabbit hutch, took off his shoes and lay down. He went at once to sleep.

It was two hours later when Marie-Thérèse woke him with her knocking on the door. She entered at once. He could see by her face that something had gone wrong.

'Raymond wants you,' she said. 'It has failed. Come quickly.'

He sat up sleepily and replaced his shoes. He walked into the main room of the apartment. They were all there except Smales. On the floor, its lid mockingly open, was the suitcase that Ormerod had taken at the Sèvres Babylone Station. It contained wads of torn-up pages from old Paris telephone directories. Ormerod whistled.

He looked around. 'I perceive that our friend Smales is absent,' he said. 'And where Smales is, that is where the loot is. Right?'

'Almost correct,' said Raymond. 'Between the time we left the bank and the time the case was delivered to you, Smales managed to make a switch. He escaped with the money.'

Ormerod looked around. They looked so perplexed, so innocent, so hurt. He wondered, not for the first time, how they would fare as resistance fighters. He sniffed. 'Well you wanted a criminal mind,' he said, 'and you got one. That's Smales all over.'

'There is a further development,' said Raymond quietly.

'What's that?'

'We have just heard from a contact who listens on the Paris telephone for us ... We have information that Smales has been picked up by the French Police and they have handed him over to the Germans.'

Ormerod felt himself go pale. 'Oh,' he said. Then slowly, 'Then in that case we had better get him back quick. It won't take Smales long to do a deal. Then we're all in the shit.'

Albert Smales had deposited his gun and all but twenty thousand of the ten million francs from the bank raid in the left-luggage bureau at the Gare du Nord. He felt happy and triumphant at the ease with which the ruse had been carried out. He was still congratulating himself on his craft when he was picked up by the French police in the suburb of Clichy that same afternoon.

Because he spoke little French and, when he was searched, the twenty thousand francs were discovered and two rounds of ammunition for a Walther pistol, the French police immediately handed him over to the German *Feldgendarmerie*, the military police.

At four o'clock that day Provost Lieutenant Huber, after questioning Smales at the *Feldgendarmerie* office in the Avenue de la Porte de Clichy, telephoned the *Abwehr*, German military intelligence, and spoke to SS Captain Ernst Heller.

'So, you have an English soldier? What significance is that?' demanded Captain Heller. Provost Lieutenant Huber, on the other end of the phone, blinked. He was cautious of the Gestapo, even at telephone distance.

'It is that we think he might have been mixing in interesting company in Paris,' he said with deference. 'He must have been sheltered and fed by somebody since he came here. He had twenty thousand francs on him.'

'How old is the man?'

'Twenty-three.'

'Probably sheltered by a woman,' said Heller. He was becoming impatient. He himself had an appointment with a woman. 'What interest is he to us? Send him back to the prison camp.'

He was about to put the receiver down when the provost lieutenant said, 'When he was picked up in Clichy he had two rounds of ammunition on him.'

'So? He is a soldier.'

'The ammunition is German. For a Walther,' said the lieutenant. He enjoyed saying that. He heard a pause at the other end.

'All right,' sighed Heller. 'I still don't think it is important but I suppose we'd better have him over here for interrogation. But don't make it official. We don't want the Geneva Red Cross and all that crap coming down on us for transgressing their beautiful convention.'

'He is in civilian clothes,' said the lieutenant, feeling better now. 'I don't see how the Geneva Convention applies. Or the Hague Convention. Or any convention. He could be shot as a spy.'

'All right,' said Heller. 'Send him over. This evening. I've got an important and busy afternoon. Make it seven o'clock. And don't lose him on the way.' The thought stayed with him. 'Perhaps we will send an escort. Yes, I think that will be better.'

'As you wish,' said the lieutenant. He wondered who had conquered France, the army or the Gestapo. 'We will expect your people just before seven.'

He put the phone down and walked along the corridor from his office to a detention room. Smales was sitting grimly at a table, guarded by a sergeant wearing the brass breastplate of the *Feldgendarmerie*. He did not bother to look up when Lieutenant Huber walked in. 'How did you get to Paris?' Huber said.

Smales looked up wearily. Huber thought what a curious face he had. He had also been crying. In his life Smales had been in the custody of the police at various times. This time he knew it was serious.

'I got a train,' he said. 'I told you before, didn't I? I lifted some money from the hospital and got on the train to Paris.'

'Why did you leave the hospital?'

'Didn't like the food.'

He regretted the remark. The German struck him across the face with his hand. 'I am asking polite questions,' he said. 'I want polite answers.'

'I just wanted to get to Paris,' said Smales, his eyes bloodshot. 'I've always been a bit of an operator in England . . .'

'What does that mean – operator?'

'Well, I've done a bit of villainy . . . in trouble with the police. That sort of thing.'

'Thievery,' said the lieutenant. He looked pleased he knew the word. 'Stealing.'

'Yes,' said Smales with a strangely embarrassed smile. 'That sort of thing. I knew there was a black market in Paris and I reckoned it would get bigger as time went on. I thought I'd get here and see what the chances were. It's easier to hide anyway. I reckon with a bit of luck you could make a fortune here.' He glanced at Huber as if thinking they might go into partnership.

'Where did the ammunition come from? It is German ammunition.'

'From the hospital at Bagnoles. I told you that. I nicked it when I nicked the money.'

'Where is the gun?'

'I haven't got a gun. Just the rounds.'

'Where have you been hiding in Paris?'

Smales looked frightened. 'All around. A night here, a night there. A couple of prossies, you know, tarts, they put me up for a week or so. I thought I might run them too. The prossies. That's going to be very big business.'

Huber smiled deftly. 'I am afraid you are going to be out of business, as you might say, for a long time.'

'What's going to happen to me?' asked Smales. 'I'm a British soldier, remember.'

'You are going to a hotel to stay for a while.'

Smales was unintelligent enough to smile. Then he saw Huber's expression. 'What hotel?' he asked.

'Hotel Lutetia,' answered Huber. The guarding policeman

looked up at Smales with something like pity. 'It is an office of the Gestapo.'

At that moment Smales made the decision he had known he was going to have to make. It was going to be necessary to come to an agreement with them.

At five o'clock the telephone rang in the apartment on the Rue des Plantes. It rang once, stopped, rang again, stopped and then sounded a third time. Raymond waited. Now he picked it up and merely gave his name. He did not say anything further until the end of the message. The speaker was in a hurry. Raymond let him continue and at the conclusion quickly said: '*Merci, au revoir*,' before putting the receiver down.

Jean Le Blanc had returned from the Unoccupied Zone only ten minutes before and was sitting noisily drinking coffee. Marie-Thérèse was there also, looking anxiously at Raymond. She had just come in with Le Blanc.

'Smales,' said Raymond grimly. 'He is with the *Feldgendarmerie* at the Avenue de la Porte de Clichy. They are taking him to the *Abwehr* tonight at seven. We will have to move quickly. We three and the Englishman will have to do it.'

Le Blanc looked up with his dull eyes over the top of the coffee cup, 'Do we need the Englishman?' he said. 'So far he has not been of great value. Englishmen never are.'

'It is because of Smales,' said Raymond. 'I made a promise he could have Smales.'

'Madness,' growled Le Blanc. 'Absolute madness. What chance has he got of doing anything with Smales, anyway? Where can he take him? Back to his police station in London? It is a fantasy. While Smales lives, we are all in danger.'

'I promised the Englishman he could take Smales. If it is possible. I want to keep that promise,' said Raymond. 'The important thing is to prevent him getting to the Hotel Lutetia.'

'They will soon make him talk there,' sniffed Le Blanc. 'What route? Did the contact know?'

'We must act very quickly, as soon as possible after he leaves the *Feldgendarmerie* post in the Avenue de la Porte de Clichy. He will be in a Gestapo car with a two-man escort. They do not know what they have captured yet. They do not realize what he can tell them. The military vehicles always take the same route from the *Feldgendarmerie* post. It is a security route. The car will turn into the Boulevard Bessières and then immediately turn into a small street, the Rue de Jonquière. That is where we must get him.'

'I say we leave the Englishman out of this,' said Le Blanc. 'He will be in the way.'

'I say we take him, we need him,' said Marie-Thérèse looking at him steadily.

'We must take him,' said Raymond. 'We need everybody. There is not time to contact the others. There are just the four of us.'

Marie-Thérèse turned towards the door to the corridor. 'I will get him,' she said.

Ormerod was sitting in the room with the rabbits, reading an eighteen-month-old English newspaper which he had unearthed in the apartment. He studied the cricket scores closely and smiled at Marie-Thérèse as she entered. 'Len Hutton's batting well this season,' he said. She hushed him. She could hear Raymond's conversation in the passage outside the room.

'Smales,' she said. 'There is something.'

He got up from the bed and touched her on the shoulder. She gave him a brief smile. 'Come,' she said. 'Raymond will tell you. Le Blanc is also here.'

'Ah good,' said Ormerod. 'I missed him.' He followed her into the room. He ignored Le Blanc.

Raymond said: 'They are going to move Smales. To the Hotel Lutetia.'

The significance of the name missed Ormerod. 'Is that a nice hotel?' he said, guessing it was not.

'A very bad hotel,' said Raymond. 'It is a Gestapo office. Once he is there he will talk very quickly.'

Ormerod thought about it. 'If he has not done so already,' he said.

'It does not seem so. Not yet. They think he is just a British deserter; he had some Walther ammunition on him and twenty thousand francs.'

'Wonder where he hid the rest?' said Ormerod, thinking like a policeman.

'That does not matter so much. What does matter is that he does not get to the Gestapo. We have one matter in our favour. The Germans will probably be careless, casual. In the first place, as I say, they do not know how valuable Smales is, and in the second they have never yet had any trouble in Paris. This will be the first time. But we *must* make sure he does not talk. After that we would not last five minutes. He has not told them anything yet. He will want to tell his story to the biggest ears. But he will not take long.'

Ormerod nodded at him. 'So we've got to get him before he gets there.' He looked squarely at Le Blanc. 'And that means you'll kill him.'

Raymond looked as if he were pondering some academic problem. He glanced up at Ormerod. 'You, monsieur, this time you cannot be a non-combatant. This time you must use your gun. We must either rescue Smales or assassinate him. He must not get to the Hotel Lutetia.'

At four minutes to seven the car from the Hotel Lutetia drew up outside the main door of the *Feldgendarmerie* office in the Rue de la Porte de Clichy. It was dusk and the streets of Paris were almost vacant. The empty trees rattled in the chill air.

Raymond himself saw the arrival of the car from a telephone kiosk almost opposite the military police post. He walked quickly to the Rue de Jonquière and joined Le Blanc drinking cognac in a café on the left-hand side.

The Rue de Jonquière runs roughly south-east from the Boulevard Bessières to the Avenue de St Ouen. It is an area devoted to specialized schools, bookshops, colleges, hospital laboratories, student cafés, hostels and hotels. It was dim and neglected, the lights of the few cafés still open reflecting morosely onto the pavement. There was only a partial blackout in Paris but few people looked for lights or entertainment out of doors in the evening. They went home early and stayed there.

Ormerod and Marie-Thérèse stood by a news-stand on the opposite side of the street from the café where Raymond and Le Blanc were waiting. Marie-Thérèse looked through a magazine, then another. Her eyes looked black in her pale face.

Ormerod picked up the *New York Times* and began to read. Marie-Thérèse reached over and took it from him, giving him a French newspaper. He grimaced and then understood. She pushed some francs across to the proprietor. He was listening to the radio and did not notice.

At five minutes past seven the Gestapo car left the *Feldgendarmerie* office with Smales sitting white-faced between two leather-coated officers in the back. The car turned into the main Boulevard Bessières and then took the predicted right turn into the Rue de Jonquière.

Over the horizon of his newspaper Ormerod watched it turn in the dimness at the top of the street. There was no doubt about it being the right car; there were no others. Raymond signalled briefly with his newspaper from the café. The drizzle was dripping from the canopy over the newspaper stand and onto Ormerod's head. He lifted the newspaper quietly in answer to the signal. He winked at Marie-Thérése. It was time. Suddenly she turned and swore at him so that everyone in the vicinity would hear and ran into the street. She collapsed on the cobbles at the centre and in a moment Ormerod was running after her. He reached the middle of the road and bent by her side. He was conscious of the Gestapo car coming nearer and then he felt the lights on him. He hoped the Germans would not spoil it by failing to stop. It came to a halt ten yards away and the driver shouted in German to get out of the way. Ormerod looked up and made helpless signs. A few people had gathered on the pavement to watch. The driver, cursing, left the car and stalked up to Ormerod and the prostrate girl.

'Get her out of the way,' he ordered in German. 'Come on, move her.' Then he tried some stumbling French. The two sentences brought him to within three feet of the couple. Ormerod eased himself up as if to speak to the man. The movement revealed Marie-Thérése lying in the road with an exposed pistol. She fired two shots, the first one of which effectively killed the driver. His face took on the usual look of a man who has met sudden death – indignation, as though he had been cheated. He sat down in the road and then rolled forward like a large doll, onto his face.

At the same instant as the Frenchwoman fired the first shot,

Raymond and Le Blanc, shadows in raincoats and trilby hats, walked briskly into the road towards the German car. Jean Le Blanc casually, like a man lifting his wrist to look at his watch, shot one of the Gestapo officers as he tried to get out of one door and the ashen-faced Raymond shot the other. The second officer stumbled across the road and collapsed against the newspaper stand, bringing down the tarpaulin canopy. He was not quite dead. He drew his pistol and fired several aimless shots as if he were trying to hit anybody in Paris as a final act of hate. Then he fell backwards and died under the unbelieving eyes of the newspaper vendor. Ormerod ran towards the rear door of the car and pulled Smales, slack-mouthed, from the vehicle. Le Blanc, who always did his killing calmly, took a pace forward and shot Smales twice through the ribs. He doubled up, conveniently falling over Ormerod's shoulder. Ormerod, staggering under the weight and with the blood of Smales all over his hands, bellowed at Le Blanc, 'You lousy cunt! You bastard French frog ...' It was inadequate and there was no time for it anyway. Le Blanc turned and ran across the road. Almost as an afterthought he turned and fired a final shot which went by Ormerod's nose and banged into the German car.

Cursing foully, Ormerod picked up Smales across his shoulder. He was not sure why he was doing it. Some instinct, he thought later. There was no sign of Marie-Thérèse or Raymond. The Gestapo car began to burn with an unhurried, almost domestic, flame. Ormerod, carrying Smales, staggered across the street towards the newspaper kiosk. He went past the Gestapo man lying beneath a shroud of newspapers and magazines. The dim, wet street had miraculously emptied of Parisians. People who had put their heads out of doors and windows to see what was going on hurriedly withdrew them.

Ormerod ran heavily, Smales a dead weight on his shoulder. He found himself in a courtyard between a café and a shop. He could feel Smales' blood warm on his own neck. He could not have run far like that. He knew he would have to be quick. He just wanted to hear from Smales.

Panting, he half fell down into a basement. Smales opened his eyes. He propped his head and shoulders against the wall.

'What you want, copper?' he said, with something like sarcasm.

'You've had it mate,' said Ormerod with a grim comradeship. 'You're dead and gone. Make your peace. Did you kill the girl? Lorna Smith. Did you?'

Smales closed his eyes as if he still refused to discuss the matter. There was blood running from his mouth and nose, bright against the pallor of his face. Ormerod shook him and Smales opened his eyes weakly. It was almost like asking a favour of him. 'Come on Smales, did you?'

'You know I fucking did,' grunted Smales. Ormerod, as if it might help him talk, wiped some of the blood from the man's mouth. 'You wouldn't have come all this way if you didn't know,' said Smales. He looked as though he might be grinning or it might have been the contortion of his features. He moved his lips for the last time. Sardonically he said: 'What you want – a bloody statement . . . ?'

He died then, a quick and simple transformation. Ormerod grimaced and put him gently back against the wall. Now he could hear the increased commotion of police whistles and vehicles in the street beyond the low buildings. He stood up, wiped the blood from his hands with a piece of stray newspaper, and walked briskly to the basement. The inexperienced Germans were a long way from throwing a cordon around the area and he walked almost casually to the Métro station in the Place Clichy and got aboard the first train that arrived.

The final pages of George Ormerod's narrative of the events of the autumn of 1940 read as follows:

'After the business in the Rue Jonquière, I hid in various parts of Paris for about a week. Even though the Germans were searching for our group it was surprisingly easy to hide. Those were now the very first days of the resistance and they did not know where to look. There were no informers and no splits inside the underground movement. It was like that at the beginning.

'At first I went back to the apartment at Denfert-Rochereau. Only Raymond was there. He did not look any different after the shootings. He still looked like a slow professor. The following day I was taken to another house in the south of Paris at Gentilly. It was another professor's house, although I did not see much of him and his family. Marie-Thérèse came there three days running and we spent quite a bit of time together. She told me that two of the French children at Moulin-en-Ceil had been blinded by the bridge explosion. There was nothing I could say about that. We talked a lot about ourselves also, for the first time since we were together in the forest, before we were taken to Villedieu to hide under the bells.

'It's a long time ago now and I don't remember much of what we said, but she was much softer to me then, much more of a woman than when I first met her and we landed in France. I suppose she had learned some things too. We were very happy together for those few days in Gentilly. Naturally she talked quite a lot about the resistance movement and how it would grow throughout France. Already there were groups forming in the Alps and other mountain places who in the following years were operating like proper armies in places where the Germans could not reach them. They had begun blowing up supply cables and trains and causing sabotage in factories. A lot of what they did was very crude and amateur, but who could expect anything else? After D-Day in 1944 they really came into their own and what they did behind the Germans' backs helped the invasion troops to get a foothold in Normandy. They ought to be remembered for that.

'Before the war was done the Germans arrested and deported thousands of Frenchmen and tortured and executed many others. Nearly five thousand were killed in Paris alone. But they won in the end.

'During the days I spent with Marie-Thérèse in Gentilly the weather became wintry, with rain and winds blowing along the streets. Very soon we would be going our separate ways, me back to England to my wife and my normal life and she to the dangers of her work in France. We spent a long time in my room in the house and we also talked about what we would do after the war. I could not for the life of me think of anything more original than still being a policeman in London. She had lots of plans for her children and the school where she used to teach. It was only daydreaming, I suppose, because she had really given up her children forever. I think the reason she moved away from her village, and apparently from France altogether in the end, was that people could not forgive her for the *violence*, even though it had all been done in a good cause. *People just don't like violence.* It must have been very sad for her to realize that.

'As for myself, I escaped from France in a very funny way. The resistance already had more than one escape network to the Unoccupied Zone in the south and then into Spain or Switzerland. Various odd methods were used to smuggle people out under the noses of the Germans. Raymond came to the house and told me I was to be moved out of the city area to Auxerre, just to the south. Marie-Thérèse came to see me in the afternoon and that was the last time we met until after the war was finished. I was sad about this, although I did not show it, because I have to admit to myself that I had to all intents and purposes fallen in love with her. That evening I went to Auxerre.

'There was a house in Auxerre which was a sort of base for smuggling people out of Occupied France. They had done it in various ways – even getting one man clear by including him in a team of cyclists and letting him pedal on over the border (with the connivance of the French border police, I have no doubt). I couldn't see me being able to ride a bike like that, but they came up with a really novel idea to get me out. I was to be taken by train to Perpignan on the Spanish border as a civilian prisoner-under-escort, handcuffed to a bogus detective. Since I was an officer of the Metropolitan Police Criminal Investigation Department this struck me as quite a joke, but it was a good idea. It overcame my main difficulty – my lack of French. If the Germans, or the French police for that matter, checked the identity cards on the train, the bogus detective, who had forged papers for both of us, would do all the talking. Prisoners-under-escort are notoriously sullen and quiet. That's all I had to do.

'The Frenchman who turned up to take me to Perpignan really looked the part, trilby hat and long raincoat. For all I know he might have been a real detective like I was. He brought a good pair of handcuffs and just before we set out for the station at Auxerre in the evening he slipped the bracelet onto my wrist. It was a very strange sensation, believe me.

'We had decided to travel by night since there would be fewer people on the train and less likelihood of snap security checks. From the time we left the house until we reached Narbonne in the morning we hardly said two words to each other. On the frontier between Occupied and Vichy France, at Chalon-sur-Saône I think it was, two immigration men, a Frenchman and a German, came into our carriage. I was slouched against the window, pretending to be asleep. I heard my accomplice murmur something to them and then they noticed the chain of the handcuffs between our wrists. They both laughed and went out without even checking on my escort's papers.

'By the time we reached Narbonne in the morning my wrist was sore from the bracelet and, indeed, in later years if I have had to escort a man in handcuffs for any distance I have always made sure that every now and then I allowed him to change wrists. It is for the comfort of the police officer as well, of course, because his wrist gets sore too. And while he is your prisoner, when you are in handcuffs, you are just as much his prisoner. It was a bit like the Germans were in France.

'Funnily enough, the people in the south did not seem so lively as those in the Occupied Zone. It was almost as if they felt guilty about being more or less free. But they certainly did everything they could to help me. I was in Perpignan for two days and then I was smuggled over the hills into Spain and taken to Barcelona. Everything was arranged and done efficiently.

'After only a day in Barcelona I was taken to the harbour and onto a fishing boat. Nobody spoke to me although they all knew I was there. We went out to sea for three or four hours and then I was called onto the deck. Imagine my feelings when, riding on the waves only a few hundred yards away, was a destroyer flying the white ensign! I waved and cheered to them from the deck of the fishing boat. The Spaniards all watched without a flicker of expression. I suppose they were getting well paid. The warship was already putting down a boat and in only fifteen minutes I was aboard and drinking a good cup of tea.

'We put in at Gibraltar and within three hours I was on an RAF plane with assorted other strange-looking people, bound for England. I think they called the plane "spy special".

'I arrived in England again four weeks and two days after I had left it. I must confess it seemed like years. From Croydon, where the plane put down, I telephoned my wife Sarah to tell her I was home from my supposed police course that day. She said she might have to go out. I said I had my own key so I could let myself in. She gave a sort of laugh and said I would not need it. I did not understand this at the time.

'It was odd going home like that on the underground. I could not help looking at the people there in the compartment and wonder what they would say if I told them that I had been on the Métro in Paris only a few days earlier. In those days, however, so many strange things were happening that this might not have seemed all that unusual to them. In any case, a lot of them were going through night after night of bombing and had their own adventures.

'The street seemed quiet, almost hollow, when I got back. A house down the road had been hit by a bomb and the houses on either side had collapsed. People were just walking past the debris, taking no notice. When I got to my house I saw that the windows had been blown out and had been patched up with bits of wood. The front door had also come off its hinges and all the plaster had fallen from the ceiling in the hall. I opened the door without having to use the key.

'Sarah was not in. She had left a note saying: "Have to do the shopping. Please try and do something about the bedroom window. It's very draughty. Hope you had a nice course. Sarah."

'From anybody else it would have been a joke, but not from Sarah. I went wearily up the stairs and found that the window had been blown out, frame and all. It was blocked up with some plywood which had come adrift. I found the hammer and some nails and fixed it the best I could. Then I sat down to wait for my wife to come home and to think what a funny world it was.'

Ormerod and Marie-Thérèse, the Dodo and the Dove, who

had shared so much, met only once more in their lives. It was after the war on the evening before the victory parade in London in 1945.

'I heard that a special contingent of French underground fighters were coming to London to the parade to meet the King,' says Ormerod in his recollections. 'I made inquiries in a semi-official capacity and discovered to my great delight that Marie-Thérèse was to be among them. I was not all that surprised because she had become quite a celebrity in France after the liberation of Paris in 1944. I even saw a photograph of her in one of the newspapers, being decorated by General de Gaulle.

'I discovered that she would be staying at a certain hotel in London with the rest of the Frenchmen and, through official police channels, I got myself a pass to go and see her. This may sound strange, having to get a pass, but the fact was that although the war was over there was still a lot of scores to be settled between all sorts of people and factions and the security at the time of the victory parade was quite tight.

'The hotel was called the Bedfordshire and I put on my best suit and went up there at seven o'clock in the evening. It was amazing but I saw her immediately. They were having some sort of cocktail reception in the main room of the hotel and almost the first person I spotted was Marie-Thérèse. She looked beautiful, really beautiful, tanned face and arms and shoulders and in a blue evening dress with a sort of sash like the Tricolor. She had a glass of champagne almost to her lips when she saw me. I was standing in the doorway and she was talking to a young man she later introduced to me as her fiancé, although she never married him as far as I can make out, so what happened to him I don't know.

'When she first spotted me she just stopped and stared for a moment, but, like in the old days, nothing really surprised her. She walked forward just as if we had seen each other the day before. We shook hands and she kissed me on the cheek the way the French do. I felt very awkward and I must have gone a bit red because she smiled at me as she stood away after the kiss. She really was lovely. You would not have thought that she had seen all the things she had seen and done all the things she had done. Then she introduced this chap, but she said something else to him quickly in French and he drifted off. She put out her hands and held mine, smiling into my face. It was all I could do to manage a grin.

' "Dodo," she said. "You are blushing."

' "Sorry," I said. "I do sometimes. Not very good for a police officer, I suppose. To blush."

' "How have you been all this time?"

' "Fine, pretty good. Usual things, police work, a bit of excitement in the bombing and all that. But nothing all that outstanding."

' "How is Sarah?" She remembered my wife's name.

' "All right. Just the same really. Not a lot happens to us."

' "You have children?"

' "Well, no. We've never had them."

' "I see. That is a pity. I always thought you would be a good father."

' "Yes, it's a shame. Your husband is dead?"

' "Yes," she said steadily. "He was fated. The Germans did it first."

' "You've been doing all sorts of brave things. I saw a picture of you getting a medal."

'Her eyes clouded. "It was for the others. For Jean Le Blanc and for Raymond and the others."

' "Oh. They're dead?"

' "Jean died in Rennes in 1943," she said. "They caught him and he died. Very bravely of course."

' "Of course. He would have done. And Raymond?"

'She shook her head. "He died on the day of the Liberation. He was with the students and they were throwing cobblestones at the Germans – tearing them up from the streets and flinging them. People say it was foolish, but it was a last gesture. He was hit by a stray bullet. It might have come from anywhere, even from our own side. But at least he lived to see Paris free again."

'It was odd but after all we had been through together and everything, we suddenly ran out of things to say. I could see her fiancé hovering at the other end of the room.

' "I think you're wanted," I said, nodding towards him.

' "Yes, I must go," she said, turning to look.

' "Me too. Early duty tomorrow. Goodbye."

' "Goodbye, Dodo," she said. I like to think she whispered it, but anyway it was softly.

'She leaned forward and for a minute my hands touched hers. We kissed on the cheeks and she turned away.

'I stood watching her. I felt very hollow, just like some sort of ghost. I suppose I was pretty upset inside. I went out of the room and down the steps of the hotel. Then I went on the District Line, home to my wife, Sarah.'

Leslie Thomas
Bare Nell 90p

Little Nell Luscombe, paddling naked in her native Devon streams, was the delight of the local GIs. She grew up into Bare Nell, learning that there was a good living to be made from her substantial charms. From servicing the Weymouth fishermen, she progressed to the pinnacle of her profession... running a high class establishment – within earshot of the division bells at Westminister...

'A most disarming heroine, guileless and open-hearted, innocent and lascivious... it is all good fun. And Nelly's a love!' DAILY TELEGRAPH

Tom Sharpe
The Great Pursuit 80p

The hilarious new bestseller from the author of *Wilt*.

'Frensic... a snuff-taking, port-drinking literary agent... receives a manuscript from an anonymous author's solicitor – "an odyssey of lust... a filthy story with an even filthier style". Forseeing hugo profits in the US, Frensic places the book with the Al Capone of American publishing, Hutchmeyor, "the most illiterate publisher in the world"...' LISTENER

'The funniest novelist writing today' THE TIMES

Dick Francis
Risk 85p

His new bestseller.

'An amateur jockey who won the Cheltenham Gold Cup is kidnapped, beaten up, bamboozled and its almost the last page before you find out why' DAILY MIRROR

'Dick Francis holds his form like a top-class chaser... a joy to see him back in the field' TIMES LITERARY SUPPLEMENT

Wilbur Smith
Hungry as the Sea £1.20

His latest bestseller.
Through shipwreck and hurricane, through the ice-world of
the Antarctic and the thundering surf of the African coast,
in the arms of the lovely Samantha and on the bridge of his
powerful *Warlock*, Berg, is a man in his element. Deposed as
top man in a huge shipping consortium, he's running a debt-
ridden ocean-going salvage outfit — fighting back against the
ruthless ambition of the arch-rival who stole his wife and son
and robbed him of an empire — hell-bent on retribution . . .

'Surges forward with a bone in its teeth'
TIMES LITERARY SUPPLEMENT

Thomas N. Scortia and Frank M. Robinson
The Nightmare Factor 90p

It began with an isolated incident: a convention of war
veterans at a San Francisco hotel decimated by a mysterious
deadly disease. Calvin Doohan, epidemics expert, finds his
investigations hampered by the very authorities he is trying
to help — news blackouts, military intervention, hints of the
most evil weapons in the armouries of the super powers. Who is
the enemy? Who can be trusted? Only one thing is certain —
everyone is a potential victim.

'Spine-tingling to read and terrifying to ponder'
PUBLISHERS WEEKLY

You can buy these and other Pan Books from booksellers and
newsagents; or direct from the following address:
Pan Books, Sales Office, Cavaye Place, London SW10 9PG
Send purchase price plus 20p for the first book and 10p for
each additional book, to allow for postage and packing
Prices quoted are applicable in the UK

While every effort is made to keep prices low, it is sometimes
necessary to increase prices at short notice. Pan Books reserve
the right to show on covers and charge new retail prices which
may differ from those advertised in the text or elsewhere